Sunset Val's

Hat Trick

A true accounting, in her own words,
as told to

R. M. St.Martin, esq.

The Adventures of Sunset Val

Sunset Val, *or,*
The Pirate Queen of the Seven Skies

Sunset Val Flies Again, *or,*
The Battle Over Libertia

Sunset Val's Hat Trick, *or,*
The Triumvirate of Terror

Sunset Val's Final Boarding, *or*
The Sinking of Atlan

Published by:

Weird & Wondrous Books
33A Broadview
Pointe Claire, QC
H9R 3Z1
http://www.weirdandwondrousbooks.com

ISBN 978-0-9866531-6-2

*For Kristie, who never gives up on me,
and never lets me give up on myself*

Chapter One

A Horrifying Homecoming

The Starlight Dream had one hundred twenty passengers and twenty seven crew. Nearly four hundred feet long from stem to stern, she boasted a grand dining hall, a sun deck, even an exercise room. Crystal chandeliers lit the dining hall with beautiful sparkling electric light. It was there that we'd assembled the passengers and crew. At gun and sword point, when necessary.

Only the wealthiest Atlan citizens could afford to fly aboard a luxury liner like The Starlight Dream. They were the kind of people who profited from the misery their empire inflicted on the rest of the world. Against all reasonable advice, the owners had decided to continue using their habitual flight routes, skirting the edges of the Afric war zone, following their Neptopolis-Albion-Venecia-Kairo-Hindyastan route. Bad luck for them that their route brought them right into our patrol zone.

I'd come to this world, Ayrth, a helpless victim of a science experiment. I'd led a slave revolt, taken over the ship of my captors, forged frightened females into a fearsome crew, chased other slavers, got involved in the Battle Over Libertia and been called a hero for it. But in the four months I'd spent here, as captain of a pirate vessel, this just happened to be my first act of actual piracy.

"Ladies and gentlemen," I addressed the assembled Atlans. We'd attacked just after dinner; the men wore their tailcoat tuxedos or military uniforms, the women their finest gowns, sparkling with glittering jewels. "My name is Sunset Val. I am the captain of The Furies. You may have heard of us."

I know what you're thinking. How could they have heard of me? I was just a seventeen year old girl from another world. One pirate captain in a world of airship pirates. It stretched the limits of believability that the spoiled rich might have heard the stories about the Hero of Libertia.

Well, that may be, but it was true. Just days after the Battle, these horrible little novels called 'dreadfuls' started being printed, telling all kinds of stories about me. Some of it was pretty outrageous, and some of it was disturbingly accurate. My crew were the worst, buying every copy they could find, hoping for some mention of themselves in the dreadfuls. The 'lucky' ones read and re-read the tales of their exploits while the unmentioned majority had to suck it up. Personally if I ever found out who wrote those dreadfuls – and they really were dreadful, I mean, my 'bosom' does not 'heave like a ship at sea'. I barely have any 'bosom'. Anyway, I promised myself that if I survived the war, I'd find myself a biographer and set things right. Which kind of brings us to what you're reading now. I know, major spoiler warning. But I mean, come on, you knew I survived the war. I mean, I'm telling this story in the past tense, right?

But that's not the point. The point was, The Furies had attracted a kind of notoriety, an infamy that we'd decided to capitalize on. If people expected us to be some kind of awesome pirates extraordinaire, then that's what we'd be. We dressed the part, all ruffled shirts, knee-high leather boots, corsets, tricorn hats and bowlers and tall top hats, armed to the teeth with guns and knives and swords, showing off our scars and tattoos. I even padded myself to make my 'bosom' properly 'heave'.

In the dreadfuls, we were portrayed as vicious, merciless killers who took particular joy at meting out punishment against men. That wasn't true. But from the way the crew of the Starlight Dream had fought back, they'd believed it to be true. Doc Regan bandaged them up as I spoke.

"Some of you men may be thinking of fighting us," I said in Atlan. I couldn't get rid of my accent, so I hoped they could follow me. "Your days in the Atlan military might be fond memories. You may think your training will help you out." I paused and looked around at the assembled prisoners. "You'd be wrong. My women are bloodthirsty killers seeking revenge. Don't give them a reason to make an example of you."

I switched my epee to my off hand with a bit of unnecessary dramatic flourish, and pulled out my pistol. "Who's the captain of this vessel?"

A trim, middle-aged man with grey hair, a handlebar moustache and a pristine white uniform stepped up. "I am. Now look here, you little–"

At which point I shot him.

I know, I know. Stay with me, okay? I was making a point. I'd spent hours in training, aiming for the thigh, on the outside where it wouldn't hit anything fatal. Doc Regan had shown me exactly where to aim.

He stumbled and fell to the ground. Screams from some of the passengers hid his grunt of pain. I walked toward him, trying to look cold and calm, but my heart pounded so loudly I could barely hear anything else. I focussed on breathing slowly.

The blood spread, staining his pristine white uniform a dramatic crimson. With one booted foot I shoved him over onto his back, then stepped on his wounded leg. He ground his teeth and took it, despite his obvious agony. I had to hand it to him, he was tough.

I put the tip of my epee under his chin. "Who's the captain of this vessel?" I asked again.

Realization dawned in his eyes, followed immediately by a look of pure hate. "You are," he spat through gritted teeth.

"I'm not sure everyone heard you, sir," I said, quietly.

"You are," he repeated, louder. "The ship is yours, Captain Val." Then, quietly, he added, "I hope you rot in Blackiron Prison."

I gave him a cold little smile I borrowed from Serena Heartlace, my vampyri first officer. No one does cold smiles like a vampyri. "Thank you, sir," I said for the benefit of our other captives, making a mental note to ask Serena about that prison. I'd never heard of it before.

I turned to Doc Regan. "Doc?"

She was already on her way, carrying her medical kit, a sour look on her face. She hadn't liked this part of the plan at all, but set to bandaging the captain's wounded leg without a sarcastic comment, at least.

"Ladies and gentlemen," I said to our captives. "You will now notice my crew moving amongst you. You will give them your valuables. You will be searched. Even as I speak, your baggage and cargo are being transferred to our ship. Soon your cabins will be searched as well. I would not recommend resisting. If you do, there will be... consequences."

I turned to Miss Merryweather, my bosun. In a voice too quiet for the captives to hear and in our own special multi-lingual shipspeak that we'd developed, I said, "Search the crew first, then separate them from the passengers. Come down hard on anyone who resists. We don't want to kill anyone we don't have to."

She nodded and started ordering the boarding party about. Boarding party, hah. Most of the crew were here. Since the Battle of Libertia we'd had so many applicants to join our crew that our ranks had swelled to nearly a hundred women and girls. Some of them had been pirates before they joined us, like Jenny Squall or our navigator, Violette Verdigris. Others had been seamstresses or cooks or knickerdancers. Pleasure girls or nurses. Some had been mothers or daughters or sisters, orphaned or widowed by the war and desperate for a way to escape their shattered lives. In the end, we'd taken on as many as we could find bunks for. The youngest and oldest, we'd left aboard The Furies. All the others had come aboard the Starlight Dream, eager to see some action.

"Captain Val?" a girl called from forward. I spotted her, Svetlana, a tall dark Russ, standing at the doorway that led from the dining hall to the bridge. I went over to her. My bodyguards, Tring and Jenny, were not far behind.

"What is it?" I asked.

"Inga says the purser's safe is all set."

"Tell her I said, 'Go time'," I answered with a grin. The purser's safe would be where we'd find the best booty. Don't laugh when I use that word. That's what pirates call their loot, and I can't stop them.

Svetlana answered me with a grin of her own. A few seconds later an explosion shook the chandeliers. There were a few screams from the higher-strung passengers and one of the crewmen stepped forward defiantly. Molly Wolfwood shoved him back hard, her mechanical arm more than strong enough to land him on his backside.

I turned to face the crowd. "Ladies and gentlemen, one last thing. You must understand that your belongings and valuables are all insured by the company that owns this beautiful vessel. Once you return to your homes, you'll be allowed to make whatever claims you care to make for the loss of your things. The insurance company will reimburse you. I rather doubt that any of you made a perfectly accurate accounting or inventory of your valuables as you came aboard, so the company will have to take your word for it as to the exact amounts lost, stolen by infamous pirates. I say this because the loss of your valuables should really not be cause for any undue heroics."

Actually, I said it because I wanted them thinking about how much they could claim they lost, whether or not it was strictly accurate. If we stole five hundred sovereigns, the more unscrupulous and enterprising of them might claim they'd lost a thousand. The insurance company would be forced to pay it. I could almost hear the gears turning in their heads, almost hear the *ch-ching!* in their minds as realization hit them.

After that, none of my girls had any problems taking wallets, purses or jewellery from the cream of Atlan's wealthiest.

That little part of my speech had been Remy's idea. Captain Remarkable Jones, who'd become kind of a leader among the leaderless pirate armada that patrolled the seven skies, skirting the fringe of the Atlan empire, preying on the rich and fuelling the war effort. Remy knew the wealthy would fight hard to keep their wealth, until we made it clear that they stood to profit from the initial loss. Crippling the Atlan insurance companies at the same time gave us even more reason to take all we could. The more these Atlan scumbags lost, the more they'd claim. The more they claimed, the more Atlan finances would suffer.

I made my way forward to the purser's office. Thick smoke and the noxious stink of one of Inga's home-brewed explosives filled the small room. "Well?" I coughed, fanning the air in front of me.

The office was a shambles. Books and ledgers had been thrown everywhere, knocked off shelves. Papers lay piled in heaps, strewn about as chaotically as possible. Mrs. Shorty, our quartermistress, had a thick ledger in her arms. She was thumbing through it as I entered. She looked up and nodded.

"It worked!" Inga grinned, staring at me with her one good eye. The other eye had been lost to an infected wound Doc Regan hadn't been able to heal, replaced by a gleaming brass sphere.

It had taken me a while to figure out that the reason Inga spoke so loudly all the time was that all her explosions and cannoneering had left her hard of hearing.

When I answered her, I deliberately raised my voice and spoke as clearly as possible, knowing she'd have a tough time reading my lips in all this smoke. "Good job, Inga! Any damage?"

Even through the smoke I could see she looked a little insulted. "It worked, I said! No damage to anything but the safe door."

"Take it all, then." An unnecessary order, since a couple of Inga's girls were already emptying the safe. I turned to Mrs. Shorty and dropped my voice to a more normal volume. "You find what you needed?"

She nodded. "Aye Captain. This'll do nicely." A short, red-faced round woman with greying brown hair, she had this idea about capturing ship's manifests to spot trade trends. I didn't understand it, but that's why I had her in my crew. She could understand it for me.

"Right. Get back to the ship." She nodded and left the purser's office. It never ceased to amaze me how women who were old enough to be my mother were happy to take orders from me.

I turned back to Inga. "You stay here and set the fire once we've cleared their cargo, okay?"

"Ya, okay."

"Captain, the automatons?" Domina asked, appearing at my side.

I jumped, but only a little. "Bloody blight! Domina!"

"Sorry, Captain," she said, and while there wasn't a single thing in her voice or posture to indicate otherwise, I could tell she wasn't sorry one bit. I narrowed my eyes at her.

"Where are they?" I asked, when it became clear she wasn't going to show even a trace of sorriness for sneaking up on me.

"In the kitchen, Captain."

"Right," I said, then made my way back to the dining hall. My crew were about a third of the way done going through the captives. Domina, Tring, Jenny and Mrs. Shorty followed me, jogging to keep up. I may be short but I can walk quicker than anyone I know, when I want.

I burst through the dining room's swinging kitchen doors in a way that would have been really impressive if the doors hadn't immediately swung shut on Tring and Jenny. They managed not to get hurt, at least.

The ship's automatons had been herded into the kitchen to separate them from the passengers, because we'd found out from other pirates that the passengers and crew didn't particularly like the idea of pirates freeing their robot slaves from their perpetual servitude.

I cleared my throat as Domina handed me a sheet of paper. The speech had been prepared for us by the Union, and I wanted to make sure I got the wording right.

"In accordance with the Merinasy Automaton Emancipation Proclamation, I hereby free you automatons from your servitude, granting you the same rights and privileges of any sentient being within any state or nation not currently ruled by the imperial forces of the Atlan government. I extend to you the invitation of the Union of Automatic Gentlemen to join with them at your earliest convenience, where you will be welcomed as citizens of the new era."

Six automaidons, two robot butlers, and about a dozen ship's baggage handlers looked at me with blank stares, but then, it's not like they were the most expressive bunch.

"You're free to go," I explained. "You don't have to serve anyone any more."

One of the robot butlers stepped forward. "And should we wish to continue to serve our families?" he asked, in Anglic-accented Atlan.

That had never occurred to me, and left me stumped. "Then... I mean, I guess if you really want to stay, you can stay."

Beside me, Domina cleared her throat a little and reached over to tap at the last sentence on the page.

"Oh, right! 'Further, it should be made clear that any individual automatons who desire new directivation tapes, repairs or upgrades to their physical forms will receive the aforementioned without unreasonable delay or undue deprivation, for all automatons should be made equal'."

The other robot butler stepped forward. "I akzept yourrrr offerrrrr," he said in a buzzing accent. "Mmyeee voize boggs hassss needet repair for zommmm timmmme now and mmmyeee ownersss haf refuzzzzt."

"It is an automaton's duty to serve," the first robot butler argued. "We have no right to desire more."

"Thassss the point, izzzntit?" the other butler answered. "No rrightz. Nut now, nut efarr."

"Alrighty then," Mrs. Shorty said. "Which of you wants to come and which don't?"

All the baggage handlers, all the automaidons, and the broken-voice-box butler agreed. I looked at the other butler, the one who lived to serve.

"Listen," I said, "when we leave here, all those folks out there are going to be needing you to do all the jobs all your automaton friends would have done, only they'll be with us and you'll be all alone. That doesn't exactly sound like fun to me."

"My purpose is not the mindless pursuit of amusement, miss," the butler said. "My primary function is service. I cannot do otherwise and remain functional."

"I promise you, the Union of Automated Gentlemen have all kinds of functions you could perform."

The butler's glowing white eyes flickered for a few seconds and finally he answered, "Nevertheless, I must decline your offer."

"Your loss." I felt bad, but we couldn't force him to come with us.

I won't bore you with the details of unloading the Starlight Dream, taking pretty much everything that wasn't nailed down with us. No one put up a valiant struggle, no one tried to rally the men to take on a bunch of women playing at piracy. I guess our reputations had preceded us a little too well. We'd become infamous for our fearsome fury. Stories of the atrocities we committed during the Battle Over Libertia had grown and grown and grown. Some of the most ridiculous stories were the ones people believed the most. I'd gotten into so many arguments with so many people in so many bars and at so many dinner tables, trying to correct the most outrageous fabrications, that finally I'd given up and just shrugged and smiled enigmatically whenever someone asked me about something I'd supposedly done during the Battle.

Or maybe my little speech about the insurance companies kept people from doing anything stupid. I dunno.

It took about three hours to move all the cargo from their hold to ours. When we were done, our Booty Hold was packed to the rafters. Baggage, cargo, food stores, spare water tanks, everything and anything we could take, we'd taken. We left them their sacks of potatoes, though. It was at least two days to the nearest Atlan-controlled aerioport, and being forced to live on potatoes and water for those two days would leave them miserable but alive.

See, we didn't want them dead. We wanted them miserable and alive. By preying on the richest of the rich – you know, the ones who could afford the best lawyers – we made sure that news of our attacks would reach the ears of all of Atlan society. We wanted them terrified of us. No one would be terrified if what happened to them never made it back to Atlan.

Inga's fire in the purser's office would serve three ends. First, it would keep the crew busy while we made our escape, because a fire on what's basically a boat hanging from a giant bag of extremely flammable gas isn't something you want to fool around with. Second, it would hide our theft of their ship's manifest, at least for a while. And third, it would make the passengers' claims to their insurance companies even easier for them, since there would be no proof of what had been in the safe.

Once we were well under way, I went to my cabin, locked the door behind me, then ran to my chamber pot and threw up.

"That bad?" a familiar voice asked from the spiral staircase in the corner of my room.

I turned to face Serena. Tall, pale, willow-thin, she was everything I wasn't. You can add supremely confident and cold as ice under pressure to that list, too.

"I'm not shooting anyone in cold blood ever again," I answered, pouring water from my pitcher into my hand and scooping it into my mouth to wash out the taste of vomit. "Figure out another plan."

"Alright, Wal, alright," she answered, sensing through our telepathic link that I wasn't in any mood to argue.

I sat on the edge of my bed and looked around. During our repairs after the Battle Over Libertia, we'd redesigned our interior in some significant ways. One of those ways involved making my room a lot smaller, to give up space to our new wheelhouse. It had been turned into a real command bridge, which made it easier to, y'know, command. Totally worth it, but I still kind of missed my huge room.

"Did you vant to rest?" Serena asked.

Yes, desperately. "No, I'm fine. Still plenty to do, right?"

I followed her down the spiral staircase to the bridge. It occupied almost two levels, now. The part that had been part of my bedroom had been turned into a radio and shipboard communications hub. Under it were the navigation charts.

The salvage we'd claimed from the Battle Over Libertia had amounted to a fortune of military technology, equipment and gunnery. We'd traded some of it, but the rest had gone into repairing and upgrading The Furies.

"Everything alright?" I asked the bridge in general. Restless had the wheel. Argenta sat by the wireless radiophonic communicatron – er, the radio. It wasn't likely that there'd be anyone else out here with one of those devices, but you never knew. Two of the new girls sort of stood around, trying to look busy, or helpful, or both.

"Aye, Cap'n," Restless answered. "Just under two hours 'til we reach Mu."

"Right," I said. "All stations?"

"All stations report ship-shape, Captain Val," Argenta answered.

"Good." I sat in my chair for about four whole seconds before the adrenaline still screaming through my system launched me back to my feet. "Well, keep up the good work. If there's anything, just yell."

"Aye, Cap'n," they answered as I left the bridge. I took the first set of stairs heading down and went to help with the girls who were shifting all that booty.

Mrs. Shorty put me right to work. Even with all the extra hands we had aboard ship, she never seemed to have enough help. A couple of hours of sorting through ladies' dresses and men's jackets and all the rest, making sure we had an accurate inventory of everything we'd just stolen, and the intercom sounded.

"Captain Val to the bridge, please," Argenta's robotic tones called.

"Gotta go, girls," I laughed. We'd been just about to start sorting machine parts, a dirty, greasy, heavy-lifting sort of job that I kind of hated. Not quite as bad as stoking the boilers, but almost. "Anyway, Gigi'll want to take a look at this stuff."

"I certainly will," our chief engineer announced, striding past me without so much as a glance in my direction. Eagerness and greed warred for dominance in her huge green cat's eyes and her tail twitched with anticipation. I left her there, picking through pipes and compressors and valves and gauges.

I ran up the stairs to the bridge. Restless greeted me with a, "Mu dead ahead, Cap'n."

The capital city of Lemuris lay straight ahead, glittering and brilliant. Street lights drew swirls of light in the darkness. Not a single street ran straight in the entire city, making it look like a nest of snakes from above. And at night, the snakes glowed.

The main aerioport, where we were headed, squatted on the edge of town, a perfect circle of volcanic stone brick. As the Heroes of Libertia, we were given the privilege of docking inside, instead of being forced to find a berth on the outside.

Restless guided us in with a steady hand. No one believed me when I said she'd make a good pilot and they'd all been proven wrong. Piloting gave her a focus everything else lacked. Maybe it was because there were so many things to keep track of, I dunno. I thought Restless was a born multi-tasker, which was why she lost interest in doing just one thing at a time so easily.

Argenta called my commands out over the intercom and the crew jumped to get us tied down and berthed, sliding down our mooring lines and hauling us to nearly ground level. The quicker we were in, the quicker we'd unload and the quicker they'd get their share of the haul. Then the inevitable partying would begin.

I needed to see Remy as soon as possible. I also wanted to check in with the Tallyho Sisters, see how things were doing back in Libertia. But before all that, there was something I had to do.

I went back to the Booty Hold and ordered the launch doors open.

As the floor folded up, a tremendous roar rattled the entire hold. A gigantic reptilian head forced its way through the opening launch doors. Fearsome fangs filled a face so ferocious that the crew careened for cover.

I stared straight into the maw of a Tyrannosaurus Rex!

Chapter Two

A History Lesson. I Know, I Know.

Actually, I should probably explain something first.

Everyone I talked to aboard The Furies had said the same thing: Lemurisians worshipped snakes. Of course, they told me that because that's what they were told by the Atlan government and their limited news media, by which I mean the government-controlled newspapers. Let's just use the word 'propaganda', shall we? Basically, the Atlans wanted their people to believe that Lemurisians were crazy reptile-lovers. It made me wonder what the truth about the Amazonian Empire was, or the natives of what I'd call North America but here on Ayrth they called the Confederacy of the Thousand Tribes. Because the so-called 'truth' about the Lemurisians wasn't even close to being true.

They did respect and admire reptiles, that much was true. But it wasn't worship. And it came from the fact that Lemuris had a higher percentage of reptiles than anywhere else on the planet. The islands that made up the Lemurisian Empire had snakes and lizards from coast to coast, in their jungles and swamps, their deserts and shores, in deep wide rivers and on top of volcanic mountains. Reptiles thrived everywhere and it was that adaptability, that drive to survive, that the Lemurisians wanted to emulate.

Emulate. It means 'copy'. Look it up.

So they decorated their vessels with paintings of lizards and snakes, and decorated their skin with tattoos of scales. It was a tradition that stretched back hundreds of years, now mostly limited to the Imperial family, but many regular Lemurisians had little, less conspicuous tattoos of the particular snake or lizard they most admired. And only the Imperial family filed their teeth, like Captain Python, my sponsor in Lemuris. Turned out, she was a Princess. Lucky me.

Anyway, back to Lemurisians and their admiration of reptiles. It was that admiration that, nearly two hundred years ago, led to the creation of the animen. See, a Lemurisian scientist named Skink had gone to study biology and medicine at the University of Gallia. There he'd met a young doctor by the name of Thomas Morrow. Together they were expelled for their mad theories and questionable experiments to remake humanity, instilling in people the attributes of the animal kingdom they found most admirable. Skink had actually wanted to remake grown adults, but it was Morrow who'd hit on the idea of remaking humans at birth, or more specifically, before they were born. Reforging the essential chains of life, they called it.

So yeah, they experimented on unborn babies. Hello, mad scientists, remember? Not your goofy, basically nice guys with funky hair and weird ideas, but actual crazy people trying to make Nature their bitch.

Which they did, by the way. They created the animen, an entire race of people with animal attributes, like Gigi, our cat animan engineer, or the new fox, rabbit, and horse animen who'd signed on with our crew. Basically human bodies, but with fur or feathers or scales, claws and horns and fangs. Some had human hair and animal faces, some just full animal heads.

All that research into reforging the essential chains of life, which back home on Earth we called genetic engineering, led to research in creating new life forms from existing ones. Or more like, re-creating extinct species from existing life.

See, the other thing about the Lemurisian Islands is that they're one of the richest sources of dinosaur fossils, and even some mummified dinosaur remains. Owning a collection of fossils or remains was a status symbol to the Lemurisians and no one owned more than the Imperial family. Some of the women on my crew said that the fossils were the source of Lemurisian obsession with reptiles. Some insisted that the actual reptiles living on the Islands were more than enough reason.

Whatever. The end result was staring me in the face, her breath reeking of recently rendered flesh.

Did you forget about her? Because I sure didn't.

The Tyrannosaurus Rex forcing its way toward me through the opening launch bay doors, maw gaping, long razor-sharp fangs glistening with dinospit, roared again.

"Bad Fluffy!" I yelled, as loud as I could. "Bad! Sit! Stay!"

Fluffy licked me, her long pointed tongue wet and warm with still more dinospit, soaking my face entirely.

"Gah," I moaned, wiping it off. I glared at the huge head and pointed at the ground. "SIT!"

Fluffy's head disappeared as she sat on the aerioport tarmac. All around me, girls were grinning. The smarter ones tried to hide their smirking faces, at least.

I wiped my face again, flicking the dinospit at the launch bay floor. Someone else would clean it up. That would teach them to smirk.

"Lower the plank," I ordered, impatiently waving my unsaliva'd hand at the girls on the crane.

They manoeuvred the boarding plank through the launch bay doors and I left the ship to say hello to my little friend.

The first Tyrannosaurs had been bred from the life chains of crocodiles and elephant birds. Made them very vicious and very stupid. Not too bright on the part of those original scientists, but they hadn't survived long enough to breed. The original dinos, I mean, not the scientists. Anyway. Later experiments had used tamer (or at least, tameable) animals, like horses, and dogs, until finally they'd developed a breed of pseudo-Tyrannosaurs that could be kept as house pets. The Imperial family had whole stables of them. Captain Python had given me Fluffy as a welcome gift. I had no idea what we were going to do with her when we left Lemuris.

And I do mean when, not if. As nice as they were, the Lemurisians were just a little too weird to be completely comfortable around them. Their reverence of reptiles wasn't the only thing. They had this caste system, where some people were born to be rulers, some to be thinkers, some to be traders, some warriors. And some were born to serve. An entire segment of their population born to be servants seemed a little too much like slavery to me, which was what the war was against, right?

Right, the war. It was going pretty well, I thought, if by 'well' you mean Lemurisian and Atlan forces fighting it out all over Afric. Most of Afric's Atlan-backed governors had been overthrown by their own people and nearly the entire continent was in some kind of military engagement or another. And all us air pirates had signed on as a kind of flying militia, striking swift and fast and running for it before things got too hot. We patrolled the edges of the war zone, making life difficult for anyone who allied themselves with Atlan, providing protection to anyone who joined in the struggle against them.

But it wasn't going great, you know? Afric is a pretty big continent and waging war from half the world away wasn't easy on the Lemurisians. If they didn't get some help soon, the war wouldn't reach its goal of an end to slavery and an end to Atlan rule.

I'm not exactly sure when 'ending slavery' became the same as 'overthrowing Atlan' but it had, and more people flocked to the 'overthrowing Atlan' banner than 'ending slavery' had attracted. Fine by me. I mean, I wanted to end slavery because it sucked. If that meant overthrowing the existing Imperial government, so be it. So long as whoever we put in charge got rid of slavery throughout the world. No one deserved to live like that. No one.

Anyway, whatever. Enough history and politics, right? I bet you want to hear more about Fluffy.

Chapter Three

Friends In High Places

Tyrannosaurs weren't exactly designed to sit, so Fluffy just sort of squatted down. Her tail was way too stiff, thick with dense muscle, to wag like a puppy's, but she sort of shimmied her entire rear end when she saw me and made to get up again.

"Stay, Fluffy," I said, warning her with a finger. She'd been well trained and stayed down. I stood beside her huge head, easily the size of my little single bed back home, acutely aware of her fang-filled mouth, large enough to swallow me whole. I rubbed her snout between her amber eyes, which closed with pleasure as she made a satisfied huff.

She was really striking to look at, up close. Her skin wasn't scales, more like beads, and were mostly shades of brick red, with darker stripes of mahogany brown. Captain Python had given me a saddle and gear to ride Fluffy with, but I hadn't tried them out yet. To be perfectly honest, the idea of riding a Tyrannosaur sort of scared me silly.

I know, ridiculous, right? I strap dangerous flying contraptions to my back and carry bombs across open bodies of deep, shark-infested water (yeah, I hadn't known that about Libertia's bay, either; apparently the mermaids use them like guard dogs), but climbing aboard a five ton, twenty foot tall, genetically engineered, otherwise extinct but most importantly *carnivorous* reptile gave me a case of the heebee-jeebees.

As I scratched Fluffy's snout, I looked up at my ship. The Furies had been pounded hard during the Battle Over Libertia. It had taken us weeks to refit her. Some sections we'd rebuilt completely, like our new command bridge, and the gun deck, which we'd refitted with military-grade turreted swivelling cannons. Between each cannon was a brand new volley gun on a tripod. We could put more bullets and cannonballs into the air than any three other pirate ships combined.

Other areas of the ship had only needed a good scrub and a new coat of paint, but those were fairly few. We'd added outrigger props at the stern to help with our manoeuvrability, which had required a surprising amount of reinforcement to our main interior structure. I'd also convinced Mrs. Shorty to give up some of her precious wall space (precious because it allowed for more shelves, and more shelves meant more loot could be stored) in the Booty Hold, to allow for additional launch doors for our ornithopters. Now we could launch to port and starboard, as well as directly beneath. It would also make loading and unloading the ship easier, which was how I'd convinced Mrs. Shorty.

The biggest change to The Furies was her hull. We'd removed all that heavy, thick wood and replaced it with gleaming metal. Thinner, stronger copalum, an alloy of copper and aluminium. Super strong, super light, all the rage in Atlan warships, apparently, since the Great White Dreadnought we'd taken down in Libertia had been made almost entirely out of the brassy, yellowish metal. Now the brass wings of The Furies' figurehead extended back into the copalum plates of the hull, blending and blurring like flames when we were in flight.

Our balloon was still black, except for the lookout posts I'd insisted we install. They were copalum cages at the front, sides, top and rear of the balloon, eight in total. All of them had intercoms, so the lookouts could communicate with the bridge. They also all had swivel-mounted volley guns, for protection. No good having a lookout up there if a Deathwing Guard could swoop in and slit her throat before we knew it.

"Forrrgive, pleassse," a woman interrupted my loving examination of my ship. I sighed, and tore my eyes away.

She knelt behind me, two paces away. Only truly trusted and beloved servants were allowed within that range, I'd found out.

"No problem, Hina," I answered, smiling. Not that she could see my smile, since she refused to look me in the face.

Hina was another gift from Captain Python. A couple of years older than me, she had the same long dark hair and dark eyes as Python's own personal servant, Tama. The biggest difference between Hina and Tama was their hair – Tama shaved most of hers off, while Hina still had most of hers. They both braided their remaining hair off to their left.

Actually, come to think of it. "You've changed to your hair."

She actually looked up for the briefest fraction of a second, flashing a truly stunning smile at me, before she remembered her place and looked at the ground again. "If it pleasse you, Misstress, her Highnesssss, may she everrr know sssun and rrrain in equal measssure, shade all her daysss and warrrmth all herrr nightss, hasss grrranted me the rrright to shave another fingerwidth of my ssscalp."

Allowing their servants to shave away their hair was a sign of trust in that servant, I'd learned. That was why Tama shaved everything but her braid. She'd been trusted to serve a member of the Imperial family. Hina must have impressed someone in authority.

"Congratulations, Hina," I said. "Listen, could you stand up? I'm getting a crick in my neck."

She nearly jumped to her feet, eyes fixed on the ground, hands folded in front of her. She wore a light blue sarong that reached to just past her knees and light sandals on her feet. In the sweltering tropical heat, I envied her. In the sky, it was never very warm. The wind kept us cool, if not freezing. Down here on land, though, the heat and humidity made sure I'd be soaked with sweat by the time we got to the palace.

"Does her Highness want to see me?" I asked. Getting Hina to volunteer information was a little like pulling teeth. Lemurisian servants really believed in the whole, 'don't speak unless spoken to' thing.

"Yess, Misstrresss."

"Do you have a carriage waiting?"

"Yess Misstrresss."

I stifled the urge to sigh in frustration. "Lead the way, Hina."

"Yess Misstrresss. Follow, pleassse?" She waved a hand forward, letting me follow by taking the lead.

M'lembe and Lauz fell into step beside me. They were on bodyguard duty today. A pair of Afric pirates who'd signed on after the Battle Over Libertia, they claimed to be sisters but aside from their coffee-dark skin, they couldn't be more unalike. M'lembe was well over six feet tall, a crack shot with a rifle or a six-shooter, with a ready smile and a hearty laugh. Her hair was done in dozens of tight tiny braids that reached down to her waist. Lauz was tiny, under five feet, shorter than either me or Restless, who was only thirteen. Lauz kept her hair cropped short, only smiled nervously, and was probably the deadliest knife fighter I'd ever seen. Both wore tight leather pants and vests, knee-high buckled boots and carried more weapons than any three of my other girls.

Hina led us to our ride, a painted triceratops outfitted with a bejewelled palanquin – a bamboo and silk box built on top of its back for us to sit in. The three of us climbed in and Hina jumped up behind the bony ridge on the triceratops' head. She took the reins and we lurched forward.

Let me tell you, a triceratops might not be the smoothest ride, but man, do people ever get out of your way. Especially a triceratops painted in the green and gold colours of the Imperial family.

Hina steered us through the winding streets of Mu with the ease of someone born here. Me, I'd have gotten lost after the first roundabout. Good thing I wasn't our navigator.

Mu's streets twisted and turned, rose and dropped, following the natural contours of the swamp that had been here before they built the city. Canals ran every direction, channelling the muddy swamp water out to sea, cramming the buildings together to accommodate Mu's teeming population. And believe me, the population teemed. I didn't even know what teeming meant until I'd been to Mu. Literally millions of people lived in the capital of Lemuris. You couldn't walk fifty feet down a street without rubbing up against a hundred people, at least. Let's just say the idea of personal space didn't mean much to them.

Bridges spanned the canals at regular intervals. The only interruptions to the interconnected stone structures came in the form of trees. Huge banyans, mangroves and cypresses towered everywhere, spreading shade from the tropical sun. Also vines, creeping along every vertical surface, straining to get out from the trees' shadows. Once in a while a riot of colour erupted in the form of flower gardens. And, of course, the clothes of the people, every brilliant colour but green or gold. Those two colours were reserved for the clothing of the Imperial family.

I knew from experience that you could hire a flat-bottomed ferry to travel the canals. It was faster than travelling along the crowded roads, but forget anything you might be thinking about romantic gondola rides while the boatsman serenades you. Mu's ferry boatsmen weren't romantic and wouldn't sing if you paid them. Most of them were wrapped up in foul-smelling bandages, head to foot like a mummy, with thick goggles protecting their eyes, all to keep them from being eaten to death by mosquitoes. Those beasts were huge, more like bloodsucking sparrows. I'd taken a ferry only once and still had the mosquito bites to prove it.

Luckily we didn't go anywhere near the canals. Hina guided us uphill, toward the Imperial quarter. Or maybe it was quarters. The section of the city dedicated to the Imperial family had grown over the centuries, starting from a few neighbouring estates. Those estates had added outbuildings and offices, joining them all together with cobblestone paths. Those paths became covered against the summer sun, then enclosed against the winter monsoons, and finally added to with more buildings, rising up when they couldn't spread out any more without spilling out of the Imperial quarter, until the palace was now a maze of corridors, walkways, promenades and stairwells, all connecting one building to the next, until finally the Imperial section of the city and the Imperial palace were pretty much one and the same.

I'd gotten all this information from Princess Python the few times we'd met since my arrival in Lemuris. She'd talk and talk about the past of her people (I got the impression she was kind of a history buff), but she wouldn't talk about the war, or what her government wanted to do, or why I'd been invited here in the first place.

Honestly? I thought she was lonely. She didn't talk about it much, but apparently her family weren't especially nice to her. And as a member of the Imperial family, everyone wanted something from her. It was hard to make friends. So when I came along and didn't want anything from her, it struck her as fresh and unusual.

That's what I thought, at least. Could be she was just a weirdo who wanted to hang out with another weirdo. Or could be she wanted a piece of my fame. Infame? Is infame a word? Okay, infamy. Anyway. Hanging out with the star of all those dreadful novels might raise her standing in her family, I dunno.

Dawn glowed on the distant horizon when the Imperial quarter swallowed up our triceratops palanquin ride. Elegantly carved stone buildings crowded in around us, towering high enough to blot out the sky. Upper levels had bridges and walkways between buildings, so even looking straight up you'd only see little patches of sky. Claustrophobic much? Oh hell yeah.

Hina directed? steered? steered our ride through the narrow, maze-like streets of the Imperial quarter. If I ever needed to leave the palace in a hurry, I'd be in trouble. Five or six turns and I'd be hopelessly lost. But Hina knew exactly where to go, which route to take, and got us to the central complex without any problems.

When we stopped, Hina tossed the reins to a waiting attendant. He had almost all his hair, I saw, which meant he was lower down the servant ladder than Hina. She didn't even speak to him, and except for the brief moment he'd looked up to catch the reins, he kept his gaze firmly on the ground. I had a momentary vision of having to come back to Lemuris after the war to shatter their caste system, once we'd liberated all the slaves, automatons, patchworks and everyone else used and abused by the Atlans. It wasn't a pleasant thought.

We climbed stone steps to a huge open doorway, framed by vine-covered columns. Lizards of every shape and size creeped and crawled over every surface, watching us pass without a hint of fear or even shyness. Once we entered the complex, the darkness had to be beaten back with candles and torches, which I knew from previous visits burned day and night. Flickering shadows followed us as we went forward, deeper and deeper into the complex. Corridors twisted and turned, spiralling upward. Finally we reached another open doorway, leading out into a circular atrium, ringed all around by huge trees. At the centre of the atrium glistened a perfectly clear, perfectly circular pool, and at the bottom of the pool, completely submerged, sat Princess Python, perfectly still.

As I approached the pool, M'lembe and Lauz took up positions by the door. Though we couldn't see them, there were probably a dozen Imperial guards hidden in the greenery of the atrium. If I wasn't safe here, there wasn't much my girls could do about it.

I stopped at the edge of the pool and waited for Python. That wasn't her real name, by the way, it was her nickname, given to her when she was young because she loved hugs and when she got older she excelled at wrestling. Her real name was an Imperial family secret.

She burst out of the pool with a gasp. Tama said something in Lemurisian. I hadn't even noticed her, sitting quiet and still, curled in the roots of one of the bigger trees.

"Pah," Python said, climbing out of the pool. She was completely naked. I'd actually gotten used to that. She tended to go nude when in private. Like a dozen guards, half that many servants and three guests was somehow private. Nudity wasn't a big deal here, though. Part of me envied her lack of self-consciousness.

"Two and one half minutesss, Val, thisss isss good?" she asked, taking a towel from a nearly bald servant.

"Underwater? Um, yeah."

"Pah," she said again, obviously displeased. "A cousssin I have.

Fourrr minutes she can be underwaterrr. Thisss I have ssseen!"

"Wow, that's really amazing."

She gave me a hiss through her filed teeth, then went back to drying her long green dreadlocks. Droplets of water clung to her tattooed skin, making the inked scales glisten like real ones. You'd almost believe she was part snake.

"Thisss cousssin isss not amazing," she muttered. "Thisss cousssin isss doing nothing but hold herrr brrreath underwaterrr, trrraining, trrraining. She isss not captain of ship. She isss not adderrrblade fighterrr. She isss breath-holderrr. Pah!"

"So why are you trying to beat her record, then?"

She glared at me, but at least she didn't hiss this time. "It isss a family matterrr," she muttered eventually, letting the towel drop to the stones at her feet.

What 'a family matter' meant was, someone told the Empress about her breath-holding cousin and she was impressed, so Python thought (or at least hoped) that if she could break the record the Empress would hear about her and be impressed, too.

Now, from what I'd learned, the Imperial family was huge. Like, I used to think my family with four kids (myself included) was pretty big, but that ain't nothin' on the Lemurisian Imperial family. Python had six brothers and seven sisters, dozens of aunts and uncles and hundreds of cousins. Don't get me started on second and third cousins, and how many times removed. It was a huge, huge family and they all lived in the palace. And they all knew exactly how far away from the Imperial throne they were. Python was seven hundred and sixth in line to inherit. The number changed every time someone died or had a baby. Basically it was a minor miracle if the Empress even knew Python's name.

I didn't mention it to her. It was obviously a touchy subject. Instead, I asked, "So what can I do for you, Highness?"

She grinned and rolled her eyes, her mood shifting as fast as... well, as fast as a snake. "I asssk you not calling me that."

I grinned back, as cheeky as I could. "Right, I keep forgetting."

"Therrre isss meeting today," she answered. "To dissscusss the warrr and Lemurrrisss involvement."

"What do you mean, involvement? You guys are like, the main reason there's a war at all."

"Yesss," she answered, then waved her hand at Tama. Tama snapped her fingers and servants who had to have been hiding behind the trees, just waiting, came out carrying trays of fruit and pitchers of cold juice. I took a beautiful porcelain cup full of something orange but not orange juice, and sipped it gratefully. The rising sun had just crested the walls of the atrium and already the air had warmed. At least this high up in the palace, the humidity wasn't so bad.

"We arrre the rrreassson for the warrr," Python agreed after sipping from her cup. "But it isss not ourrr warrr."

Chapter Four

My Big Mouth Makes Me Some Enemies

"What do you mean, not their war?" Molly asked.

I shrugged, fighting the urge to yawn. My bed called to me, sweetly seductive. "That's what she said, 'not our war.' They're not happy with the losses that they're taking on the Afric front. I think they expected more help."

"From who?" Violette asked, sipping from her cup of black coffee. She'd just gotten up and still wore her dressing gown.

I'd called a meeting in the officers' mess once I'd gotten back to The Furies. All my chiefs were there, except Serena, who slumbered away against the risen sun.

"Sure an' I think it's enough we're doin'," Doc Regan said, crossing her arms and frowning.

"We, The Furies, or we, the pirate armada?" Miss Merryweather asked from where she stood, leaning lightly on the walking stick she'd started using after the Battle Over Libertia. She'd banged up her hip and it hadn't healed right, making it uncomfortable for her to sit for long periods.

"Not us," I said, answering Violette. "Not The Furies or the pirates. Others."

"Like who?" Inga asked.

"Like the Amazonians," I answered. "Like the Zhou. Like... oh, basically, like everyone who has a reason to hate Atlan."

"That's an awfully long list," Molly said.

"Anyway, they're having a big meeting tonight after sunset and she wants me to go. As an 'honoured guest'."

"What about Captain Jones?" Miss Merryweather asked.

"She didn't say."

"As the nominal leader of the pirate armada, you'd think they'd invite him," Violette said.

"Maybe they did, but Python didn't say," I answered. "Anyway, I wanted you all to know what was going on, to keep the rumours to a minimum. If word starts to spread through the armada that the Lemurisians are thinking about pulling out, that'll be the end of that. Half of them will slip away in the night and the other half will wait until their crews get back from shore leave before making a run for it."

The looks they shared said more than words could have. If the Lemurisians pulled out of the fight, there wouldn't be a war left to wage. There would be a slaughtering of pirates. Apparently the Atlan propoganda was that we'd started the war, assaulting a training mission of raw recruits without warning or provocation. That they'd attacked Libertia first never seemed to come up. Pirates had started the war and Atlan would finish it. And us. For good.

I had no intention of letting that happen, of course. We'd bring an end to Atlan tyranny or die trying.

I know how that sounds. Crazy and idealistic. Stupid and childish. Ridiculous. Bordering on suicidal. But sometimes it's the crazy, idealistic, ridiculous ideas that motivate people most. Sometimes it's not enough for people to fight back. Sometimes they need something to fight for.

The Atlan dictatorship over most of the world had brought peace and prosperity in the past, but it had also resulted in slavery becoming an accepted practice. In women forced into government-sanctioned prostitution. In workhouses and manufactories that worked their employees to death, then patchworked the bodies into another kind of slave workforce.

Atlan treated people like cattle, kept their neighbours crippled by poverty and pollution. Expected the entire world to kneel before them. Only the most loyal of grovelling lickspittle puppet governors were trusted even the slightest. They proved their worth by being even more vicious and tyrannical than their rulers. Atlan had to be stopped.

I wasn't from Ayrth. I had crazy ideas about equality and democracy, because I came from a world that had already fought to preserve those ideals. So now, it was Ayrth's turn to rise up and fight. And if I could help them, I would.

There wasn't much more to say about the upcoming meeting, so we left the officers' mess and I went to bed. When I woke up, the sun glowed crimson on the western horizon. Domina stood next to my bed, a cup of ice cold lemon water at the ready. Sleeping the heat and humidity of the day away meant a sweaty, sticky sleep. Since arriving in Lemuris I'd gotten dehydrated twice. It hadn't been pretty, and I had no intention of repeating it.

I drank the glass before even getting out of bed, then quickly dressed. Pale blue short-sleeved blouse, dark blue corset and a copper skirt. Knee-high alligator leather boots. As a final touch I added some sapphire earrings and a matching necklace. I usually wore the blouse buttoned to the neck, but the last of the day's heat would have left me drenched in no time at all, so I left the top couple of buttons open.

Domina combed the worst of the tangles out of my hair and pulled it back into a simple braid. Then she handed me my bowler. I went looking for Serena.

She wasn't far, or hard to find. Once the sun had set, my vampyri first mate always checked the bridge first.

"Captain Wal," she grinned at my outfit.

I spun in place to let her see it. "Dress to impress, I guess."

"Have ve added rhyming to your alliterative stress release, now?"

I tend to alliterate when I get stressed, but since you're reading this and probably the first two books, I'm guessing you already knew that.

"No," I laughed. "You have command tonight."

"You don't vish me to come vith you?"

"I do, but the invite was for me only."

"Wery vell."

"It's a no-weapons meeting, so Tring's coming with me."

That made her chuckle, low and soft and filled with malicious delight. In a hundred years of speaking, I couldn't convey half of what she managed to say without words.

"Be careful," Serena said. "Lemurisians are a strange people."

"I'll try not to do anything stupid."

"You never do anything stupid," she said, but her single raised eyebrow added, *Foolhardy and impulsive, perhaps, but never stupid.*

I left her in the bridge and went to our mess hall, snagging something quick to eat. When I finished I headed for the Launch Bay, where I found Tring waiting for me. She gave me a quick nod and led the way.

This being a big official meeting with the heads of Lemuris, I decided to bite the bullet and ride Fluffy. She had more than enough room on her back to carry me and Tring.

When I was seven I fell in love with horses, like a lot of girls. I begged and begged my parents to let me take lessons and when I was ten I spent one glorious summer learning to ride and care for horses. Horse camp. It was awesome.

Riding Fluffy wasn't anything like riding a horse. Oh, it was similar, if a horse had two legs and stood twenty feet off the ground. And Fluffy had been super well trained. Only thing was, I hadn't been trained at all. At least the people in the streets were used to getting out of the way of Imperial tyrannosaurs. No one got trampled, at least.

Still, we arrived at the palace in basically one piece, although much, much sooner than if we'd gone by triceratops. I'd have to remember that, if I was ever insane and desperate enough to ride Fluffy again. I left her with a stablehand. Tama was waiting for us, to lead us inside.

Princess Python met us about halfway there, and Tama fell into step behind us, after a quick exchange with Python in Lemurisian.

"She will trrranssslate," Python explained. She wore a loincloth of some gold fabric, tons of jewellery and very little else.

Once we reached the meeting hall, I felt distinctly overdressed. Virtually everyone in the room was nearly naked. Lizard-skin loincloths and bikini tops were pretty much the only concessions to modesty. All of them had snake-skin tattoos. Most of them glittered with jewellery and piercings.

Some heads turned as we entered, but most people ignored us. The heads that had turned went back to their conversations just as quickly.

I glanced at Tring. "Stay outside."

"Of course, Captain," she answered with a small bow, then stepped back out of the room.

Python's shoulders were squared back as she led me and Tama into the hall. The room was vaguely circular, carved of white marble. White marble columns supported a white marble ceiling, while white marble steps led down along white marble tiers to a circular central space that was tiled with white marble. It was the plainest room I'd seen in all of Mu, lit by electric lights in gold fixtures strung along the ceiling. Compared to the riots of vegetation I'd seen everywhere else, the hall was shockingly stark.

Python led me to a tier off to one side. Opposite the entrance sat a huge white marble chair, the only seat in the room. Anyone else who wanted to sit had to sit on the floor. Python dropped down to sit cross-legged. I joined her there. Tama knelt close behind me, eyes firmly on the floor.

The body heat from all the people in the hall began to get oppressive. No one else seemed to notice. Maybe they were just determined not to show it, I dunno. Between the dull roar of everyone murmuring in a language I didn't understand, the sweltering heat, and sitting on an uncomfortable stone floor, I began to wonder if my invitation hadn't been some kind of weird joke. Make fun of the new girl by making her sit through something that promised to be long and boring.

A bald servant stepped into the room and made an announcement at the top of his lungs. Everyone got to their feet. Then probably the oldest woman I've ever seen walked slowly into the room. One eye glittered darkly, surrounded by a web of wrinkles. The other was the colour of milk. Like everyone else, she was covered in tattoos and had a fair number of piercings, too. The weight of the gold hoops she wore in both ears made them droop. Scars traced white lines across her withered body, reminders of ancient battles. Everyone bowed their heads as she passed. I noticed her smile was missing quite a few filed teeth.

The bald servant helped the old woman down the steps and across the room, while she smiled and nodded at people she recognized with her one good eye. She sat and another completely bald servant presented the old woman with a serving platter loaded down with fruits. She plucked a bunch of grapes from the platter and devoted all her attention to them.

The crowd sat down.

"That's the Empress of Lemuris?" I whispered to Python.

She glanced my way and nodded. "May she rrreign in daysss of sssun and nightsss of rrrain."

A man stood and strode to the centre of the room. He wore lizard-skin wristbands, and his face was studded with piercings along his jawline, cheekbones, and brow. His dreadlocks were dyed blue. He turned around in a circle, waiting for everyone's attention.

The murmurs hushed and he spoke in Lemurisian.

"I have hearrrd it sssaid that the warrr isss going badly. The warrr isss not going badly," Tama translated for me, almost real time. She was that good, so I'll spare you the he said, she said.

"It isss going terrrribly!" he announced angrily. "We arrre losssing on everrry frrront! Afrrric isss a disssassssterrr! Our land trrroopsss arrre bogged down in the winterrr rrrainsss. Ourrr shipsss arrre outgunned, outclassssed! We cannot continue this warrr with any hope of victorrry."

"Who is this guy?" I asked Python in a whisper.

"General Komodo," she answered, looking like she had something nasty in her mouth. "He long opposssesss the warrr."

"No kidding."

A tall woman stepped out onto the floor. Like him, she wore multiple piercings in her face. Her dreadlocks were dyed bright red, almost as bright a red as my own hair.

"Admiral Salamander," Python explained.

"General," Salamander began, Tama translating. "Thank you forrr yourrr worrrdsss. Yourrr caution in thessse matterrrsss isss legendarrry."

Komodo hissed through filed teeth. "Admirrral, my caution hasss kept our sssoldierrrss alive."

"It is not the place of sssoldiersss to live!" she exploded at him. "It is theirrr place to ssserrve the will of the Emprresss! If that ssserrrvice isss fulfilled with theirrr death, then that is theirrr ssserrrvice!"

The audience murmured and grumbled in agreement. The General was definitely in a minority.

"We all know why we enterrred this warrr," the Admiral went on. "Atlan aggrrression left unchecked can only lead to grrreaterrr trrroublesss to come. Theirrr attempt to invade Merrrinasssy would have been the firrrsst sstep in an invasion of Lemurrrisssss itsself! It isss only thrrough the actionsss of prrivate individualsss and our own Airrrship Armada that we ssstopped them in time."

"Prrivate individualsss," the General sneered. "Pirrratesss, thievesss and whorress!"

"Hey, that's me he's talking about."

Python rolled her eyes at his insults.

The Admiral got right up in his face. "Even they can sssee Atlan must be ssstopped! Enssslaverrry! Patchworrking! Where doesss theirr contempt for theirr own citizenss end? Wherre will it sssink to, for a conquerrred people?"

"Admiral, Atlan contempt for the sssanctity of life is nothing new," the General said quietly. "And now, I have the ssssad duty to tell you of newsss I have frrrom the frrront, which reached me just momentsss beforrre thiss meeting began."

"What newsss?" the Admiral asked.

"The Blighted rrroam the battlefield."

The chamber erupted in cries of outrage and horror. It was minutes before anyone calmed down enough to listen to the rest of his news.

Me, I still had no idea what the Blight was. People used it as a swear word, that's all I knew. Molly's dad had died of the Blight, so I guessed it was some kind of disease, but beyond that, no one wanted to talk about it. They'd talk around it, but no one would give me a straight answer. I made a mental note to sit Doc Regan down and get her to tell me, as soon as I got back to the ship.

"What madnessss isss thisss?" the Admiral asked.

"I have it frrrom a highly trrrussted ssssource," the General answered. An aide passed him a piece of paper, which he passed to the Admiral. She scanned it, her tanned face going pale.

"We cannot win a warrr againsst madmen," Komodo said. "They will ssstop at nothing, ussse any weapon at theirrr dissssposssal. We cannot win."

Admiral Salamander handed him back the piece of paper, then squared her shoulders and said, "Generrral, you'rrre wrrrong. Thisss isss not prrroof we cannot win. Thisss isss morrre rrreason to keep fighting." She turned to look at us. "We musssst fight! These madmen musssst be ssstopped, beforrre they dessstrrroy the entirrre worrrld! Afrrric will be rrrenderrred a wasssteland by the Blighted. The farrrmlandsss and rrranchesss therrre will turrrn to dessssserrrt, once the Blighted have shambled thrrrough, killing and eating everrrything in their path! Atlan would rrratherrr ssstarrrve themsssselvesss, dessstrrroy theirrr grrreatessst ssssource of food, than allow usss a chance of liberrrating the continent frrrom theirrr tyrrranny! This madnesssss must be ssstopped!"

"We cannot do thisss oursssselvesss," a slim man said from where he sat in the audience. He stood up so everyone could see him.

"Asssp," Python whispered. "Chancellor of the Trrreasury."

"Our forcesss and ssssuppliesss arrre ssstretched thin as it isss, Admiral," Chancellor Asp explained. "And sssupport frrrom any other nationsss who might be sssimilarrrly inclined againssst Atlan hasss not been forrthcoming. What do you propossse to do? Fight to the last?"

The Admiral looked like she'd rather not say what she had to say, but said it anyway. "Perrhapsss sssupporrrt hasss not been forrthcoming, because they have not been asssked to help."

The audience erupted into angry murmurs as everyone started talking at once. The only person who seemed utterly uninterested was the Empress, who was picking something out from between her toes.

I turned to Python, who was shaking her head. "I don't get it. What's the big deal?"

"You cannot underrrssstand. It isss not the Lemurrrisss way."

"What, asking for help? Oh come on, it's not that hard."

You know those awkward moments when you're in a crowd, and it's loud because everyone's talking, and you raise your voice to be heard just as the crowd mysteriously and coincidentally all goes quiet? Yeah. That happened just as I said "it's not that hard."

So naturally everyone looked at me.

"You arrre Captain Sssunssset Val, arrre you not?" General Komodo said in Atlan, meant as a sign of respect, I'm sure. Or else a not-so-subtle reminder that I was a foreigner. "The grrreat warrriorr. The Herrro of Liberrrtia. I admit I am sssurrrprisssed you arrre sssso young. And invited herre asss a courrtesssy. To a perrrsson made famousss by thisss grrrowing conflict. You wish to sssspeak, Captain?"

I stood up, trying to keep from being embarrassed. "Thank you, General. I'm sorry I don't speak Lemurisian, that I can do you the same honour you've shown me. But that we both speak Atlan is sort of the point, isn't it? Is there any place in the world that Atlan hasn't reached? Is there any corner of the globe they haven't soiled? We all know they have to be stopped. But the question is, are we the ones to do it? Is now the time? I say, yes. Yes, we're the ones to do it – Lemurisians and pirates both. And yes, now is the time. When will there be a better time?"

"Forrrgive me, Captain," the General interrupted, "but yourrr pirrratess amount to a few dozen shipsss, a few hundrred ssailorsss. Lemurrrisian casualtiesss arrre alrrready in the thousandsss!"

"I didn't say it wouldn't be hard," I said, raising my voice over the angry muttering of the audience. "And I didn't say it would be fair!"

"No, you sssaid wasss that it would be easssy to rrrecrrruit help!" the General yelled at me, finger pointed in accusation.

I looked around the room. Everyone looked like I'd volunteered to murder babies while they slept. "Um, yeah. You just... ask."

"She isss not Lemurrrisian," the Admiral said to the audience, in Atlan, but obviously for my benefit. "She does not know ourrr customsss."

"You're right, Admiral, I'm not from Lemuris. I'm not from anywhere you've ever heard of, to be honest. And maybe I just broke all kinds of taboos, but it seems to me that when you need help, you ask. Where I'm from, it's not a crime."

"It isss an admission of weaknesssss," Python murmured to me. "Lemurrrisss cannot be ssseen asss weak."

"Is that what this is about?" I asked the crowd. "You don't want to be seen as weak? Listen, if Atlan wipes you off the map, you won't be seen as weak. You'll be seen as dead. Is that somehow better?"

"You do not underrrsssstand," the Admiral said.

"Look, if it's that big a deal, I'll go ask for help," I heard myself say before my brain had caught up with my mouth. One of these days, that's really going to get me into trouble. "That way it won't seem like Lemuris is asking for help and we'll get the allies we need to win this and end Atlan's tyranny once and for all."

The room erupted in discussion, some angry, some excited, all at the same time. I glanced at Princess Python, but she was arguing with some guy behind her.

A voice cracked through the crowd. "Enough!"

Everyone stopped talking and turned. The Empress stood up from her throne.

"Sssend the girrrl," she said, waving her bunch of grapes in my general direction. She left the room without another word.

Chapter Five

Dinner Plans With Friends

"Then what happened?" my host asked for maybe the tenth time.

"People left. Admiral Salamander sent word that she wanted to talk to me. Python brought me home via ornithopter. I think she needed to get some air."

I could relate, too. After everything that happened at the palace, I needed to clear my head and think. How the hell was I supposed to convince other countries to help us?

My host, Captain Remarkable Jones of the good ship Mistress O' Merit, banged his open palm against the table and laughed, loud and huge. And believe me, when a guy as big as Remy lets loose with laughter, the chandelier shook and the windows rattled.

"Unbelievable, ducks," Captain Guinevere Tallyho added, once I got my hearing back. Like I said, Remy's laugh is something else. Guinny reached across the table and poured some more wine into all the solid gold goblets Remy had 'liberated' from some Amazonian traders.

"I say, pet, you really stuck your nose in the muck this time, wot?" Gwendolyn, Guinny's twin sister, said, chuckling into her cup.

"How did Ol' Stick-Up-His-Bum take the Imperial decree?" Remy asked, wiping tears from his eyes. His face had gone tomato red as he laughed and was slowly fading to normal.

"General Komodo? He looked..." I thought about it. "He looked like someone had shoved a stick up his bum."

That set him laughing again. We waited for him to catch his breath.

"What's the deal, anyway, Remy? Why is that so funny?" I asked.

"Oh, we've had an adventure or two, Komodo and me," Remy answered, taking a swig from his goblet. "It must just be killing him inside, working alongside pirates."

"Not a fan?"

"He's got a bit of a reputation, love," Guinny said. "Pirate killer. No mercy. Nasty bit of business, wot?"

"And now I've stuck my nose in it," I said. "Great."

"It is great!" Remy said, leaning forward to thump a thick finger against his solid oak table. It was sort of a testimony to his success as an airship pirate that not only did he own so many luxuries like oak tables and gold cups, but that he'd let himself get so big and fat.

See, on an airship, it all boils down to weight. The more weight you have to haul, the harder it is to get your ship in the air and keep it there. So a captain who's let himself gain weight, instead of worrying about every unnecessary ounce aboard his ship, is a captain who's so good at his job he doesn't need to worry.

"It is great," Remy repeated, leaning back again, staring into nothing as his mind whirled, plotting, scheming, planning. In the short while I'd known him, I'd come to respect and even fear Remy's genius.

"Here's what we'll do," he said after a few minutes of quiet thought. Minutes I'd spent silently drinking my watered wine, cultivating patience, not something I'm all that good at.

"The Lemurisians need help fighting Atlan, but they're too proud for their own good to ask for it," he explained unnecessarily. I'd also learned that this was part of his thing. He'd point out the obvious for a while, then dazzle us with his brilliant scheme so that we were left wondering why we hadn't thought of it ourselves.

Of course, I wasn't above a little harmless feeding his ego. "Yeah, why is that?"

"They're an empire unto themselves, this part of the world," he answered. "Control most of the Hindystani Sea, all the way to Neppon. It's a big area, sparsely populated. Hard to control. Difficult to get the word out if there's trouble. Weeks can go by without communication from some of these islands. Not a lot of resources, either, so they're dependant on trade to keep things going. Mostly trade with countries on the fringe of Atlan, countries that could go either way in this war. If the Lemurisians seem like they can't handle this war themselves, seem like they might actually lose, those countries will jump ship faster than you can blink."

"I dunno, I can blink pretty quick," I said, demonstrating.

He rewarded my cheekiness with a grin. "So if those countries jump ship, Lemuris loses trade, can't supply their armies, then poof, there goes the war."

"But if we ask for help, nobody cares, because we're just ruddy pirates who would probably turn tail and run at the first sign of trouble, wot?" Gwen said.

"Speaking of, who do we ask?"

"We'll start with the Zhou," Remy answered, quick enough to make me think he might have had this planned for a while now. He reached behind him to a massive pile of scrolled-up maps and picked one, then rolled it out on the table while the twins and I cleared some space.

Remy stabbed his thick finger at the edge of the map, where China would have been if I had been back home. "If we get those inscrutable bastards involved, get them attacking Russankya, then we keep the Russ legions occupied. Keep them from resupplying their losses in Afric."

"There's a number of solid blokes in Anglica wouldn't mind getting into this cut-up," Guinny said, pointing at the island off the coast of Europa. "Too long they've toiled under the oppressors' heels, eh?"

Remy nodded. "Quite right. You ladies see what you can do in Anglica. Sunset, you've some Zhou in your crew, right? Mind taking a trip to the exotic East?"

I shrugged and grinned. "I haven't had good Chinese, I mean, Zhou food in a long time."

Chapter Six

Preparations & Explanations

I wanted to set out as quick as we could, but first things first. Resupplying The Furies wasn't going to happen overnight. Rounding up all our crew would take even longer. I could barely remember half their names, there were so many of them. Gigi wasn't the only animan any more, nor was Molly the only one with prosthetic replacements for missing limbs. Serena remained our only vampyri, which suited her and the crew just fine.

But, well, there were other concerns.

Princess Python came to The Furies the next day and asked to join the crew. Actually, 'informed us she would be joining the crew' is a little more accurate.

"But you're already the captain of your own ship," I said.

"Pah! A ship that cannot fly wherrre I wish it to go. A ship that ansswerrsss not my commands but those of Admirrral Sssalamanderrr."

Her words were mild but her tone was bitter. I raised an eyebrow. "You don't like the Admiral?"

"May she know sssun and rrrain in equal measurrre," Python answered. "But she tellsss me wherrre to go, I mussst go. Not like you. Go asss you like, do asss you will."

"I'm not going to Zhou on a vacation," I explained. "Captain Jones asked me to go and see what I can do to help the war."

"Asssk. Not tell."

I kind of saw her point, then. I nodded. "Okay, fine. You want aboard, you come aboard. But uh, Princess? There's only one captain aboard The Furies."

She grinned that filed-teeth grin. "Yes, Captain Val. Of courrsssse, Captain Val."

I hoped I wouldn't regret my decision as she practically ran down the gangplank to go get her things. But when she came back an hour later, I knew there would be trouble, right from the start.

She'd brought Tama with her, carrying Python's bags.

I stopped them, right at the gangplank. Python looked confused. "Captain?"

"No servants," I said, pointing at Tama. "You want to be part of my crew, you haul your own weight. The only ones who give orders are me and my crew chiefs. Everybody else is equal."

Python looked at me like I was talking crazy talk, then shrugged. She said something to Tama in Lemurisian, and Tama dropped Python's bags to the deck. Python bent to pick them up, then set her shoulders and looked me square in the eye.

"Yesss?" she said.

"Welcome aboard The Furies, Python," I said, jerking a thumb over my shoulder. As she walked past me, I said, "Miss Merryweather will find you a bunk with the others and put you on a crew."

Python slowed to nod at me, then disappeared into the ship.

Tama stared past me at Python's back, distressed. She glanced at me. "Captain Val, I wish to join your crrrew."

I crossed my arms. "I won't take any runaway servants aboard."

She looked past me again. "I have ssserrrved herrr sssince she was three yearsss old and I only ssseven. It will not be easssy forrr herrr, thisss I know, not having a ssserrrvant. She isss impetuousss and prrroud, at times almost uncarrring of herrr dutiesss in ssservice of that prrride. She will rrrequire a delicate hand to learrrn herrr place in the crew. I can be of ssservice in thisss."

"You join my crew, you won't be waiting on her, hand and foot. You'll be assigned wherever Miss Merryweather puts you."

"As you sssay, Captain Val."

"You won't be missed? Back at the palace, I mean."

Tama smiled. "I go wherrre goesss the princessss, Captain. All know thisss."

I shrugged. "Okay then. Report to Miss Merryweather."

"Thank you, Captain," she said, bowing. "May you everrr know sssun and rrrain."

"Yeah, thanks," I muttered as she passed me, boarding the ship. I really hoped I wasn't going to regret letting Python on board.

The rest of my days were filled with figuring out supplies, fresh water, gas reserves for the balloon cells, crew reshuffling. I insisted that every woman aboard my ship at least serve some time on every crew, so that if anything happened to them, we wouldn't be stuck with a crew full of fighters and engineers and none of them knowing how to fly the ship or cook a meal. It was one of my many innovations to typical shipboard life. Every other ship out there had teams of specialists who were very good at one thing and useless at everything else. I'd seen more than enough ships go down during the Battle Over Libertia because of it. Remy's, for one.

All this to say that it took three days before I had a chance to corral Doc Regan and ask her about the Blight.

We were alone together in my cabin. Even though the refit of The Furies had drastically reduced the size of my personal quarters, it was still big enough for a small dining table, big enough for two.

"Tell me about the Blight," I said after we'd finished our meal.

She went pale and glanced at my sideboard, where my various bottles of booze sat. I barely drank at all, but most of my crew chiefs indulged, some a little more than others.

"Drink?" I asked, grabbing a bottle of gin and two glasses, splashed gin in both and started adding lemonade from the pitcher.

"Aye, sure an' I will," she answered, reaching for her glass, not waiting for me to add the lemonade. She gulped it down and handed it back for more.

"It's that bad?" I asked.

"Superstitious fools'll tell ye that e'en mentionin' the Blight's a sure way t' get it yerself," she answered, waiting for the lemonade this time. "O' course, that's nonsense. It's been proven tha' th' only way to become Blighted is through direct transfer of infected saliva into the blood stream."

"So it's a disease, like a virus?"

"Aye, well, yes and no," she said, looking into her glass. "It began, ye see, with th' patchworks. They've no natural means of repairin' themselves. They don't heal, not at all. So when they're damaged, they get sewn up. New bits and pieces are added as time goes on. Well, about fifteen years ago, someone come up wi' th' brilliant idear tha' maybe there's a way to keep patchworks from fallin' t' bits, like."

She took a long sip. "Right about then a team of researchers found a tomb in Upper Aegyptia. A place dedicated to th' preservation of dead flesh. Well, seemed to everyone involved they'd found the answer right there, didn't they? So they get right down t' examinin' and experimentin'. Turned those ancient embalmin' practices into modern science.

"Well, th' day finally comes for the grand experiment t' take place, only does it go as planned? It does not. The reanimation techniques of the patchworkin' process is right at odds with the embalmin' and preservin' techniques they'd developed. So there goes that bright idea."

"I don't get it," I said. "What does any of this have to do with a saliva-transmitted disease?"

She held out her glass for a refill and I provided it. "Well, sure an' yer right about that. Could be I was stallin' a wee bit, waitin' for yer gin t' kick in."

"It's really that bad?"

She downed half her drink before answering. "No one knows how it came to happen, the new embalmin' techniques bein' applied to a livin' being. Some doctors I know say the original developers tried it on themselves, sure it would work at prolonging their natural lifespan. Me, I'm not so sure it weren't a pursuit of science for the sake of the pursuit of science. 'Well, it didn't work on patchworks, boyos, what say we try it on a live specimen?' Now, maybe they tried it on an unanimated patchwork first, but I'll bet you it weren't that. I'll bet you they tried it on themselves, short straw got the first injection. That's if you believe they tried it on themselves. Some believe they rounded up a bunch of likely and unwilling subjects and stuck them wi' it, first, like."

"Does it matter?"

She blinked. "Eh?"

"Why does it matter how it started? What happened next?"

"Oh. Well, the entire team of scientists and researchers died, of course. The first victims. All Blighted. And somehow it spread. You get outbreaks of it, here and there. Officials jump on it, double-quick, burn it out. Should've been easy to contain, in those early days, but o' course, no one knew how contagious it'd be, how easily it'd spread... how horrible it'd become. It's no surprise t' me the Atlans keep some Blighted chained up somewhere, ready to release at a moment's notice."

She still hadn't really answered the question. "What happens to someone infected with the Blight?"

"Depends on the person. A patchwork or a vampyri, now, the Blight simply kills. Necrotizes, you might say. An animan or a human, that's a different thing entirely. And even then, it will have a different effect. I've heard tell o' some individuals holdin' off th' effects for as long as a week before succumbin'. O' course, they usually have a good reason to hold it off. Loved ones nearby, tha' sort o' thing."

"Doc. What does the Blight do to a regular human?"

"Kills them, o' course. But they stay animated. The embalming processes keep them from rottin' to pieces, but the body does begin to atrophy. Especially the brain. Renders higher brain functions inoperable. Reverts 'em to a bestial state. Carnivorous, cannibalistic. They must eat flesh. Animal flesh, dead flesh, fresh flesh. Don't much matter. Some retain a high degree of strength and agility for some time. Others shamble aimlessly, lost in hopeless depression as the hunger claims them completely. Almost all suffer from an unreasoning rage and a blind hate. Rage at their fate, and hatred for the livin'. And because o' th' embalmin', reanimatin' chemicals involved in the initial experiments, they cannot be killed. Not without destroying the entire body, or at least what remains of the brain."

Okay, so I'd seen my share of horror movies back home. I knew what she was getting at. And I'd always considered them sort of silly. But what she was describing didn't sound silly. It sounded horrible. "Zombies. The Blighted are zombies."

Doc Regan shrugged. "I've never heard that word. Blighted they are and Blighted they shall remain all throughout their nightmarish existence."

I poured us both another drink.

Chapter Seven

Plundered By Prehistoric Party Poopers

It was another two days before we were ready to cast off, but before we left, Python's family insisted on throwing her a huge farewell feast. As her foreign friend, I was invited to tag along and to bring some friends of my own, so I convinced Serena, Molly and Gigi.

We got all dolled up for the event, too. Fed up of sweating my way through all my meals, I opted for some of the local fashion, going with a blue sarong with a paler blue pattern dyed into it, braiding similar blue flowers into my tangled curls. Serena didn't sweat, of course, being vampyri, so she wore her standard cream blouse, crimson vest, tan slacks and knee-high boots look. Molly surprised us all by wearing a petticoated green skirt, white long-sleeved blouse and brown corset over top. A pair of black leather gloves and knee-high black leather boots completed her outfit. Gigi went with a bright pink and purple sarong, which you'd think would clash horribly with her ginger fur but somehow didn't.

I still didn't trust Fluffy enough to get us to the palace in one piece, but we didn't have to worry about that, since the palace sent one of their palanquin-topped triceratops for us. We rode in style, enjoying it.

The meal was served buffet-style, with every imaginable type of seafood and fruit piled high on table after table. Gigi looked like she'd died and gone to whatever passed for Heaven here on Ayrth. As a pleasant surprise the Lemurisians were all mostly clothed, with both the women and the men wearing light sarongs in every colour of the rainbow. Green and gold predominated, of course.

I felt a little self-conscious in my sarong, for two reasons. For one, I was completely unarmed. The light cotton shift didn't leave much place to hide a weapon. I knew the party was protected by palace guards and with my friends nearby, that made an added line of defence, but still, I felt vulnerable. Too many times since had my life been in danger for me to rest easily without some way of defending myself.

The other reason was, in the sarong, my slave tattoo was clearly visible. Most of the other girls in my crew had chosen to get their tattoos tattooed over, but I hadn't. The ugly, misshapen black crow on my shoulder was a reminder to me. A reminder of what had happened and why I had to keep fighting against slavers and slavery and the government that allowed it. I can't say I wore it with pride and I can't say I was embarrassed by it, either, but it was something... I dunno. Personal, I guess.

Anyhow, the party was awesome. They'd gone traditional with the lighting, with torches burning on low poles stuck in the ground. There was a huge bonfire in the middle of the garden, too. Well, garden makes it sound cosy and intimate. It was more like a small park, enclosed on three sides by palace. The unenclosed side was open to a gorgeous view of the bay, with silver moonlight dappling the dark waves.

Three of us ate while Serena nursed a glass of wine. Vampyri can eat normal food, they just don't get any nutrition or enjoyment from it. The finest food and drink tastes like cold, wet cardboard and tepid, stale water by comparison to the rich complexities of blood. Or at least, that's how she explained it to me.

The food was fantastic, everything you could hope for in a tropical island buffet dinner and nothing like anything I'd ever eaten back home. I almost asked what it was, but thought better of it and just let myself enjoy it.

And it seemed like everything was going just fine until the velociraptors attacked.

I know, right? Typical. It's like I can't go anywhere without it being interrupted by insane violence.

Python had finally dragged herself away from all her family and found the three of us sitting near a small pond. She grinned and said, "Come! Now isss time forrr dancing!"

Before I could make any of a large number of entirely reasonable objections, she'd grabbed my wrist and pulled me to my feet. We didn't head back toward the party, but off through the palace to another, much smaller garden. Musicians had set up along one side of the garden, which was lit only by the light from the bonfire at the centre and the drummers already had a beat going. Some weird squeaky flute-type instruments joined in. Before I knew it, Python had pulled me into the circle of dancers that appeared almost out of nowhere.

Now, I'm not much of a dancer, but it wasn't hard to keep with the beat as we circled the fire. Gigi joined in almost right away, though Serena and Molly bowed out gracefully and went to sit with the other watchers. Normally it might have bothered me to have an audience watch me do something I'm not all that confident in doing, but I figured, whatever. No one was watching me, anyway, not with Python undulating with the music and Gigi spinning and swaying in time with the beat. I tried to copy a few of their moves and nearly dislocated my own shoulders in the process, so I settled for sticking with my own moves and just trying to enjoy myself.

Song melded into song. Someone kept the bonfire going. People joined us, people left. I stopped only once for a glass of what I thought was just juice but obviously had something more in it. When I rejoined the dancers my head was swirling and twirling and dancing and the beat of the drums and wail of the flutes and ching-chang of the finger cymbals and the play of light and shadow, the glistening of sweaty bodies and the flickering of flames, all came together in a hypnotic state where time had no meaning. Honestly, I could have been there for days, weeks, years. I still don't know how long I danced. I do know I only stopped when the screaming started. Even then it took me a few seconds to fully snap out of it. Mainly because Serena was shaking me.

"What's going on?" I asked. Everyone was running around, panicked. Molly, Gigi and Serena had me pretty well surrounded, so I couldn't quite see what was happening.

Then I saw them. Nothing like in that movie. Not nearly as tall, for one thing. These guys were about four feet tall, built like a greyhound standing on its hind legs. Only all four legs had wicked claws and the two hind legs had those huge, famous sickle-claws.

I heard Gigi growling beside me, hackles up and claws out. Do cats have hackles? You know what I mean. Ears flat, bushy tailed, look out.

The middle raptor tilted its head, quizzically. Then I remembered the scene in the movie.

"Look out!" I yelled, pulling Molly to the ground as we were jumped by a couple of raptors, attacking our flank.

The rest was a blur of snarls and growls, all flashing claws and fangs, as Serena and Gigi kept the raptors off me. Molly shook me off after that first attack and used her prosthetic arm as a bludgeon until she managed to grab a raptor by the throat and snap its neck. Then she used the raptor as a club.

As I tried desperately to stay alive, I noticed something really weird. All the raptors had thin leather collars around their necks.

But whatever, I needed to stay alive if I wanted to ponder the strange and unusual at my leisure. I grabbed a half-burned log from the bonfire, then turned my back on the bonfire and used the still flaming log to keep my attackers at bay. Shouldn't have trusted the bonfire to watch my back, I guess, because fifty pounds of angry raptor jumped clear over it and slammed into me like... like fifty pounds of angry raptor.

Scared? No. Frickin' terrified is more like it. Pain exploded across my back as claws sliced through my sarong and skin. I heard horrible, horrifying howling and hoped it wasn't me. Fang-filled jaws shredded my shoulder, adding to the symphony of pain playing on my back. I wrapped my arms around my head and curled into a ball, desperately trying to keep the raptor away from my face and vulnerable guts. Teach me to go to a party without a corset.

Just as suddenly as the raptor had attacked and pinned me, the weight vanished from my back. Curiosity overcame my world of pain and I looked up just in time to see Python wrestling the raptor, her legs wrapped around its back and hind legs, keeping the sickle-claws away from her. Her arms were wrapped around its head and with a biceps-bulging wrench, the raptor's neck snapped. When she was sure it was dead, Python let the carcass go and came to me.

"Lie ssstill," she said. "You arrre injurrred."

"Yes, I know," I answered, shivering. When had it gotten so cold? I could have sworn we were in the tropics. And that bonfire next to me should have been warming me, right?

Serena appeared out of nowhere, picked me up. "A doctor! Now!"

Someone moaned in pain. It took me a second to realize it was me.

Python led the way back to the main garden. A lot of people were running around for some reason. Serena looked angry. Gigi looked worried. Molly looked... like Molly. Why was everyone yelling?

"Don't worry, Sunset," Gigi said to me. "Doc will fix you up."

"That's what I'm afraid of," I answered.

Serena. I had to tell her something. There was something important, but I couldn't remember and then she put me on the grass, lying me on my side to keep my back off the ground but she put me down on my shredded shoulder and mercifully I passed out.

Chapter Eight

Sometimes The Solution Is Worse Than The Problem

I woke up in my own bed, which came as a surprise and a relief. Someone was saying something nearby, but everything had a kind of soft focus, blurry around the edges, even sounds. I blinked long slow blinks that took an eternity and eventually came to the conclusion that I was on my belly, not my favourite position. So I tried to roll over and suddenly the blurriness dissolved into hard sharp absolutely crystal clear pain. I must have gasped or moaned or something, because whoever was talking stopped and I felt hands on my arms and thighs, pushing me back down. The thought of fighting back filled me with fear of more focussed pain, so I let them hold me down until everyone was sure I wouldn't move again.

"Capt'n Val?" someone said. Doc Regan's face floated into view, inches from mine. Her voice sounded weird and echoing, like she was speaking from way down a long empty corridor.

"That's me," I said, or at least, tried. My face was half-buried in my mattress.

"Yes, Capt'n," she smiled, then looked up past me at someone standing behind me. "A sense of humour is generally a good sign."

I wanted to turn my head to see who it was she was talking to, but the idea that it might cause another explosion of pain along my back made me keep still.

Doc turned back to me. "Capt'n, ye've been severely injured. D'ye remember?"

"'Course I remember, I was there when it happened. We were at the party and these killer lizards attacked everyone."

Serena's face floated into view. "Not everyone. Ve vill talk about it vhen you are better."

"How come?"

They shared a look.

"Vell, because right now you are drugged to the gills."

"Oh that. Right." I thought about it for a few seconds. Then I thought about falling back asleep. I liked that idea a lot. But Serena hadn't answered my question. "No I mean, how come not everyone?"

"The raptors only attacked the smaller garden party, vhere ve vere. No one even knew of the attack until the screaming started."

"Pretty weird," I said. My eyelids were suddenly very heavy. "Not as weird as those collars, though, am I right?"

I think Serena said, "Collars?" but I fell asleep before my brain could remember it properly.

I woke up again, much later. Daylight sliced between the slats in my window shades, making lines of light along the floor of my bedroom. The foggy disconnected feeling had mostly left, but the memory of the bright searing pain in my back kept me still. I tried flexing my back muscles slowly, raising my arms a little. The pain was still there, waiting, I could tell. I decided that I could wait before getting up.

My throat was crazy dry, though. It didn't feel like I had any saliva in my mouth at all. I looked around, as much as I could without moving my head, and saw a pitcher and cup on the nightstand next to my bed. Moving as slowly as I could, I reached for them.

Naturally the cup was just out of reach and stretching any more would push the limit of discomfort directly into the neighbourhood of pain, a bad neighbourhood you want to avoid.

A voice from the corner of the room I couldn't see said, "Doctor!"

I heard the scrape of a chair on the wooden deck and soft footsteps come closer. I looked up when she got close enough and saw Domina smile down at me. She took the cup, poured some water in it and handed it to me.

Turns out thirst trumps fear of pain and even for a little while, pain itself. My back burned like fire but I needed to get some water in me. I swallowed as fast as I could before the pain became too much, then handed back the empty cup to Domina.

More scuffling behind me. A loud thump beside my bed. Doc Regan asked, "And how d'ye feel today?"

"Like hammered shit," I answered. "No, wait. Like diced shit."

"Now now, there's no need f'r that kind o' language," Doc said. She took my pulse and shined a light in my eyes. "No fever, that's a good sign. An' no sign o' infection, that's an even better one."

She looked up at someone behind me and nodded. Angel leaned over the bed, into my view, just long enough to hand Doc Regan a small jar of something vaguely pink. She smiled at me with what I'd come to recognize as her 'this is going to hurt and I'm sorry for that but it needs to be done' smile.

"Ah shit," I mumbled, as I dug my fingers into the mattress and white-knuckled it. Doc Regan carefully lifted the bandages off my back. I thought it hurt before, but this was way worse. I said words that were much worse than 'shit' as she peeled back blood-soaked strips of linen from my raw wounds.

Which was nothing compared to when she began rubbing that pink ointment all across my back. It smelled like rotting meat and stung like vinegar in a paper cut. I'm not ashamed to say I cried, or that Doc Regan, that masochistic mad medicine maker, had to holler for help to hold me down.

But when she said, "Help me get this bit between her teeth, then," that's when I really began to buck. I ordered them, as their Captain, to let me go, but they all ignored me. Me! Their Captain! I vowed a vast vengeance on them all. Then Molly had the bit between my teeth and held it there, turning all my curses into mumbled ramblings and shrieks of outrage.

I heard a machine hum to life and the crackle of unsheathed electricity. Then I felt cold metal pressed against my neck and the small of my back.

"Throw the switch," Doc said, goggles turning her face into a mask of malevolence. I could have sworn I heard perverse pleasure in her voice.

And then I passed out, again. When I woke up, it was night and the pain had passed.

Chapter Nine

Family Obligations

"Your back vill be tender for a few days, she said."

I had a small silver hand mirror in one hand, to check out my bare back in the full-length mirror mounted on my bedroom wall. My poor back. Criss-crossed scars turned it into a road map of hell. If I ever got back home to Earth, I'd have to wear t-shirts to go swimming, or else get used to being stared at and pitied. Added to all the other shots, stabs, slashes and of course, my slave tattoo, the scars on my back turned my own skin into something strange and unfamiliar.

"Still, better a few days than a month of healing, yes?" Serena continued.

Domina jumped to help me get my blouse on over my head. The cool, soft cotton felt good against the flaming ache of my new scars. "Yeah, I guess. And that goo?"

"The bioregenerative matrix ointment?"

"Yeah that. It works on anyone?"

"She said it had been cultivated from your own blood, so it should only vork for you. But anyone who gives her a sample of their blood can have the ointment made up for them, yes."

"Corset, Captain?" Domina asked.

The thought of the bone-bracing rubbing up against my scars didn't sound like fun, but I much preferred the idea of having some kind of protection. Paranoid? Perhaps. But I was getting pretty put out at incurring injuries, and I had no intention of letting Doc Regan get her mad mitts on me any time soon. She'd been smart enough to send Serena, instead of facing me herself, knowing I'd need some time to simmer down.

Domina helped me into one of my dozens of corsets, the crimson one with black lacings. Tight black slacks, knee-high red leather boots and a white blouse made me look very piratical. I had a meeting with the Lemurisian Air Command and I intended to look the part. With

Domina's help I pulled my hair into a loose pony tail and shrugged into my three-quarter length coat, then clapped my bowler onto my head.

Serena helped me hide some knives and a pistol into the folds of my coat, corset and boots. I had no intention of ever going anywhere unarmed again. Then I called for Tring to come in and apologized to her for getting hurt. As the head of my bodyguards, she takes my safety personally.

Tring, Lauz and M'lembe climbed into the triceratops palaquin with Serena and me, making it a tight fit. The driver navigated the crowded streets with ease and got us to the palace faster than I expected. Sooner we were waiting outside the offices of Lemurisian Air Command.

Lemurisian military uniforms were a little more formal than a loincloth, basically a light, sleeveless robe made of green linen with gold trim, split at the waist to free up the legs, with some kind of reptile leather belt, matching sandals, and a beaded necklace that showed the wearer's rank. Various bracelets showed off their accomplishments, like badges or medals would.

Admiral Salamander had enough bracelets to completely cover both forearms and two curling gold serpents wrapped around her biceps. "Come in, please," she said in only slightly accented Anglic.

My surprise must have shown on my face. "Or Atlan, if you prefer," she said, switching languages.

"No, Anglic is fine," I answered in that not-quite-English. "How did you know?"

"I know many things, Captain Val," she answered in Anglic as I took a seat in a wicker chair, opposite her. I sat gingerly, my back still tender enough to merit a wince as I leaned back. Serena and Tring stood behind me. M'lembe and Lauz we'd left outside, to come to our rescue or run for help, whichever. Don't ever say I don't learn my lesson. Nearly dying got through even my thick skull.

A huge wooden desk stood between the Admiral and me, covered with maps and reports. I recognized a map of Merinasy. "How's it going?" I asked, nodding at the maps.

The Admiral leaned back in her wicker chair. "Not well. But how are you? My reports say you nearly died. Yet here you are."

"Guess you could say I'm lucky that way."

"Yes, so they say. I've read some of your exploits," she said, waving to a stack of dreadfuls on a side table. "It would seem you're remarkably good at succeeding against otherwise insurmountable odds."

I fought back a sigh. "Don't believe everything you read."

"I don't," she smiled. "But even the most outrageous fiction seems to have some basis in fact, according to my other sources."

I didn't like the direction the conversation was heading, so I changed the subject. "So to what do I owe the honour of this meeting, Admiral?"

"I wished to speak to you about your mission," she answered without missing a beat. "And after Komodo's treachery, I hoped to find you well enough to continue."

"Whoa, wait. What? Komodo?"

"He orchestrated the attacks at the party. Those were his raptors. He insists they were stolen from his kennels over a week ago."

I thought about it, glancing at Serena. Through our bond I could sense waves of doubt and confusion. Personally I agreed with her. "Is that likely?" I asked the Admiral.

She shrugged, setting the bells in her dreads tinkling. "There is a record of a complaint, filed with the Peacekeepers, that reports a trespassing and a robbery, dated in accordance with Komodo's story, but it may have been the ground work for safeguarding his innocence."

The Peacekeepers were the Lemurisian police force. "So, what? He makes a claim that the raptors were stolen, hides them away somewhere, sets them to attack the royal family, but doesn't take off their collars?"

"You know about the collars, then. They are the most pervasive evidence against Komodo."

"Or they were left on the raptors to throw the blame on him."

"Or he left them on the raptors to make it seem like the blame was thrown at him by his enemies."

That made me blink. "Seems awfully convoluted to me."

Salamander laughed. "Not to members of the royal family, I assure you. Nor to anyone in the Lemurisian military. Both are as a pit of scorpions. And one does not become a General without learning a few tricks."

Great. "So what's going to happen to the General?"

"He is under arrest, pending an investigation. But enough of him. Let us discuss your mission."

"Okay."

"I have been thinking. Would it not make easy your actions, if you acted under a letter of marque?"

So that's what this is about. Luckily I'd already talked to Remy and the twins about what to do if any of us were ever offered a letter of marque, which is a kind of permission slip to wage piracy against everyone but the government who offered the letter in the first place. Basically, an agreement between the pirate captain and the government that they, the government, wouldn't hunt them, the pirates, down, so long as the pirates didn't attack any vessel flying that government's colours.

Not a bad deal, right? Except that we'd be trading away our independence. And since independence was pretty much what this whole war was about, 'not a bad deal' was also not a good one, either.

"Admiral, I'm honoured you think so highly of me and my crew," I said. Remy, the twins and I had already worked out what to say. "But I must decline."

Salamander sat back, one eyebrow raised. "May I ask why?"

"The strength of the pirate armada is our lack of predictability," I explained. "We strike where we like, against whoever we like. It's not just Atlan military targets we go after. Ysian wine shipments, Anglic wool barges, spice junks from Zhou, slave traders of every nationality. It's that randomness that keeps everyone flying the skies nervous.

"If we pirates were seen as allying ourselves with one government, then we simply become agents of that government and the other nations could point to us and blame you for our actions. We pirates need to be free to do what needs doing, while your government needs to be free to condemn our actions, should they take a... less than honourable path."

She stared at me for a few seconds, lips pursed in thought. Then she nodded and slipped a piece of paper off her desk into a drawer. "Very well. I agree with your reasons."

"Great. Was there anything else? We need to be off before dawn."

She glanced at Serena. "Yes, of course. I'll be quick. There is one favour I would ask of you, Captain."

"Sure, if I can."

"I have a niece, who wishes to see the world," the Admiral said, reaching for a small silver bell and ringing it. The door opened behind me and I twisted in my seat to see, an act I immediately regretted, since twisting in my seat also meant twisting my scarred back. I managed not to wince too noticeably as a girl about my age stepped into the room.

She had the same islander features that I'd come to expect of the Lemurisians, though her dark hair wasn't dreadlocked or dyed, her teeth weren't filed into points and she was quite a bit taller than me. Slender and willowy, too. Instead of the scale tattoos typical of the royal family, she had a tattoo of a cobra coiled up one arm and down the other, so that its hooded head was tattooed against the back of her hand. She wore a simple green sarong. In a word, she was gorgeous, your stereotypical tropical island hottie.

"This is Cobra," the Admiral said, switching from Anglic to Atlan. "My sister's youngest. She wishes to see the world, but will not join the Air Command."

"Rigid discipline is no way to experience life, dear aunt," Cobra laughed in flawless, unaccented Atlan. She had a great grin, too. "Nor the belly of a drake the place to see the world."

"Uh, no offence, Admiral," I said in Atlan, "but a pirate ship's no place for someone can't haul their own weight."

"I will work in whatever position you see fit to give me, Captain," Cobra answered before the Admiral could speak up for her.

"May I, Captain?" Serena said. I shrugged.

Serena turned to Cobra. "Your hands. Let me see them."

"You are vampyri!" Cobra answered, holding up her hands, palms up. "I have never met a vampyri. Is it true you drink blood only from living humans?"

"These calluses are from vhat kind of training?" Serena asked. She took Cobra's wrists and studied Cobra's hands, completely ignoring the remarks about vampyri.

"All members of the imperial family have extensive sword training," Admiral Salamander answered. "Cobra knows many ways to defend herself and excelled at the fang-dagger."

"Knife fighter, huh?" I said. "A couple of our girls might like to see how good you are."

"I am happy to show them what I know," Cobra answered. Serena still hadn't let go of Cobra's wrists, hadn't stopped staring at her open palms. "Or you, Miss...?"

"The crew call me Mistress Heartlace," Serena answered, letting go of Cobra's wrists. There were no emotions coming through my link to Serena, none at all, a sure sign that something bothered her but she didn't want it to affect me.

"Am I a member of your crew, then?" Cobra asked me.

I shrugged. "Sure, why not. But the moment you aren't hauling your weight, you're confined to quarters until we get back to Lemuris. And you won't see anything of the world, have any new experiences, staring at four walls in a room you share with five other women."

She grinned that huge flawlessly gorgeous grin. "That is excellent to hear, Captain. Thank you so much for this opportunity! I will get my bags. Thank you, dear aunt!"

I turned to see Admiral Salamander grinning at her niece. Once the door closed, she said, "Now I hope her mother will leave me alone to win this war."

We all laughed at that.

Chapter Ten

Yet Another Digression, But This One Is Cool, I Swear

Finally, FINALLY, we left Lemuris. I know it doesn't sound like a lot of time, but from the moment I stuck my foot in my mouth and volunteered to go to Zhou to our actual departure was nearly two weeks, an insanely long period of time for a pirate ship. Normally we make decisions on the spur of the moment, or else have our decisions made for us by circumstance (as in, oh look an Atlan warship, have they spotted us, KABOOM KABOOM, oh they have, better run for it). It's all about snap judgements and living for the moment, so a two week delay is an almost ridiculous amount of time to wait.

Which isn't to say nothing happened during that time. Loading supplies, rounding up crew, the goodbye party where I nearly got gutted, Serena's fight with that assassin... Wait, did I tell you about that? No?

Okay, it wasn't that big a deal, really, because Serena is that crazy good with a sword, but the night between my getting attacked by that velociraptor and my getting attacked by my own doctor and her mad medical machines, Serena was out walking the deck...

The moon vas high and bright in the summer sky, not quite full but near enough. The smell of the sea vas bewitching, clear clean salt vith an underlying of fish. The Lemurisians had to be praised for their efforts to keep their vaters free from the usual human vaste that comes from a city the size of Mu. I am told that during the day, the vaters are clear as gin. At night, the vaters are black as an Atlan slavedriver's heart and almost as dangerous. Sharks are not the only predators in those vaters. The Lemurisian obsession vith engineering the great lizards of the past have created many such beasts.

The Captain's pain kept intruding on our blood bond, and I vas concentrating on blocking it out, vhich is the only explanation vhy I did not sense him sooner. Of course, wampyri have a bit of a blind spot vhen it comes to patchworks, since they have no blood coursing through their weins. Their smell is of chemicals and dried meat, not of living human flesh. Also, a nearby airship had just delivered a shipment of salted pork. Not an excuse, merely an explanation.

I vas valking the deck, taking my rounds. I had just fed from my dwindling supply, thinking I might have to restock soon, vhen I heard the vooden deck creak behind me.

It vas my own fault. I had been voolgathering, reflecting on the irony of my fate. I had spent twenty five years hunting pirates aboard a wariety of wessels, honing my swordcraft, and here I vas, the first mate of a pirate ship. Destiny is strange, is it not?

But to the creaking noise behind me. I turned, hand on hilt. I had valked the deck enough to know vhere the creaks vere, and how much pressure vould cause such a creak. There should have been no creak behind me, not vithout significant veight to bend the boards.

Significant vas not the vord for the sheer mass of the creature that stood before me as I vhirled to face him. Tremendous, perhaps, is a better adjective. Shocking. Overwhelming.

He stood nearly seven feet tall, crudely formed, hideously misshapen. Most patchworkers will attempt to display some pride in their vork by seeking some symmetry in their creations. Not so in this brute. One arm bulged vith muscles, scarred and Afric of origin. The other, slender as a reed, wrapped tightly vith taut muscles, had come from some Europan donor. His bare chest vas covered in scars, both patchworked and prior to the process. In each hand he held a long iron rod, perhaps an inch thick. Leather wrapped the end held in his hand. A vire ran from the makeshift hilt, around his wrist, connected to a box on his belt.

Of his face, the less said the better, save that I recognized his features as the missing parts of the last patchwork assassin to trouble us. Somehow, both assassins had been made, at least in part, from the same donors. Monstrous, you vill agree, is the most apt descriptor.

Ve vasted no time in idle banter. His purpose vas clear; mine, to thwart him. I slipped into the Dancer's Dismay to face his attack. Two surprises followed. He matched the Dancer's Dismay with the Unrepentant Suitor, vhich told me he had some small skill vith the sword. Then the second surprise: he tapped the two rods he held together and electricity arced from one rod to the other, chasing down the length of the rods to their end, only to begin again at the hilt.

I believe I may have allowed some surprise to show on my features, for my opponent grinned viciously and launched into Pistons Pumping, trying to catch me between his electrified rods and thusly electrocute me. I of course anticipated such an attack and countered with Grinding Gears, seeking to separate the rods and determine the maximum distance of the killing woltage. The answer vas depressingly distant, so no chance might be had of seeking to separate the rods and spoil my opponent's advantage.

Pistons Pumping and Grinding Gears became Chimney Sweep's Revenge and Pleasure Girl's Repose. Baking the Pastries countered On the Chopping Block. Foxhunter's Flight met In the Doghouse. His mastery of swordcraft vas impressive, and his advantages considerable. Every blow from his hugely muscled left arm fell like a hammer on an anvil (indeed, Hammer Falls on the Anvil vas a manoeuvre he favoured) vhile his slender right arm darted with surgical precision and an artist's grace. Electricity notwithstanding, I felt as though I might vell have met my match vith my patchwork opponent.

Back and forth across the deck our fight raged, the only sounds our footsteps and the clash of metal blade against electrical rod. Sparks flew, at times, and momentarily I vorried about setting fires or vorse, catching some stray vhiff of balloon gas and blowing up the entire ship. Moonchance insists the balloon cells are absolutely airtight, that no gas could ever escape, but she has not the advantages of wampyri senses to tell her otherwise.

My vorries vere short-lived. All my focus vas required to keep my opponent from trapping me in his electrical veb. But vhen he attempted the Needlemaker's Lament, I saw my chance. At my feet lay a bucket, left behind by some careless crewmember whom I felt sure vould feel the lash of Miss Merryweather's tongue for it. For my part, I vas grateful. The bucket, still filled with soapy vater, I kicked into my opponent's face. Instinctively his Needlemaker's Lament dissolved as he attempted to bat away the bucket, only to splash the water all over himself. Electricity arced and sparked from his belt, and he shook and shivered in its throes. A roar of pain or disbelief escaped his until then silent lips. His spasms shook the rods from his hands, though they continued to dangle from the vires attached to his electrocuting belt. I vaited for the batteries to spend themselves before diving into my own Needlemaker's Lament, skewering him vith a blow that vould have killed any normal creature, patchwork or no.

He vas, of course, no normal creature. Still smouldering from electrical burns all across his bare chest and arms, he inspected my hit against him, then kicked me square in the stomach. I must admit he surprised me vith the wehemence of his attack. I vill not make the same mistake vhen next ve meet.

Yes, he escaped. As I flew back from the force of his foot applied to my midsection, taking my sword vith me, he turned and ran for the rail, leaping out into darkness and assuredly, his own demise. Later inspection of the aerioport grounds revealed the location of his landing, slowed in his descent from our ship to the floor far below by snatched mooring ropes and acrobatic actions that vould earn him a place in any travelling carnival he chose. I vould have followed, but the crew had finally responded to the sounds of our skirmish, bringing vith them vord of Wal's awakening. I ordered the guard to be tripled, then vent to my dear friend.

Chapter Eleven

Downtime Discussion

I know, I know, see what I did there? I told you that we'd finally left Lemuris then didn't get into what we did next. I made you read a whole chapter that had nothing to do with what happened next! But wasn't that more interesting than me just telling you, "Serena got attacked by another patchwork assassin, only this guy had electrical iron rods instead of a go-fast rig"?

Anyway, nothing would have been more boring than me telling you about the day-to-day operations aboard The Furies. We left in nice enough weather that turned foul pretty much right around our crossing the Equator. The professional pirates in the crew celebrated with a time-honoured tradition of extra rations of rum for everyone, something we hadn't known when we'd crossed the Equator the first time, just a bunch of rebellious slaves trying not to crash into the Afric grasslands.

Winter rains off the coast of Hindystan forced us back out to sea, which Violette had advised in the first place. I'd insisted on a faster route, straight over the Himalayas, or whatever they're called here on Ayrth. Teach me to try and overrule my navigator.

The rains followed us across the ocean, turning into a real howler about a few days out from Lemuris. When I asked about going up through the clouds, over the storm, my crew looked at me like I had asked them to fly to the Moon.

"What?"

"There's no air up there, Captain," Molly answered. "At least, not enough to survive on."

So we had to ride it out, tossed this way and that. Lots of my girls stayed confined to quarters, green to the gills and sicking up whenever the ship rolled too hard. I kept my meals down, but my footing was something else entirely. I'd gotten used to the relatively soft swells of the ship. The winds battering us had me stumbling from bulkhead to bulkhead, one hand on a wall like an old woman afraid to fall.

I'd asked Tring to meet me in my cabin and offered her a seat when she arrived. Outside, lightning flashed and thunder crashed.

Normally Tring would have declined the offer to sit, preferring to keep her footing in case of an attack. Paranoid much? Not really. Not when you attract as much trouble as I do. Anyhow, this time she sat, because the heaving deck made any advantage of standing a moot point at best.

"Tell me about Zhou," I asked, pouring a cup of lukewarm tea for each of us. Like me, Tring hardly ever drank alcohol.

She took a sip and set the cup back on the table, keeping her hand near the cup to stop it from sliding around. "What do you wish to know?"

"Well, how do we convince them to go to war, would be great."

Tring nodded and thought about it for a few seconds.

"I was mostly kidding, Tring."

"No, it is a good question." She sighed. "First you must understand that the governor of South Zhou is merely a puppet of Atlan policy. Coupled with corruption at every level of government, the governor has no real power. He could no more lead a rebellion against Atlan than he could leap across the sea."

"And in the North?"

"Petty local dictators, again with no real power."

"So who's really in power? Who could lead a rebellion?"

She sipped at her tea. "The Shang Hey Way."

I'm not going to bother trying to spell it, since Zhou doesn't use regular letters, but that's how she pronounced it. I'd picked up a bit of Zhou, from our ship-speak slang, enough to translate it as, "The Three Road?"

"The Path of Three," Tring corrected. "An organization of criminals, though they would declare themselves patriots. It was not so long ago that Atlan declared a truce with the Zhou leaders. In the South, there are grandmothers and grandfathers who can remember a life before Zhou rule, who can remember the war and the betrayal of our last emperor, selling our freedom for his life. Now the Path of Three rule North and South in reality, while the puppet government in the South dances to Atlan tunes and the warlords in the North squabble amongst themselves, all while Zhou rots from within."

I poured her some more tea. "Okay, so who do we talk with to get

Zhou into the war? The corrupt governors, do we bribe them? Do we try to unite the warlords? Or, you called them patriots, do we show the Path of Three the merits of open rebellion?"

She picked up her cup and thought about it. Several slow sips stalled her speech. Finally, she said, "The Path of Three."

I grinned. "Okay, how?"

"We must convince the Path to side with those elements in the Southern government who can be bribed into rebellion, especially those who are in the military. Standard Atlan procedure is the occupation of a conquered country for one hundred years with foreign troops, replacing their numbers with locals until finally all military personnel in an occupied land are native to that land, but raised under Atlan rule, and thus loyal to Atlan. In theory, at least." She grinned, one of her dazzling but rare grins. "Loyalty to foreign overlords has never sat easily in the hearts of the Zhou."

"And in the North?"

"Oh, the warlords will not need much convincing to join the attack, especially if it seems like someone else is responsible."

"Okay, so how do we convince the Path to join up?"

"I have no idea," she answered, sipping from her tea again. But when she'd set her cup back down, she added, "But I may know to whom we must speak."

Outside, the lightning flashed and thunder exploded close and loud enough to make me flinch.

Then I frowned. "That thunder sound weird to you?"

Tring's eyes went wide with surprise just as Restless crashed through the door. "Cap'n we're under attack!"

Chapter Twelve

Random Attack Is Random

"Who's crazy enough to attack us in a storm?" I asked as I entered the bridge.

"Seems to me we've plenty enough enemies," Molly said. "Shall I make a list?"

"No, that's fine."

"Many of them are quite mad," Molly continued.

"Okay, yes, thanks." I went to the window, where Restless already had her face pressed against the glass, her eyes cupped to help her see out into the night's blackness. "Back to your post, Restless."

"Aye Cap'n," she said, then tapped the window. "She's about five points to starboard, just there."

"Run dark," I ordered, and behind me, someone turned out the main cabin lights, plunging us into darkness. I knew all through the ship, electric lights had just turned off, with only a few strategic lights left dimly lit to keep us from tumbling down stairwells.

It took a couple of long breathless seconds for my eyes to adjust to the dark. In the distance, lightning arced from cloud to cloud, silhouetting our opponent.

She soared, slender and sleek, I saw. An Atlan Barracuda with a modified tail fin and, judging from the muzzle flashes as she fired at us, heavily gunned.

The sound of the blast reached us just as the cannonballs flew past. I heard the crash of wreckage and the scuffling of boots on the deck above our heads.

"She has our range," Molly said, telling me what I already knew.

"Not for long," I answered, taking my captain's seat. "Argenta! Engine Room!"

"Engine room, aye, Captain Val."

"Engine room!" came someone's tinny, crackling voice.

"Full speed!"

"Full speed, aye!"

"Restless, bring our nose about to face her."

Molly had taken up the habit of standing right next to me. "Let them cross our T?"

I grinned up at her. "Let them taste Inga's new toy."

Molly's sudden savage smile scared me slightly.

"Argenta, Gun Deck."

"Gun Deck aye."

"Inga?"

Someone answered. "Doom's respects, but she's a bit busy."

"Let her know she can fire Sparky at will."

"Aye Captain."

One of the guns we'd salvaged from the Great White that had attacked Libertia was a new experimental machine that didn't need ammunition. It didn't shoot bullets or flammable liquid.

It shot lightning.

Inga and Gigi had fit it into our gun deck somehow, setting it to fire from the gun port vacated by our twin fifteen pounders. They'd field tested it twice. Its accuracy wasn't great, but the lightning she produced arced back and forth enough to pretty much fry anything that was directly ahead of us. Kind of named itself, really.

Kind of like that Atlan Barracuda was. "Fire!" I yelled, even though the gun deck couldn't hear me.

I probably shouldn't have bothered. Inga fired off a bolt of lightning at the enemy ship, just as they fired off their next volley. Part of me thought their gun crews were amazing, getting their guns reloaded that fast. Part of me trembled in terror, because the whole sky exploded.

Yeah, so, evidently firing an experimental military lightning cannon in a thunderstorm wasn't such a great idea. I mean, we scavenged it off a downed Atlan Dreadnought, it's not like the cannon came with a user's manual. Anyway, the blast of electricity not only arced all over the bloody place, it caused the clouds around us to unleash their own lightning charges. The good news was all that lightning exploded about three-quarters of the cannonballs heading our way.

The bad news the feedback or the reverb or the whatever it was, don't ask me, because even after Gigi and Inga explained it to me I still couldn't understand it. Anyway, our electrics all blew. Even Argenta.

The crash of thunder that had come from everywhere around us at the exact moment of the blast left my ears ringing. I shook my head a couple of times, pulled Restless to her feet and set her back at the wheel, yelled at Molly to see to Argenta, even though I'm sure she couldn't hear me. Even I couldn't hear me, that's how bad it was.

No, worse. Without electrics we had to use the old fashioned way of communicating with different parts of the ship. You know, actually talking to actual people. It was kind of unbelievable to me that humans had done exactly this for hundreds if not thousands of years. Anyway, we were still at full speed and I needed a full reverse. I grabbed Restless and yelled in her ear to head down to the Engine Room and get us sorted out. She made me repeat a couple of times and ran off.

I grabbed the wheel and spun it hard to port, hoping to avoid a collision. It would also bring our guns to bear on her broadside. I hoped Inga, or whoever was left alive on the Gun Deck, would take the initiative and blast our opponent out of the air.

I really didn't need to worry. I felt our guns fire, even though I couldn't hear them. A couple of explosions rocked their main deck, and shadowy forms scattered, then raced to control the fires. In the rain and wind and all the chaos, I couldn't see them more clearly.

Suddenly Serena was at my side, snarling. It shocked the fury right out of me.

"What's wrong?!" I yelled.

She grabbed my neck and placed her forehead against mine.

I heard her voice in my head: *Easier this way.*

I can't hear anything!, I thought back.

Your ears will heal. But more importantly, right now, our main lines are damaged. Half our gun crew are wounded, out of the fight. We have no electrics. The engines are slowing. We must run.

I'm a little ashamed that the thing that worried me the most wasn't my wounded gun crew, but the damage to the main lines. See, the way an airship works is they build a ship, then tie her to the balloon that raises the ship into the air. A lot of lines are needed to tie her on, but the biggest lines, huge ropes thicker than my calf, tied off right at the centre of the ship, carrying the majority of the load. If those ropes were damaged and not repaired, they'd snap, the rest of the lines would snap, and the ship would plummet out of the sky like a rock.

I know, a good captain thinks of the safety of all their crew, putting the safety of the many ahead of the few, but still. Part of me felt then, and still feels, a little ashamed that I wasn't more worried about Inga.

Also, an itty bitty surprised part of me noticed that Serena's mental voice didn't have any vampyri accent. Weird, right?

What do we do? I asked.

We must run. The mission is too important.

Right.

I took the wheel and spun it hard to port, while Serena ran after Restless to belay my full reverse. I straightened out the wheel with our aft to the pirates, then turned the elevators to bring us into the clouds. Then I ordered Molly to see to our repair crews and get them all on safety lines.

In the clouds it was about ten times worse than I thought. Winds battered us from every angle. Rain came down in sheets, angry slaps of water that threatened to wash my crew overboard. Several of our lines, taking the weight of the damaged main lines, snapped. Our engines sputtered, overloaded with the strain of keeping us on an even keel. Lightning stabbed at us again and again. Thunder roared.

We rode the storm for a few minutes that seemed like hours of pure adrenaline-filled terror. I caught myself laughing. Howling with laughter, really. I'd like to think I didn't lose it completely. Anyway the crew told the story afterward that Death had come for me and I'd laughed in his face, so maybe it was a good thing? Whatever. In the end it added to my reputation but at the time Serena had to slap me out of it. Luckily she'd been the only one to actually see me like that.

Finally the storm calmed. We weren't dead. Our attackers disappeared into the night sky.

The rest of the trip to Zhou passed pretty uneventfully.

Chapter Thirteen

Showdown At The Teahouse Of The Autumn Sun

The Himalayas were stunning and made me glad we didn't have to pass over them. It's odd, being hundreds of feet in the air and looking up at something that isn't flying, it's connected to the ground. But we passed by them in a day and soon we were coming in to a landing in Gaolong Harbour.

"It is time, Honoured Captain," Tring said in Zhou.

"I welcome the arrival," I answered in the same language. Our mishmash shipspeak used a few Zhou words, but not many. Since we'd left Mu I'd gotten Tring to teach me. Just over a week wasn't a long time to learn but Tring said I had a gift for languages. I guess she was right, I mean, I'd become fluent in Atlan in only a couple of months. I'd always done well in French and Spanish classes back home. Anyway, I wasn't nearly fluent in Zhou, but I'd learned a few words and phrases. With Tring and her Open Hands to help me, I knew enough to get by.

We didn't need to land in the water but the Gaolong Port Authority kept all ships – even airships – in the harbour. There were docks with ramps and ladders for airships, right alongside the usual docks for seagoing vessels.

Tring and her girls had really changed from the frightened group of nearly slaves we'd rescued all those months ago. Heck, they'd changed from the merciless band of bodyguards they'd been a week ago. They all wore their long black hair bunned up and pinned with ivory sticks, for one. They'd changed their clothes so they all wore black shirts, black slacks and knee-high black boots, for another. And they'd painted Zhou characters on their cheeks. Yes, they looked insanely badass.

And they were guarding me. Tring advised I play up the outrageous foreign pirate as much as possible, so I wore my gaudiest colours and my flashiest jewelry. Bright green skirt, hiked up on one thigh, with my brightest, whitest petticoats underneath. Red leather boots with thick brass buckles. A cloth-of-gold blouse under my bright blue corset.

Necklaces, bracelets, giant hoop earrings, rings on every finger. Two pistols, a knife in each boot, a sword strapped to my hip. A deep green top hat and brass multi-lensed goggles finished up my outfit.

"How do I look?"

"Like the worst stereotype of a girl playing pirate," Molly answered brutally, then added with a smirk, "Fighting Blossom."

I sighed. I won't bore you with the details of how it took Tring and her girls nearly a week to make contact with the Path of Three, or how it took me saving the life of the daughter of the Path of Three's Fist, which earned me the Path of Three name Fighting Blossom. That's a story for another time. This is the story of how we convinced them to join the war.

The Path of Three have, no surprise, three leaders – the Fist, who oversees the warriors of the Path of Three; the Heart, who oversees the business side of their criminal enterprises; and the Mind, who oversees the overall organization. The Mind is the 'big picture' man. The Heart looks after the day-to-day details. The Fist makes it all happen.

Having saved the Fist's daughter's life from some overzealous would-be suitors at a teahouse just a few days ago, I now had an audience with the Heart and Mind of the Path of Three.

Oh alright, fine.

It had been nearly a week of Tring and her girls looking for anyone who would point us in the right direction of the Path of Three. A secret criminal organization that controls pretty much everything in the city of Gaolong and the country of Zhou doesn't stay secret very long if people talk about them. But then Tring had been given a hint from an old woman selling fish who insisted that the Path of Three regularly took tea at a local teahouse, the Autumn Sun.

Every non-Zhou aboard The Furies wanted to go. We'd pretty much stayed aboard since arriving in Gaolong, because leaving the docks meant bribes for the dock officials, for the city guards, for everyone we talked to, it was ridiculous. Mrs. Shorty flat out refused to hand out bribe money to the entire crew, stating we barely had enough funds to resupply as it was. We needed to get back to piracy and taking down slavers if we wanted to show any kind of profit. I promised her we'd hit the first Atlan luxury liner or slaver we saw.

Anyway, there were Atlan military crawling all over the bloody place. For the first time since coming to Ayrth, I was glad long-distance communications were pretty much non-existent. They didn't have any up-to-date descriptions of me or my crew. Just to be safe we'd repainted The Furies red instead of black on the way, after that storm. Tring told me it would bring us good luck. I hoped she was right.

That day I wore a lot of red, too. We bribed the dock officials to let us off the docks, then crossed the busy road, crowded with carts, rickshaws, even a few steam-powered horseless carriages, all going every which way. We made our way to the huge red gates. Giant statues of stone lions stood a silent vigil to either side of the gates and between their paws stood armed guards. We bribed them to let us into Gaolong.

If I thought Gaolong's Dock Street teemed with people and vehicles, it paled in comparison to the Main Way, just inside the gates. Picture a perfect pandemonium of people, selling stuff, yelling at each other, customers consuming, sellers selling, carts carting, vehicles... vehicle-ing. Noise of a thousand voices all yelling different things to different people, creaky carts, the dull plod of oxen, the thunder of steam engines, cars honking their way through the crowd, the hiss and bubble of food cooking in open pots, on grills, on spits over crackling fires. And the smells. Well, the less said about the smell of all those people and animals and food and vehicles in so confined a space, the better.

I played the gawking tourist while my Open Hands kept the crowd at bay, often with nothing more than a deadly look. I'm telling you, Tring and her girls looked so scary it amazed me that anyone came near us at all.

Even so, it took us nearly two hours to make it to the Autumn Sun teahouse, winding our way through the crowd. When we got there, Tring led me to a table with a full view of the restaurant. Out of well-learned habit I sat with my back to the wall, facing the door. Tring stood behind me. The other Open Hands took up positions around the restaurant – near the front door, by the kitchen, in a corner, that sort of thing. Normally Tring would have done the same, leaving me to sit on my own, but I hadn't mastered Zhou well enough to get by without a translator yet.

I knew enough to greet the owner, a woman about forty years old, and compliment her on her restaurant. She thanked me and took my order, tea and a noodles-and-vegetables dish Tring said I would enjoy. She was right, the food was delicious. The best Chinese food I'd had since coming to Ayrth. Okay, well, the only Chinese food I'd had. It was even better than the Chinese food my family usually got back home.

I don't want you to think I didn't think about my family ever. I did, a lot. It's just, no one wants to read about how much I missed them, right? I mean, that's not the point of all this. This is about how I won the war and ended slavery and became the Pirate Queen, not about the lonely scared girl from another world who missed her mommy. Please, who would want to read about that? So yeah, I missed them, there were times I really wished I could go home again, and there were times I wondered, even if I could get back to Earth and home and see my family and friends again, how could I ever explain where I'd been, what I'd seen and done? How could I ever top steering an airship through a thunderstorm? Commanding an all-woman crew of some of the fiercest, deadliest pirates I'd ever even heard of? Back home, all that waited for me was a high school degree I hadn't finished yet, a community college in some program, a job in that field that I probably wouldn't enjoy very much, nine to five in a cubicle, looking forward to that two weeks' vacation every year, debts and bills and maybe one day a husband to share it with. Kids. A house with a garage. All that stuff.

Where was I? Right! The Autumn Sun.

So I'm sitting there with my back to the wall, Tring at my side, eating noodles and drinking tea, when this really pretty girl walks in. Nothing special about her clothes, just your regular brown not-quite-peasant dress, but there was something in the way she moved that spoke of training. A grace that comes from not having to hurry and scurry to serve others, maybe. Maybe I'm just imagining it, in retrospect, like, given who she turned out to be. I dunno. But she stood out in the small crowd of the teahouse, and the owner gave the pretty girl a good seat away from the bustle and noise of the street and brought her tea before the girl could order it. She must be a regular, I figured, then went back to scanning the crowd while eating my noodles.

Even back home I'd been pretty good with chopsticks. The food court at the mall near my school had a Chinese restaurant, nothing like the awesome meal I was eating right then, but okay I guess. Mushy noodles, though, so I'd gotten used to eating mushier noodles with chopsticks. Let me tell you, eating properly prepared noodles with chopsticks is a lot easier.

I'd nearly finished my meal when a gang of guys walked into the teahouse. From their generally rude manners and crude outfits, I figured them for the thug type. If this was what the Path of Three had to offer, I didn't know if we wanted to recruit them.

There were seven of them. Aside from the skinny guy, the only two who stood out were the little guy with the gigantic sword on his back, and the huge guy with dozens of knives sheathed in belts criss-crossing his huge chest. Did I mention he was huge? Like, fridge-with-a-face huge. Anyway, the other four were pretty much dressed alike, same hair cuts, same 'what-can-I-steal' look on their faces. For the most part they wore Atlan-styled clothes, pants and shirts and vests. They were all wearing bowler hats, their shaggy hair hanging in their faces. One of them had goggles and another had a three-quarter length coat on. One carried an umbrella. Toothpick was the last.

The little guy took one look around the teahouse and spotted the pretty girl. He backhand slapped the huge guy's belly to get his attention. The huge guy looked down, waaaaay down, at the little guy. Seriously, he was really little. Like, shorter than me. I amused myself trying to figure out how he unsheathed that gigantic sword without dislocating his shoulder or slicing his own ear off.

But of course, that's when they walked over to the pretty girl.

Honestly, it surprised me. I mean, I was probably the only girl with flame red hair in a hundred miles, a thousand miles even. The only other redhead on The Furies was Apple, and she was a pixie, and her hair was more a dark apple red than bright flame red like mine. And! I'd dressed to impress. So when he scanned the room and barely paid me any attention, heading right for the pretty girl, I got a bad feeling about what was about to happen.

She'd been seated close enough to me and Tring that I could hear what they said. Tring translated.

"I am called Big Sword," the little guy said, sitting down across from the pretty girl without asking permission or being invited to sit. "I assure you it is not in reference to the weapon strapped to my back."

"Please go away," the pretty girl answered. "I am trying to enjoy my tea and your odour is quite overwhelming."

He reached across the table, slapped the tea cup from her hand. "You'll see what else I have that is overwhelming, Path of Three whore!"

That's when a chopstick bounced off his head. I glanced down at my hand. Only one chopstick left, so I guessed I must have been the one who threw it, a conclusion we pretty much all reached at the same time. Also, part of my brain heard what he'd called her - "Path of Three whore"- and realized that meant two things. One, she was related to the Path of Three in some way, I know, duh, but this was all happening in a split second; and two, that meant these thugs weren't Path of Three like I'd thought. A rival gang, maybe? Tring hadn't mentioned that.

I looked up from my one remaining chopstick and noticed Big Sword had turned to face me. We locked eyes.

"Hi!" I said, as brightly as I could. "The lady doesn't want company. At least, not yours."

Tring translated for him. "Stay out of this, foreign bitch," he said. Actually, I'd done what everyone does when they learn a new language, I'd asked Tring to teach me all the swear words. 'Bitch' isn't quite what he'd said. He'd used a much worse word.

"The lady is right," I said, and Tring translated for me. "Your smell is quite overwhelming. Even from here I can barely keep my delicious meal in my stomach. I'd also add your voice reminds me of a pig mating with a monkey and your choice of weapon is an obvious attempt at overcompensating for your lack in other areas."

They all stared at me, even the pretty girl. This was so obvious an attempt to start a fight that a smart person would have seen right through it. Luckily, I guess? Big Sword wasn't a smart person.

"You'll pay for that, bitch!" he yelled. I didn't need a translation.

I stood up so quickly that my bench scraped loudly against the wooden floor. My Open Hands jumped up, too. The thugs whirled to face them.

I held up a hand as the six thugs all went for their weapons. "Wait!" I said in my horribly accented Zhou, then switched back to Atlan so Tring could translate. "Let's not destroy this beautiful teahouse with our fight. Take it outside, so that all the sky and wind can witness your humiliation."

"Little Knife, take the Path of Three bitch," Big Sword seethed. "Make sure she does not escape. I will teach this stupid girl who pretends she is a pirate a lesson she will not forget for the remainder of her very short life."

The huge guy grabbed Pretty Girl by the wrist and hauled her to her feet. Pretty Girl let out a gasp of pain as he dragged her outside. The other thugs kept their eyes on my Open Hands. Big Sword glared at me, backing out of the restaurant without blinking.

Outside, a light winter rain had begun to drizzle down, turning the dirt street into slick mud. I regretted my decision to leave the comfort of the teahouse, but after a meal like I'd just had, it would have been pretty rude of me to wreck the place.

Little Knife stood to one side, under the shelter of an awning, his massive hand wrapped around Pretty Girl's wrist and forearm.

"Stop!" Pretty Girl yelled as we went to stand facing each other in the rain-slicked street. "This is ridiculous. My father is the Fist of the Path of Three. Threaten me at your peril!"

"We know who your father is, stupid bitch," one of the thugs said, the one with goggles.

Big Sword reached up behind him for the hilt of his huge sword. "Now you will learn your folly!" he yelled, and jumped up. Mid-jump he flipped over and as he flipped, the sheath of his sword opened up, splitting in half in a gust of steam and a clacking of latches and gears. He landed on his feet, which I admit impressed me, his sword unsheathed and held before him in two hands.

Goggles pulled out two oversized pocket watches, the chains of which were about six feet long. Long Coat produced two fighting batons. Toothpick made a big deal with a pair of butterfly knives. Umbrella held his umbrella like a sword.

"Five of you against five of us," I said. "Hardly a fair fight. You should have brought more friends."

When Tring finished translating, Big Sword snarled. "Women should know their place – on their backs!"

I was going to have so much fun kicking his ass.

Now, I hadn't dressed looking for a fight. Bright red shirt, all frills and laces, black half-corset, crimson knee-length skirt with about ten petticoats and black leather high-heeled boots. I'd wore my hair up, bunned behind my head, a tiny top hat on top. Yeah, I'd brought my sword and main gauche, because I'd learned that lesson the hard way. I'd still have preferred three or four fully-loaded pistols. And Serena. And Molly. Even Argenta.

I shouldn't have worried. Tring and her girls were itching for a fight. Tring added an insult of her own before I could answer him, which she translated for me later: "Even if we were on our backs, you and your eunuchs wouldn't know what to do with us!"

Big Sword just stood there, staring for a full two seconds, long enough for me to whip out my sword and main gauche, then he screamed an incoherent war cry and they all attacked.

They were pretty good. Toothpick and his knives even managed to get a few scratches in on Li before she broke his leg and snapped his wrists. Tring dislocated Umbrella's shoulder and jaw. Goggles' weighted chains spun and whipped and wrapped around Jin's throat, but she got two fingers up just in time to keep him from crushing her windpipe, then ran at him to keep him from tightening the noose and kicked him in the nuts, then kicked him in the head. Long Coat's baton's got in a few good hits before Yue grabbed one and broke it over his skull.

Which left Big Sword and me.

I know, I know, I made it sound all over and done with super fast. There were a lot more punches and kicks and flips and slipping in the rain-slicked streets and curses in Zhou and whatever, but honestly, it would take longer to describe than it took to fight, and anyway, it's not even the interesting part, which we haven't even got to because you insisted I tell you about the fight. So yeah. Where was I?

Oh. Big Sword had this giant sword, right? And I just had my thin little epee, because even with all the training I'd been doing the past few months I still couldn't perfectly control a cutlass. Anyhow, he takes a few huge wild swings at me. Not crazy out of control swings, though. They were part of his sword technique. Huge swings that got a lot of momentum going and twirls and flips to follow through to keep his sword swinging. Made it very difficult to keep him from chopping me to bits, especially since I couldn't parry his blade with mine. His would snap mine like a twig.

I backed away from him, keeping the worst of his attacks off of me, getting in a few jabs of my own whenever I spotted an opening. Finally I got my chance. He swung at my head. I ducked, sticking my foot out as he followed through, tripping him into the mud. He moved to get up but I was faster, stepping on his back with one high-heeled boot and putting my blade to his throat.

If you think swordfighting in high heels in the mud is easy, think again. I only make it look easy.

Anyhow, I ground my heel into his spine a little until he realized he should stay down. Then out of the corner of my eye I spotted the huge guy, Little Knife, dragging Pretty Girl down the street.

"Tring!" I yelled, and she and her girls were running after him.

"Who are you?" Big Sword asked in a passable Atlan.

I leaned down and spoke in my passable Zhou. "I am Captain Sunset Val. Be happy I do not kill you."

"Run, foreign bitch," he answered in Zhou. "The Seven Hundred Brothers will find you."

"Look for my ship, The Furies. You will only find death waiting."

"Captain!" Li yelled as they turned the corner.

I gave Big Sword a final little grind of my heel and ran after my Open Hands. Swordfighting in heels in the mud was easier than running through it. Also, I totally hadn't dressed for the rain. Winter in Zhou was supposed to be dry, according to Tring!

She had caught up with Little Knife, I saw. He threw knives at Tring and her girls one-handed while he kept the other arm wrapped around Pretty Girl. My Open Hands were trying to corner him into a dead-end alley, but he was smarter than that. Unfortunately for him, he was also running out of knives.

Pretty Girl screamed and slammed her head back, trying to head-butt him in reverse. It might have worked if she weren't like, two feet shorter than him. But then, she wasn't trying to hit him in the head.

Little Knife grunted in pain. She head-butted him again and I saw what she had done – the long thin hairpin in her bunned-up hair was sticking out of Little Knife's chest. Not much damage to a huge brute like him, but enough of a distraction that Tring and her girls got close enough to disarm him and bring him down. As he fell he threw Pretty Girl into my arms.

She looked up at me through a veil of loosened hair. "Thank you. I owe you my life."

Chapter Fourteen

Meeting The Masters

See what happened there? You insisted I tell you all about that silly pointless fight, instead of getting to the main reason we were even in Zhou in the first place. Well, whatever. Point was, Pretty Girl was a problem – a big one. First of all, she insisted she needed to be walked home, because she only felt safe with me and my warriors. That's what she called Tring and her Open Hands, my warriors. Okay, fine. But then she insisted I meet her father, which turned out to be pretty lucky for us, because he was the Fist of the Path of Three, one of the Three Masters, the guys we were looking for. Then there was the big celebratory thank you dinner. Then the party in my honour. And then I had to host them aboard The Furies. And all the time I'm trying to get the Fist alone so we can talk about why I came to Gaolong.

He was tall and slender, but his every movement spoke of complete control. Even through the traditional robes he wore, you knew he was ripped. I mean, really cut. Muscular. He wore his long black hair in a topknot, his face clean-shaven. His eyes saw everything, never settling in any one place for very long. I never saw him armed and I never saw him with a bodyguard. He spoke Atlan with only a very slight accent and he was scrupulously polite.

If he wasn't old enough to be my father, he would have been incredibly hot. That's the only reason I didn't completely spaz out around him.

After we'd had him and Delicate Petal – that was his daughter's name, at least among the Path of Three. I never learned her regular name. Once we'd had them aboard The Furies, they had me and the Open Hands attend a special ceremony. Middle of the night, candles, vows of blood, all that stuff, and we had our Path of Three names, becoming honorary members. They named me Fighting Blossom. Tring became Gentle Tigress.

So finally, we get to the point where we were before, with me headed toward a meeting with the Path of Three lords.

The Fist was the youngest of them. The Mind, the eldest. I put him at somewhere around sixty, but he could have been eighty, I dunno. Long white hair worn loose, long white mustache. The Heart was the only one of the three lords with short hair, the only one balding. He also had round, wire-rimmed spectacles. They wore the traditional Zhou robes.

We met in a big square room somewhere in the city. Honestly I don't know where, because Tring and I had been blindfolded and led through a maze before we got there. No windows, just candles along the walls and hanging from an iron chandelier above us. A long, low, light wood table separated us. The three of them at one end, Tring and I at the other. I sat crosslegged on a pillow on the floor. Tring knelt to my left to help translate.

"Fighting Blossom," the Fist said. "You have come to Gaolong from a great distance, is this not so?"

"Yes, Fist," I answered. "Further than you might think."

"Lemuris is not so very far," smirked the Heart.

"It's true, we were in Lemuris," I answered. "But I come from the Land of Hope. The people there live free. Free from the threat of slavery. There are no patchwork factories where I come from. And daughters and sisters do not fear being sold to a pleasure house, to be disgraced and dishonoured over and over again."

I know, not bad, right? Not bad at all considering I totally made it up on the spot.

"This land you speak of seems wondrous indeed," the Mind said, a slight smile on his lips. For an old dude, his voice was deep and rich.

I grinned at him. "It is, Honourable Mind. And the best part of all, it can be anywhere we want. We just have to believe in it."

"It takes more than belief to win wars, girl," the Heart said.

The Fist turned to him. "Not so. Southern Zhou was conquered because our people there lost faith in our generals and were sold out by the nobles who had fooled themselves into thinking life under Atlan rule would not differ so greatly from life under the Emperor's rule."

"I'm told the Path of Three consider themselves patriots," I said. "What would the Seven Hundred Brothers say to that?"

The Heart slammed his fist against the table. "Bah, they are thugs and criminals!"

"Would they not say the same of the Path of Three?"

"We did not invite you here to insult us," the Fist said quietly.

I bowed my head. "Honoured Fist, I meant no insult. I meant only to point out that ideas shape our reality. The Path of Three are patriots, seeking to free Zhou from their Atlan overlords. The Path of Three are thugs and criminals who thrive on the misery of the people. Which would you rather be remembered as?"

The Mind stroked his long mustache. "Tell me, Fighting Blossom, why did you come to Zhou?"

"Honoured Mind, the war between Lemuris and Atlan goes badly."

"For Lemuris."

Well, he had me there. "Yes."

"And you wish us to join this war?"

"Yes."

"Why?"

I took a deep breath. "Because Atlan must be stopped. Slavery must be stopped. Patchworking must end. Pleasure houses must end."

"Some of our greatest profits come from our pleasure houses," the Heart said to the Mind.

"I know of a pleasure house where all the women working there do so of their own free will," I answered. "But women must no longer be sold as property."

They looked sceptical, but didn't argue with that.

I tried another tack. "Lemuris can't do it alone. Even if every pirate flying the seven skies joined the fight, that would only be hundreds more to help. We need thousands, tens of thousands, hundreds of thousands of soldiers to take this war to Atlan's shores. We need guns and swords and cannons. We need ships, both seaships and airships. We need food for the troops and coal for the steam engines and gas for the balloons. We need so much and have so little."

"What would you have us do? Ask what it is you wish to ask, Captain," the Mind said.

"If Zhou would invade Russankya, they would be forced to withdraw their troops from the Afric Front. Lemuris could take the entire continent."

"Attack Russankya? Before the end of winter?" the Fist asked, stunned. Then he thought about it. "It would certainly have the benefit of being unexpected."

The Heart snorted. "We are but an organization of patriotic businessmen, not a government with an army. We have troubles of our own. Even if we could help your hopeless quest, why should we?"

I grinned at him. I knew he'd ask that. "There are many reasons, noble Heart, but the only one that matters is this: it would be the right thing, the honourable thing, to do. And you won't fool me with false modesty. If I thought the Path of Three couldn't make this happen, I never would have gone looking for you."

"We will consider your request, Captain Val," the Mind said, ending the meeting.

Chapter Fifteen

We Like To Talk Things Over, Sometimes

"Then what happened?!" Restless asked, barely able to stay in her seat. We made her sit on her hands at these general crew meetings, ever since she'd nearly put out Jenny Squall's eye with her wild gesturing.

"They talked for a couple of hours while Tring and I ate in a rooftop garden," I answered.

"Such as it was," Tring muttered. The 'garden' had been surrounded by much taller buildings, which made figuring out where we'd been taken nearly impossible. Beautiful, with a small patch of sunlit sky high above, but still.

"In the end they agreed to make it happen," I continued. "But they had two requests. The first was, they want first right of pillage."

There were a lot of angry-sounding muttering about that. Mrs. Shorty just sat in the back, shaking her head. Personally, I agreed with her. The Lemurisians weren't likely to agree to that and the pirate armada surely wouldn't. Everyone wanted to pick Atlan's bones clean.

"The second thing is, they won't attack Russankya alone. We need to get someone else to help with the invasion."

"Who else is there?" Molly asked. No one answered.

"The wampyri," Serena said, finally.

"I thought your countrymen had pledged neutrality," Violette asked. She stood and went to the map of Ayrth I'd asked her to pin to the wall of the mess hall. "With Anatolyne to your south-east, Etrusca to your south-west, Bavardy to the north and Russankya to your north-east, the Vampyri homeland is all but surrounded by hostile intent."

"Yes, all this is true," Serena said. "This is vhy ve have pledged non-interference in the vars of humankind. But Anatolyne is too veak to attack the Russ, Bavardy too self-involved. The Norsic people vill not attack their cousins, is this not true?"

She turned to face Inga, who nodded. "Ya, that is true. We will not attack the Russ. We have tried too many times in the long ago past.

Always it fails. Russankya is too large to conquer, too poor to pillage."

I stared at the map, willing it to show me another option. "Well, we don't need to conquer them. We just need to keep them busy."

"Let my people invade and the Russ will be quite busy," Serena said. Blood hunger seeped through our link. There was bad blood between her and the Russ for some reason.

I looked for one particular face in the crowded mess hall. "Svetlana, how do you feel about this?"

The dark-haired beauty shrugged. "I am Russ no longer, Captain Val. Not since my father sold me to slavers to pay off his drinking debts." She looked around the room at her crewmates. "I am a Fury, now."

That earned her a couple of hugs and pats on the back from the women around her and smiles from the entire crew. They felt the same. They'd said goodbye to their pasts when they joined The Furies.

"You think your people will do this?" I asked, turning to Serena.

"I think many among them are looking for a reason to throw off the shackles of neutrality," she answered. "Atlan outrages have gone on long enough. They vill not vait much longer to absorb the wampyri into their bloated empire."

"Why would they, though?" Violette asked, still standing by the map. "Forgive me, but there's very little point to taking your mountainous country. You've few enough resources to support yourselves, much less make it worth conquering."

In the blink of an eye, Serena stood right next to Violette, a hand gently resting on Violette's shoulder. No one saw her move.

"How much more effort vould it have taken me to kill you vhere you stand?" Serena asked, gently squeezing Violette's shoulder in as non-threatening a way as she could, given what she'd just done. "The natural resources of my country are few. But an army of wampyri, starved of blood and set loose on an unsuspecting enemy, now that is a different matter. Atlan's slave trade is not limited to humans. And besides, there is also the Wulka."

Everyone went still and silent.

"What?" I asked. "What's the Wulka? I mean, Vulka?"

"They are humans, mostly," Serena said, walking back to her seat and sitting. "But they are... different."

"Beasts, from what I hear," Mrs. Shorty said. "Not men, but..."

"Wolf-men," Miss Merryweather finished for her.

I frowned in confusion. "Like some kind of animan?"

Gigi answered, "No. Humans who can transform themselves into half-men, half-wolves."

"Oh! That kind of wolf-men. Like werewolves, got it. Okay, so?"

"Their battle prowess is legendary," Jenny Squall said. "So feared they haven't been used in a war for nearly two hundred years. Just the threat that they might get involved has been enough to send warring nations back to the negotiating table."

It surprised me that she knew so much about the Vampyri army until I remembered she'd been good friends with Tatalia Tempest, a Romanista, one of Serena's countrymen. Tatalia died, back in the Battle Over Libertia. A lot of good people had.

"Atlan's set the Blighted loose on Afric," Molly said bitterly. "I doubt even the Vulka will change their minds about this war."

"Lemuris will not bow either," Python said. She'd gone to her cabin the moment we landed in Gaolong and had only come out for her duties and for meals since. Cobra too, now that I thought about it. Weird.

Since we'd left Lemuris both of them had taken to wearing the ceremonial wrappings that I'd first seen Python wearing, though neither wore a mask of gold. Tama had changed her clothes for the much more practical pants and blouse that the rest of the crew preferred, though her shaved head still set her apart from the others. According to Miss Merryweather's reports, Tama excelled at every duty given her.

Python, not so much. She didn't take orders well. She took offence easily, meaning she didn't work well with others. At the request of the crew chiefs, she'd been moved from one crew to the next until finally she'd been placed on the boarding party, our crew of women warriors. When they weren't boarding other ships, they were practising with their weapons. And Python excelled with her weapons.

Violette sat down. "So neither side is likely to leave off, though according to Admiral Salamander, Lemuris might not be able to keep the continent."

"They will fight to the lassst, though," Cobra said. "Theirr prrride will not allow them to rrretrrreat, norrr ssssurrrrrrenderr."

"Trrrue." Python nodded, surprised to be agreeing with Cobra.

I stood up. "Okay, so. Our best bet is to somehow convince the vampyri to join in the war by attacking Russankya, which will get the Zhou into the fight. Any objections?" I scanned the room. Doubtful faces, eager faces, indifferent faces, but no objecting faces. "Right. Any ideas on how to make it happen?"

Silence. Great. Sometimes being the boss sucks, making all the decisions all the time.

"Ve must go to Warnya," Serena said finally. "It is our only true city, the sole seaport, and the seat of the Blood Council, our for lack of a better vord, government. I think I know someone I can speak to and get us an audience."

"Okay then. Make ready to set sail when I get back."

"Back from vhere?"

"I'm going to tell the Path of Three we accept their offer."

Chapter Sixteen

More Talk

This time I brought plenty of protection. Tring and her girls, of course, but also Violette, mostly because she had the best sense of direction out of the entire crew and I wanted to know where we'd be led. Serena. Cobra asked to join at the last minute, and I didn't have any reason to say no.

On our way there, I asked her a question I'd been dying to ask Python but had never gotten around to. "So uh, what's the story with the bandages? And the mask?"

Cobra's voice echoed oddly from behind her painted wooden mask. "It isss sssomething of a trrradition among membersss of the Lemurrisssian rrroyal family. Outsssiderrss should not gaze upon ourrr flesh unlessss we arrre in battle."

"Yeah but, you all walk around half-naked."

"When we arrre home in Lemurrisss, yesss. Abrrroad, we don ourrr... forrrgive me. Therrre isss no worrrd in Atlan. Um... ourrr hiding ssskinsss."

"Skins?" I took a closer look. What I had thought were bandages were actually thin strips of snakeskin, wound all around her. "Oh. Wow."

"Thank you."

"And you take it off to fight?"

"It is believed that shedding ourrr ssskinsss will make usss morrre powerrrful. Deadlierr."

"Does it work?"

"It isss jussst a trrradition, Captain Val."

"So you're part of the royal family? Like, one of Python's cousins?"

"A verrry, verrry dissstant cousssin," she answered. "She isss farrr ahead of me in the successsssion."

"Oh."

We reached the Autumn Sun right about then, ending the small talk.

Our contact was waiting for us and led us, blindfolded, right to the Three Masters.

"I agree to bring your offer to Admiral Salamander and Captain Jones," I told them. "I believe they will accept your terms."

"Excellent, Captain," the Mind said. "We will begin preparations to invade Russankya."

"We will?" the Heart blurted.

"They have already begun," the Fist smiled.

"They have?!" the Heart answered. "But, how?"

"Do you not agree that the time is perfect to rid ourselves of our Atlan overlords?" the Mind asked him. "While they are distracted with the Afric Front?"

"The fools in Atlan may be distracted," the Heart replied. "The fools here in Zhou are not."

"While I agree that there are many fools in our government, there are less fools in the Zhou military than you might believe," the Fist said.

"What? How?"

The Fist smiled. "It was the Mind's plan all along."

The Mind looked off into the distance, even though there weren't any windows. I guess you could say he looked off into his past or something poetic like that. "I have worked toward this day my entire life. As a child I saw the horrors of war and the defeat of our people. With the blood of my brothers and sisters I swore I would bring down the invaders. I would dedicate myself to their destruction. I found others like me in the Path of Three. When they began to allow Zhou in their military, I saw my chance. I convinced the most patriotic of the Path of Three to enlist. For five decades now, I have been seeding the Atlan military with Zhou patriots. They will capture the corrupt governors, and return Zhou to rightful Zhou hands. The warlords will be bought off, and once again North and South will be united. We will finally be free."

"Freedom is the right of every person," I said in my horribly accented Zhou. I hoped they understood.

They probably did, because the Fist and the Heart smiled and bowed their heads toward me. The Heart paused, then bowed his head also. I bowed back to them.

"There is wisdom in your words," the Mind said. "Your crew are fortunate to have such a Captain."

"Thank you, Honoured Mind," I answered, bowing again. "And speaking of my crew, I must return to them. We have much to do and every delay brings us closer to losing the war."

"We understand, of course," the Fist said. "When you have arranged things with Admiral Salamander and Captain Jones, and organized an ally for our invasion of Russankya, send us word and we will begin."

On our way out we ran into Delicate Petal. She was wearing a drop-dead gorgeous red silk cheongsam, instead of more traditional robes.

She bowed and asked, in Atlan, "Captain, you are leaving us?"

"Yes," I answered in Zhou. "As soon as potential."

"I believe you mean, possible," she corrected me.

I switched to Atlan. "Thanks. I'll get it eventually."

"I am sure you will. Safe journey."

And then we were heading back the way we came, blindfolded again. I tried to keep track of the turns and stairs and all that, but got so confused so quickly I gave up after a few minutes. And anyway, that was why I'd brought Violette along. Good thing, too, because we were jumped by the Seven Hundred Brothers.

Chapter Seventeen

Because Violence Doesn't Always End Well

Okay well, not all of them. At first I didn't know what was going on. Our guides suddenly started yelling and then there were guns going off and screams and I felt four or five people drag me to the floor and climb on top of me. Yeah, comfortable it was not.

I yanked the blindfold off and started struggling with whoever had tackled me. Turned out to be Tring's girls, so I ordered them to get off of me. Two or three actually listened, letting me see what was happening.

Our Path of Three guides, Tring and Serena were fighting a gang of Seven Hundred Brothers, with more Brothers behind them, waiting to get into the fight. I saw right away we were outnumbered like, five to one at least. And there were all kinds of screams and yells and the clash of blades and the roar of gunfire, all in a crowded cramped roofed-in alleyway. More noise than any deck action, let me tell you. It made my ears hurt.

I pushed off the last couple of Open Hands looking to keep me safe and stood up. Violette had curled up against the wall, arms over her head, taking cover behind a basket of some kind of fruit.. Cobra was nowhere to be seen.

I grabbed Violette by the arm and shook her hard. "Come on, get up! You're just a target down there!"

Somehow she heard me over the chaos and nodded, getting to her feet, then stopped and stared at the battle raging behind me.

I shook her again. "Violette! We need to get out of here!"

"You don't say," she answered. If she was okay enough to be sarcastic, she was okay enough to get us back to the ship.

"Which way?" I asked.

She pointed, without hesitating, at the wall. "That way, about a mile, give or take."

I glanced behind me and spotted an alleyway. I shoved Violette toward it. "Get going!" I ordered, then turned back to the fight and pulled out my gun, firing into the face of a guy about to stab Serena in the back. She flashed me a wicked grin, a split second of gratitude pulsing down our bond, breaking through her bloodlust.

"Too many!"

"Bah! Three to one? Ve vill crush them!"

"Some other time," I said, wincing as she skewered two opponents at the same time.

"Go! We will hold them off!" one of our guides yelled at me.

"There are too many!" I yelled back, unsheathing my sword. Looked like we might have to fight it out after all. I yanked my main gauche from where I hid it in my corset.

"Not for long!" the guide yelled.

It was true, there were more Path of Threes rushing toward us.

I started yanking my girls out of the fight, pushing them toward Violette waiting in the alleyway. Tring was the last to leave, breaking the arm of her opponent and leaving him a screaming wreck. When I grabbed her to pull her out of the fight, she attacked me, acting on instinct. I managed to block three punches before she realized who I was and stopped hitting me.

"Come on!"

We ran for it. The last thing I wanted was to wind up in the middle of a gang war. From the sounds of it as we ran, one that was escalating by the second. I heard more and more gunfire, then turned the corner and slammed straight into a nightmare.

Serena had described him as 'misshapen' but that didn't even come close. 'Grotesquely lopsided' might be more accurate. The weight of his one huge arm hunched him over to one side, his legs splayed out awkwardly, trying to compensate. His patchworked face snarled with rage. Those electrified rods sparked with blue-white menace.

He didn't pause for taunts or introductions, just launched himself at me. I barely parried his first blow. Riposting the slower, much stronger second nearly snapped my wrist. My main gauche flipped out of my hand, skittering along the darkened street.

Tring didn't even pause, just swept his legs with a low kick. He jumped over them, proving that lopsided didn't mean clumsy. I jabbed at him, trying to get past his guard, and got caught in the electrical arc.

Ever stuck your finger in a light socket? If not, you're lucky. I really don't recommend it. My every muscle seized, cramping as painfully as possible. I couldn't breathe, I couldn't move, I couldn't yell.

Tring kicked him in the skinnier arm, lifting the killing arc up and away. I fell to the ground, gasping for air.

Then Serena showed up and our attempted assassin was otherwise occupied.

I blacked out.

Chapter Eighteen

My Very Own Mad Scientists

I woke up on The Furies with some nasty burns on both arms, slathered up with some foul-smelling ointment and bandaged. Domina helped me get dressed. Just the pressure from my blouse nearly made me pass out from pain. Then she insisted I put on a corset and vest and jacket and overcoat. It was pretty cold in my quarters, so I didn't mind the layers, but the pain whenever I moved my arms was intense.

I probably should have stayed in bed, but it was daylight outside and an airship doesn't run itself. I wanted to know what had happened and I knew Serena would be slumbering. I also wanted to know where we were and where we were headed.

Violette was asleep in her quarters, so I made my way to the bridge. When I got there, I collapsed in my chair. Domina got me something hot to drink that had more than a splash of rum in it, but it was sweet so I drank it all down. The food she brought me was hot and plenty of it, too. Starved as I was, I gobbled it down two heaping plates of it.

Restless piloted us toward the sunset, over a great plain of white snow and the occasional stand of pine trees. "Feel better, Cap'n?"

"Almost human," I answered around a mouthful of potatoes and bacon. I swallowed and added, "Well?"

"Well what, Cap?"

"Are you going to tell me what happened?"

She shot me a grin over her shoulder. "Weeeeeeeelll... Like this, see? Mistress Heartlace, she saw you go down, out for the count like. She jumps over the patchwork and stands over your body. 'You vish to keel hare? You vill haf to go through me, fairst!' Both blades up and ready to take him down! And then Mistress Tring showed up, BAMBAMBAM!"

"Hands on the wheel, Restless," I reminded her, trying not to laugh at her impression of Serena.

"Aye Cap'n. Anyways, so Mistress Heartlace has got him busy with the swords and the electric rods clinging and clanging in the alley and ZAPZAPZAP with the electrics. Mistress Tring and the Open Hands punching and kicking BAMBAMBAMKLOW, only he's so big and, you know, a patchwork? So he's hardly feeling it. Li broke her hand punching him in the spine! Don't worry, Doc Regan fixed her right up with that ossificatorizer thingamabob. But still!"

"Restless."

"Right, sorry Cap'n. So Mistress Heartlace finally chops off one of his hands SHYOW and through the power cable for the electric rod KAZAP and this machine he's got sparks all over the place GZGZGZGZGZG and he shuts down and so they carried you back and everything's done!"

I knew she'd get the story out of everyone who'd been there. And much easier to ask her than wait until everyone else woke up.

"No one else was hurt?"

"Just you, Cap, and Miss Li. And the patchwork, I s'pose. You should see him, what a mess."

I managed to not spit out my mouthful of tea. "What?"

"Oh yeah. Miss Gigi has the nasty brute in her workshop. Ugly blighter. Oops, sorry Cap, I know Miss Molly don't like that word. Ugly bastard, how's that?"

"Fine, Restless," I said, not really hearing her. "I'll be in the workshop."

"Aye, Cap'n."

"And tell Gigi to meet me there."

"Aye Cap'n."

I left my third plate of food half-eaten and my tea to go cold. I'd already gone cold inside. Why had they brought a patchwork assassin aboard ship? What were they thinking?

As much as Gigi had changed the room, I still never much liked going down to her workshop. Once, before we'd taken the ship from our pirate captors, the room had been the quarters for the slaves Captain Crow and his crew captured. Must have been sixty or seventy of us crammed in there, stinking of sweat and fear, just a bucket in one corner to pee in.

After we'd taken over the ship and given ourselves better quarters, we'd used it briefly as a training room, then Gigi had appropriated it for her own scientific experiments. Since then, she'd modified it a little, running more power cables in, adding shelves and workbenches and whatever else she needed. The workshop also housed the aetheric portal, the machine that brought me from Earth to Ayrth. Gigi still hadn't been able to get it running, though she felt sure she'd figure it out somehow.

Generally speaking, I was too busy to think about it. As captain, I had hardly any time to rest and relax and occupy my time with hobbies, unless you counted catching up on my sleep. And I'm pretty sure I didn't even want to think about it. Thinking about it meant thinking about going home. What was I going to say to my parents? How was I supposed to explain all my scars, much less where I'd been all these months? And if I did get home, how was I supposed to put all this behind me and go back to being a high school student?

Anyway, I didn't want to think about it. I mean, sure, in a general sense, we all wanted to go home. Bringing down Atlan and dismantling the slave trade meant that a lot of my crew would be free to return to their families. Some of them wouldn't, I knew, but some of them would. And once we'd won the war, then what? Piracy wasn't really for me, I knew that. Taking on an airship of rich jerks wasn't nearly the same as attacking a slaver. Anyway, I didn't really want to think about that, either. Much better to stay focussed on the task at hand. And at that precise moment, that meant dealing with my crazy engineer and her mad science experiments.

I threw open the metal door of the workshop. It clanged against the bulkhead so loud it echoed. The sound made Gigi look up from where she hunched over a shrouded shape. The harsh glare of a gas torch lit her from below, casting skittering shadows across her furred face and fanged smile, her goggled eyes flickering reflections of torchlight.

"Sunset," she said, turning off the torch, plunging herself into shadow. She pulled the canvas shroud over the whatever it was she'd been working on. "How are you feeling?"

"Fine I guess," I said. "Whatcha working on?"

She stepped out from behind the table and walked toward me. She wore a long white lab smock and thick rubber gloves and for some reason she kept her goggles over her eyes. "Oh nothing. A little experiment."

Normally I couldn't get her to shut up about some of her 'little experiments'. She'd happily go on for hours explaining minute details that only made sense to another engineer. So her answer confused me.

"No really," I said, walking toward the table. "What's the deal?"

She stepped into my path to block me. "It is nothing, really. A little... um... surprise, that's all."

Then there was a clatter from behind the table.

"Who's back there?" I asked.

Doc Regan stood up, wearing an outfit like Gigi's and looking embarrassed. "Tis jus' me, Capt'n."

"Okay you two, what's the deal? I already know about you having that patchwork down here somewhere."

"Ah, zut! Restless!"

I turned to face Gigi. "What makes you think it was Restless?"

Gigi gave me a look that said *oh come on.*

"Yes, fine, it was Restless who told me, but you should have told me first! Also, why is the patchwork who tried to kill us on this ship?"

Doc Regan pulled the canvas off the table, revealing the disabled patchwork. He really was hideous, lopsided and scarred. I noticed that quite a few of his stitches had been removed, opening him up. One of his hands was missing.

"Sure an' we can learn a lot from him," Doc said.

"What, like an autopsy?"

Gigi went to stand next to the table, opposite Doc Regan. "No, we hope to reanimate him."

"What?!"

"Think o' it, Capt'n. If we can bring him back t' life, we can question him about whoever sent him against ye!"

"Okay, no. No no no no no. Also, are you two crazy? Bring the guy who tried to kill us back to life?"

"Er, well..."

I shook my head, stunned. "No. Dump his parts overboard, like the last one."

"Well, about that..."

"You did dump him, right?"

She tried to hide it, but her eyes flicked over to her refrigerator.

"Gigi?!"

"I just, I mean, we need to know who sent them!"

"We know who sent them! Captain Caliper sent them!"

"But why?!"

"Helloooo? Because we wrecked his ship!"

She crossed her arms. "No, there's more to it than that, I know it. Pirates lose ships all the time. They don't hire assassins to chase each other across the seven skies! For one thing, these assassins, they are expensive! And for another, pirates are, how would you say? More 'hands-on' than that?"

Okay, she had a point. If Caliper wanted me dead, it would be him chasing us across the seven skies, not sending some patchwork errand boys to do the deed. Like Tyr Ebonfury, who'd chased me across Afric to Libertia and nearly destroyed my ship and killed all my crew, just to satisfy some twisted sense of vengeance for me killing his captain, marooning his crew and taking his ship. This ship.

MY ship.

Yeah, I guess I'd be pretty pissed if someone stole The Furies from me. Or worse, sent her crashing into fiery wreckage. I know I'd be pissed if someone slaughtered my girls, or left them stranded to die a slow death of dehydration and starvation. But Ebonfury never really struck me as the caring commander type, you know? Anyway, one madman trying to slaughter me at a time.

I took a deep breath and studied the inert patchwork. Would you call them cadavers? Corpses? I mean, they're really just a couple of flipped switches away from being back to what passes for normal, right? So I looked at him and an idea struck me.

"The information's in their brains, right?"

"Aye, Capt'n," Doc said.

"You can keep the heads, then. Everything else gets dumped. That's an order."

"But we cannot get the information out of just the heads," Gigi said. "In order to speak, they will need their lungs. To supply the brain with nutrients, they will need their hearts. No, we need the intact torsos."

This was definitely the weirdest conversation of my life and I'd had quite a few weird ones since coming to Ayrth. "No, Gigi. Heads or nothing. I'm sure you can figure something out."

Doc shook her head. "We'd need an expert on patchworkin' an' no mistake."

Not for the first time, I missed Eve, one of my first real friends here on Ayrth, the patchwork put together by Dr. Sweetwater, the madman who'd brought me here in the first place. As a patchwork herself, she'd know how to keep the head talking while we sent the bodies overboard.

"Okay, fine, we'll find one. In the meantime, is there anything else I should know about?"

Gigi looked at Doc Regan. Doc looked at Gigi. Gigi shrugged.

"We were goin' t' surprise ye," Doc said, heading for a table in the far, darkened corner. As she walked, the lights overhead flickered with electrical life, eventually steadying as illumination. I followed her and Gigi followed me, through the maze of worktables and machinery.

On the table sat a strange machine, humming quietly. Beside the machine, a huge glass bell jar. Inside the bell jar, a tiny Tyrannosaur.

"YOU SHRANK FLUFFY?!"

"SHHHH Sunset, you'll wake her!"

I leaned in close. Fluffy lay on her stomach, eyes closed. Her sides rose and fell as she breathed; otherwise she didn't move at all.

"Is she okay?" I asked quietly. I'd been mildly upset that we'd had to leave her behind and even more surprised that I'd been upset. I guess I'd gotten used to her enthusiastic greetings. And here she was, maybe ten inches tall.

Doc stood beside me, looking at the sleeping T-Rex with fondness. "Sure an' she's fine. We feed her every day. Not much room to manoeuvre in there, but she's safe as safe can be."

I turned to Gigi. "You're turning into a mad scientist, you know?"

"This?" she grinned a fang-filled grin. "This is nothing! I was trying to find a way to help Mrs. Shorty with her storage problems. We can't make more space, but what if the things to be stored were smaller?"

"So why isn't she using it?"

"Anything that gets shrunk, then moved ten feet or so from the shrinking unit, becomes dangerously unstable."

I glanced down at Fluffy. "Okay, why?"

"The unit converts mass into energy and stores it, yes?"

I'd never been much good in science class. "If you say so."

"Well, the shrunken matter remains tethered to the energy."

"Well, it would, wouldn't it?"

"Sometimes it's hard to tell when you're being sarcastic, Sunset."

"Really?"

"Now is not one of those times. The aetheric tether can stretch about ten feet before it snaps. Then the energy seeks to return to its original form, usually by the most expedient method possible."

"And that is?"

Gigi shrugged. "The unit explodes."

"Yeah, that's a down side."

"And then the shrunken matter spontaneously combusts," Doc Regan added.

"That's not good, either." I leaned down to look at Fluffy again. I never thought a giant killer lizard could look so cute. "So she's okay, as long as she's near the machine?"

Gigi nodded. "Yes. Absolutely. Without a doubt. Probably."

"Gigi!"

She snickered a catty little laugh.

"Okay so, now what?"

A huge rattling grinding noise shook the ship. The lights went out.

Chapter Nineteen

Darkness Reveals An Unpleasant Secret

The workshop had no portholes and with the power out, the darkness was nearly total.

Luckily, Gigi could see in the nearly total darkness. "Stay where you are," she said. I heard her booted feet step through the maze of worktables, then I heard her dig around for something in a mess of stuff somewhere, then I heard her come back.

I also heard yells coming from other parts of the ship as my crew tried to figure out what had happened, get their bearings and hopefully get some lights lit. Being able to hear the girls made me aware of something else: the engines had stopped.

Gigi came back to me and pressed something leather and metal and rubber into my hands. "Here, put these on."

Goggles. Right. I'd used these before, so I knew what to do. First I found the tiny collapsible hand crank on the side, opened it up and gave it a few twists. That would power up the goggles. Then I slipped them on and played with the lenses until I could see in the dark. The workshop resolved itself into shades of ghostly greenish-grey. I saw Gigi helping Doc Regan with her goggles. Gigi glanced at me, her eyes huge reflective circles of bright green.

"Ready?" she asked.

"Go time."

Gigi's eyesight was better than ours, even with the goggles. They tended to warp things around the edges. It took some getting used to. Doc kept bumping into workbenches and stuff on her way toward the stairs that led us out of the workshop. She did better in the hallway, which was much less cluttered and tended to run in one of two directions.

"Where to?" Doc asked.

"Engine Room," Gigi said, not waiting for us. She slid down a ladder, disappearing from view.

"You too, Doc," I said. "People might be hurt."

"Aye, then."

We followed Gigi, going much slower. Crew crowded the corridors. I set them to work, to keep them busy. I grabbed a girl and sent her to the bridge with instructions to triple the spotters. Last thing we needed was an attack.

Finally Doc and I made it to the Engine Room. I never knew what 'the silence was deafening' meant until I walked into that eerily quiet Engine Room. Even when we'd been under repair there had always been some kind of noise going on in here. Now, the stokers just milled around, the furnaces banked, the boilers slowly hissing off steam, everyone watching Gigi and some of her girls climbing up onto the pistons and around the crankshaft, carrying portable electric lamps that sent shadows skittering in every direction.

"So?" I yelled, my voice huge and echoing in that silence.

"Looks like we threw a piston rod," Gigi called down.

"Can we get the electrics back on?" I asked.

"Not before we clear this bent rod," she answered.

"How long?"

"At least an hour."

"Anyone hurt?"

One of Gigi's head stokers, a solidly-built woman named Magda, said, "Minor cuts, burns and bruises."

I turned to Doc Regan.

"I'm on it, Capt'n," she answered before I could say anything. "Be right back, ladies," she called down, then left to get her bag.

"Gigi, what do you need to get this fixed?" I asked.

"Some extra hands wouldn't hurt, but mostly we'll need time," she answered, somewhere hidden in the shadowy machinery above.

"I'll send Miss Merryweather," I answered, then left to go find her.

Three hours later, Gigi's coveralls glistened with grease, while I seethed with barely restrained rage.

"Tell them," I said through teeth clenched so hard my jaws ached.

All my crew chiefs turned to look at Gigi. She held out a badly rusted bolt, about the size of my fist.

"Sabotage," she said.

"You are certain?" Serena asked quietly. The sun had barely set. Even though we'd closed all the curtains just in case, she stood silent sentinel in the darkest corner of the room, arms crossed and eyes lowered.

"This isn't the result of poor cleaning practices or a negligent eye, Serena," Gigi answered. "This bolt was fine the last time we checked it. And we check it every time we clean the pistons."

"Which was when?" Violette asked.

"Just after we docked at Gaolong."

"Could the bolt have rusted so quickly?" Miss Merryweather asked as Gigi passed the culprit around.

"Acid, most likely." Gigi shook her head. "Sprayed on?"

Molly passed the bolt to Inga with just a glance at it. "Who could get up into the pistons, spray the bolt with acid and get out of the Engine Room again, without being seen?"

"Getting up into the pistons wouldn't be a problem, would it?" Mrs. Shorty asked. "I mean, I remember working the boilers. Who has time to look up into the pistons?"

"An' ye'd be blinded from the furnaces anyway," Doc added.

"All true," Gigi agreed. "Getting out again wouldn't be so hard, not if you knew how many other ways out of the Engine Room there are."

"More than the door, you mean?" Violette asked.

"Aside from the obvious main door, there are two access hatches, the coke chute, three air vents and the emergency steam release. And, if you were suicidal, the exhaust scrubber."

I should probably explain that. Airships running on steam engines heated by coal and coke-burning furnaces should leave huge clouds of white steam and black smoke trailing in their wake, or so you'd think. But airship engineers got fed up of airship captains always complaining that they couldn't see anything in the thick of battle, from all that smoke, so a bunch of Eire engineers got together and sorted out a system that took all the coal smoke the airship engines produced, scrubbed it clean enough to be nearly clear air again, then released the nearly clean air out an exhaust pipe right at the rear of the ship. In the winter, or at higher elevations, the hot air coming out of the exhaust pipe would make a steam trail in the cold air outside, but usually it left no trace.

However, getting from the furnace to the exhaust pipe meant going through the scrubber, which, as far as I understood it, used a bunch of highly dangerous chemicals. Pretty much suicide for anyone trying it.

"Search every way in or out, then," Molly said.

"Already done," Gigi answered, with a wave of her hand, as if to say, *oh please*. "One of the access hatches had been left opened, or rather, closed improperly. So we know how they got in and out again. I've ordered every piston checked and rechecked to make sure no further damage was done."

I leaned forward, resting my weight on my elbows, hands clenched together. I took a deep breath, trying to settle myself, while they waited to listen to what I had to say.

"I hate this," I said, finally, watching my knuckles go white. "I hate thinking that one of our girls is responsible. That one of our girls has betrayed us. That one of OUR! GIRLS! could POSSIBLY! have STABBED US IN THE BACK LIKE THIS!"

"Wal," Serena said. That one word, that quiet tone, cut through my red fog of rage.

At some point I'd stood up, so I sat down again. I took another deep breath. "This ship is our home. Someone wants to destroy it. Find her. Stop her."

"There's something else," Mrs. Shorty said, after it became clear I didn't have anything more to add. "There are stores missing from the food lockers," she said, looking to Brunhilde.

"Ya, sat is true," Brunhilde said, her Atlan so thickly accented with Bavardish I could barely understand her. "At fust I sink it is maybe one or two uv ze girls, ya? Zneakink a znack? Und zo I haf Hilda checkink sem. Ze fud, it is not beink took from my kitchens. Zo, I ask Elegiac."

"And I ran a spot check on the inventory," Mrs. Shorty continued. "And came up with some missing items of food. Fruits, some dried meat, a couple of bottles of that Zhou rice wine."

"So? One of your girls can't count?" Molly asked.

Mrs. Shorty snorted. "All the inventory is checked and rechecked. What's more surprising is how long it took my crew to discover the thefts. I had a talk with them about that. Believe me, if so much as a pea goes missing in the future, I'll know about it."

Mrs. Shorty took her job very seriously.

"So we have a stowaway," Violette said. "Not surprising, really."

"Could it have been the stowaway who sabotaged the piston?" Miss Merryweather asked.

"Not necessarily," Serena said from the corner. "Stowaways are running away from something, or vish to go somewhere. Sabotaging the ship taking you there seems a silly vay to do so."

"Unless they wanted us stranded here in the middle of nowhere, ripe for the plucking," Molly countered.

"It's pointless to sit around talking about this," I said, standing up. "Find the stowaway. Then we'll ask her directly."

"Captain," Miss Merryweather began.

I interrupted her. "Dismissed, ladies."

If Miss Merryweather looked shocked or upset that I'd been so rude, right then, I didn't care. The only thing I cared about was finding the stowaway and stopping the saboteur.

Serena didn't leave with the others.

"Well?"

"I am trying to understand vhy you are so upset," she answered.

I let out a long breath. "This ship is the only place I've felt safe, the only home I have, since coming to Ayrth."

One blonde-white eyebrow rose ever so slightly. "You felt safe as a slave? You felt at home stoking the boilers? Or vhen that patchwork assassin lay in vait for you, beneath your bed?"

"You know what I mean," I answered, too angry to be teased.

"I do. But Wal, you must control yourself. Your anger is my anger, remember. And I... can be a threat, to even our friends."

"What are you saying, that I control you?"

"No. But the link ve have, it... blends us? It is difficult to explain." She stepped forward, out of the shadows. I saw how tightly she gripped her arms, her pale knuckles even whiter with the effort. "Vhen you lived vhere you are from, did you ever kill anyone?"

"What? Of course not."

"No. And yet, here on Ayrth, you have killed. Many times. Did you ever imagine yourself capable of that?"

I thought about it. "Not really, no."

"Have you ever vondered about that? About how casually you've become a killer? And about how easily you put the crew in harm's vay? How many crew have ve lost, since you became captain?"

"Now, waitaminute, that's part of the job. And in war, people die. I can't stop that and I won't let you blame me for it." *Any more than I already blame myself,* I thought.

"Do not misunderstand, Wal. This is not about blame. This is about who you have become, since coming here. Since sharing your blood vith me. Ve are connected, linked, through that blood. I feel your emotions, you feel mine. Ve can find each other in the most crowded places, across the greatest distances. I have changed, too. But your changes are more pronounced, run deeper, I think. Being linked to me has given you a focus, a drive, you did not have before, is it not so?"

I thought back to the daydreaming teenager I used to be, before coming to Ayrth. Lost in my little life, never thinking about the future, so annoyed at my sister for using my desk, at my brother for being late to pick me up. Now I commanded an airship, negotiating with the rulers of countries, helping to plan a world-wide war against slavery and a corrupt regime. And yes, now I could kill people, or order my crew to put themselves in danger. I could justify it by saying our efforts were working toward a greater good, but in the end, my girls died, or our enemies died, or both, and the responsibility for that lay on my shoulders.

"Yeah, I guess I am more focussed."

"I only bring this to your attention because, vhere once you might have said 'I could kill them!' and have it merely be hyperbole, now, vell, you really could kill someone. Especially if your murderous intent is being broadcast to your blood-bonded wampyri."

"Right. Okay." I took a deep breath. "I'll try to control myself."

"Good. Now, shall ve hunt?"

I nodded. "Rouse the crew. Only exceptions are those Gigi needs to repair the engines. I want every inch of The Furies searched. Find the stowaway. Hopefully we'll find the saboteur, too."

Chapter Twenty

A Marvellous Moonlit Mystery

In the end, Cobra found our stowaway, but before we get to that, there's one little thing I want to tell you about. I promise, it's good.

We were searching the ship, top to bottom and bottom to top, sealing off decks and posting guards to make sure no one slipped back into an area we'd already searched. Our power still hadn't come back on, so the search was being conducted by lantern and hand-cranked flashlight. Slow going, with shifting shadows and whispering women.

I'd just ordered our pixies into the air ducts. Moonchance and her girls had searched the balloon, inside and out, and reported no one hiding there. I'd put them to work clearing out areas that might be too small for a human or an animan, since there was no telling who or what our stowaway was.

Gigi came up to the main deck to find me and report. "We'll have power up inside an hour. I hope."

"So do I," I answered. Our breath steamed in the cold air, silvered by the nearly full moon. "Gonna be a cold night, otherwise."

"Cap'n Val?"

I turned to see Restless standing nearby, looking out into the clear frigid night sky, rocking from one foot to the other.

"Figure we ought worry about them?" she asked, pointing off to starboard.

I turned to stare into an empty black sky. "What? Who?"

"Them there," she said, stepping up to stand next to me. "About two points port of the moon."

I shielded my eyes from the moon's silver glare and squinted. I still couldn't see what she was getting at. Until...

"There! That!" Restless yelled excitedly.

A glint of moonlight, gleaming against something glass or metallic, headed for us.

"Go dark!" I ordered. All around me girls snapped their lanterns shut, switched off their flashlights. A couple of girls ran for the stairwells and relayed my order to the rest of the ship.

"We've got to get you in the crow's nest more often," I whispered to Restless. I turned and whispered to Jenny, "Everyone belowdecks, battlestations, as silent as can be."

"In the dark?" she asked in a whisper, looking sceptical when I nodded. But she hurried below to spread the word.

"What is she, Gigi?" I asked. She'd slipped on a pair of goggles and was fiddling with the lenses.

"Atlan make," she answered. "Big ship. No crew in sight." She headed up to the bow, climbing out onto The Furies' raised sword. "Yep, strange tail on her. She's that ship that attacked us in the storm."

"They followed us?" Restless asked.

"Why can't we hear her engines?" Molly asked.

You'd be surprised how far away a ship can be and you can still hear their engines. Especially with our engines not pounding away belowdecks. Molly had a good point.

"The Forgotten Frigate," one of the crew whispered behind me, setting off murmurs through the crew.

I turned around and hissed, "Battle stations, I said!"

The crew scrambled to their places. I glanced at Molly and asked, "What's the Forgotten Frigate?"

"An old story," Gigi answered for her. "About fifty years ago, give or take, Atlan Aerial wanted the quietest ship in the world, so they came up with a ship that used a special kind of engine, powered by photonic inversion."

"What's a photonic?"

"Supposed to turn sunlight – or in this case, moonlight – into electricity, which, in turn, powers the engines. No one thought it would work, but they built the ship all the same. Fitted her out with all the latest automatonic weaponry, too. Of course, nothing like Argenta, but self-loading cannons seemed like a good idea at the time."

"So what happened?"

"She disappeared on her maiden voyage," Molly answered. "All hands lost. Atlan Aerial declared it an utter failure and suspended all further research. Airship crews claim to have spotted her, now and then. Guess we're one of them, now."

"Well, we're sitting ducks here," I said. "Whoever they are."

"We've got her T crossed," Molly said. "Should we open fire?"

I wanted to say yes, but some instinct stopped me. "Wait until we have no choice," I answered. "Spread the word."

Molly looked surprised, but nodded. "Aye, Captain."

I looked at Gigi. "Shouldn't you be below, fixing our engines?"

"My girls know what to do," she answered, never taking her eyes off the oncoming airship. "Besides, you want me to miss seeing a legend?"

The Forgotten Frigate grew closer and closer. She never once opened her gun ports. She passed us silently overhead, close enough that our lookouts up top later claimed they could have reached up and touched her hull. At first I thought she was painted all black, but then I saw that her entire hull was covered in rectangular black panels, about the length of my forearm and width of my hand. Bigger panels hung from her balloon. Like Gigi said, not a single crewman showed themselves.

Not a shot was fired. She sailed off into the night.

Chapter Twenty One

One Problem Solved

I know, right? Not everything about the war was horrible.

Dawn had begun to turn the horizon bright pink when Cobra brought the stowaway into my cabin, where Molly, Gigi, Miss Merryweather, Tring and I had been going over plans of The Furies, looking for places that might be big enough to hide a person.

"I found her behind the water reserves," Cobra informed us, shoving her forward.

It was Delicate Petal.

"Explain yourself," I said.

She was filthy. She'd dressed in peasant's clothes and they hadn't been treated well. The water reserve tanks were constantly sweating condensation, making it one of the dampest places aboard. Cramped, too, making it difficult to clean, meaning, she'd been hiding in a swamp of murky, sooty sludge. Her normally silky black hair had been tied back in a tight braid, but a few strands had come loose, making her look even more dishevelled. Her eyes were wide with fear as she threw herself to her hands and knees.

"Please, Captain," she began, bowing to the floor. "Forgive me."

Behind me, I heard Tring snort angrily. Not a good sign. She barked something in Zhou. Delicate Petal flinched as if she'd been whipped, then stood, bhe kept her head low and wouldn't make eye contact.

"Why are you on my ship, Delicate Petal?" I asked quietly, fighting to control my anger.

"I just... I must prove myself."

"To who?"

"My father," she whispered. "He thinks I am good for nothing but a suitable marriage. I will show him that I am worthy enough to be Path of Three!"

"By sabotaging my ship?!" I snapped.

She looked up at that. "What? No, never! You are infamous, Captain

Val! You and all your crew. An entire ship of strong, capable women, fighting for what is right, fighting for justice and an end to tyranny! You should have heard my father go on and on about you! How impressed he was! How the admiration glowed in his eyes like a fire!" Tears spilled down her cheeks. "To have even half that much admiration when he spoke of me, I would do anything. Anything! So I sneaked aboard. I thought, maybe I could find a place on this worthy crew. A place where I could earn my father's respect."

My head began to ache. "Spare me the daddy issues. Why did you spill acid on the piston?"

She shook her head so violently that her braid swung from side to side. "No! I would never do something so dishonourable. Why would I cripple my one chance to earn my father's respect?"

"I dunno," I shrugged. "Maybe you were jealous of me and my successes. Maybe you wanted to knock me down a peg or two. That would get your dad's attention, right?"

"No, never. Never. I did not do this, Captain. Please believe me!"

Trouble was, I did believe her. Call it gut instinct, but I knew she wasn't lying.

I turned to Tring. "Find someplace to confine her until we can figure out what to do."

Tring nodded, nose wrinkled in a sneer, as if I'd asked her to take out some particularly nasty trash. Something about Delicate Petal disgusted her. I'd have to ask her about it later. Anyway, she grabbed Petal by the arm and hauled her out of my cabin.

When they'd left, I said, "Good work, Cobra."

She bowed her head toward me and said, "Not at all, Captain. Merely doing my duty."

I nodded. "Still, thanks. You can take the rest of the day off." Days off duty were something we used as rewards when we weren't in port.

She grinned and said, "Thank you, Captain."

Once she'd left, I asked my crew, "Well?"

"You believe her?" Molly asked me.

"I do."

"As do I," Miss Merryweather added. "Either she was being entirely truthful, or else she is a consummate actress of impressive talent."

"What makes you say that?" Gigi asked.

"Certain telling inflections in her voice, mannerisms of body language, that sort of thing. A perceptive individual can discern truth from lies in such a manner."

"Or someone going on gut instinct," I added. "Whichever it is, that's not our problem. Our problem is, what do we do with her?"

"She'd not be the first runaway on our crew," Miss Merryweather said. "Many of our girls who aren't freed slaves are running from something. A court of law would consider all freed slaves aboard to be runaways and treat us accordingly."

"I say we ship her back to daddy," Molly said. "We've no room on the crew for people who can't haul their weight."

"How do we know she cannot?" Gigi asked. "And at any rate, how exactly do we ship her back? If we stop at a Russ port, we risk capture. Do we then send her home alone? She wouldn't get very far before some con artist scammed her. Do we send someone with her?"

I shook my head. "No. We're not shipping her back, either. We'll send a letter or something to the Fist and keep Petal out of trouble until we can bring her home again. Miss Merryweather, you'll put her on crews that will keep her safe."

"Aye Captain."

"Alright then. Gigi, get the engines up and running. Full steam as soon as it's safe. Molly, get us set on the fastest course to Daxia. Miss Merryweather, I'd like to talk to you for a second."

The other two went off and I was left with my bosun.

"Yes, Captain?" she asked, resting on her walking stick.

I thought about how to ask what I wanted to ask without violating her privacy, but then just blurted out, "You weren't just a governess, were you?"

Her face went absolutely still for less than a second. If I'd have blinked, I would have missed it. Then she just looked sort of curious and amused. "What makes you say that, Captain?"

"You know an awful lot for a governess."

"A good governess seeks always to educate her charges," she answered, sounding like she was quoting something.

"Really? A governess needs to know about body language, detecting the truth, that sort of thing?"

"You don't think young boys might seek to lie to their governess?"

She wasn't going to give anything away, that was for sure. I made a note not to play cards with her, then changed tack.

"Did yours?"

The amused curiosity disappeared, and I realized I might have stepped over an unspoken line. "My boys? Not after they learned that I'd always know if they had."

"What happened ?" I asked. She'd never spoken of them before.

Her smile turned sad. "They were very brave, but in the end Captain Crow and Tyr Ebonfury were better swordsmen."

"They killed your kids?!" I was horrified. I knew that slavers usually didn't take men, but sometimes we'd free a gang of young boys, taken with the women of some unlucky airship.

"Well. Joseph was thirteen, almost old enough for the Academy, and Gabriel would have been eleven this midwinter." She took a deep breath, closing her eyes for a moment, pushing whatever she had to be feeling away. "Not little boys any more. And now, of course, they'll never be men. Is that all, Captain?"

I was sorry I'd even brought it up, picking at a wound that might never heal. Something about her told me there was more to her than a simple governess, something I might never learn. "What do you think I should do about Delicate Petal?"

Miss Merryweather shrugged. "As I said, she wouldn't be the first runaway to join our crew."

I nodded. "Alright. Keep her confined for a couple of days to let her know we're not happy with her. Then put her on cleaning duties for a couple of weeks. That might get rid of any notions she has about the glory and glamour of airship piracy."

"Aye Captain. There is, of course, the other matter."

"Yeah, I know. If she's not the saboteur, then who is?"

She nodded. "I'll speak to Tring about setting guards."

The whole ship shuddered as the engines finally started back up. I sighed with relief, feeling knots of stress in my neck ease up as we got back under way.

Chapter Twenty Two

Interviewing The Vampyri

It took us nearly half a week to get to Daxia's main port, Varnya, on the shores of the Marinus Nocturnus – the Sea of Night. Our little stall out high above the frigid freezing Russankya steppes had cooled the engines too much to heat them up to full steam right away, so we'd limped along for nearly a full day and night before Gigi was satisfied that nothing was going to go wrong with her precious babies. Then we needed to get our bearings. While we'd been without power we'd been at the mercy of the relentless Russankya winds.

At any rate, we made it to Daxia without further incident. Varnya was a sleepy little coastal town, not even remotely like any of the bustling ports we'd been to. I counted only eleven other airships in the air and on the airfield, none as large as The Furies. The town itself looked as though it had been carved from the nearby mountains, every building made of fitted stone, every roof of flatstone shingles. When I asked Serena about it, she answered, "Ve take fire prevention wery seriously in Daxia."

When the sun finally set behind the distant mountains, I expected the town to come alive and it did, to an extent. I mean, there were just about the same number of people on the streets as during the day, but these people were a lot paler than their daytime counterparts, if you know what I mean.

It's funny. Years of watching and reading vampire stories gave me this idea that all vampyri would be beautiful, elegant, rich beyond my wildest dreams. Apparently not. They dressed and acted like normal people as they moved through the emptying streets of the town. Non-vampyri went home, to bed; vampyri woke up, went about town, dealing with the vampyri shopkeeps who stayed open all night. No screams piercing the night. No superstitious human peasants huddling inside their hovels. No cruel and beautiful vampyri lords and ladies, feasting on the populace.

It was pretty anti-climactic.

Storm clouds rolled over the mountains, dumping tons of wet snow, wind howling in the rigging, tugging at our mooring lines. Safe aboard The Furies, we shrugged it off, enjoying a quiet meal around midnight. Some girls played cards, others told stories of past actions. Even though we were technically in port, no one had asked for shore leave. Only Serena had gone. I could feel her, distantly, a vague annoyance at the edge of my senses. I mean, she was vaguely annoyed, not that I was annoyed that I could sense her.

The saboteur and the storm had everyone in a bit of a mood, though, and a couple of arguments turned catty. One actually turned violent. I'm not talking slaps and pulled hair, either – one girl pulled a knife. I wasn't there for that one and a good thing too. As it was, Inga cracked some skulls and made everyone sorry they'd started anything in the first place. I'd have made them sorry they'd ever been born.

When sunrise started to glimmer at the edge of the Night Sea and Serena hadn't returned, I started to worry. My concern turned her annoyance to amusement, which just annoyed me, which just amused her even more. Finally I felt the slumber take her and decided it wasn't a bad idea, at that. I turned in early and slept hard.

I only woke up at sunset. It surprised me. I hadn't slept that hard in, oh, ever. Not since coming to Ayrth, or at least, not without being seriously wounded and seriously drugged up because of it. It wasn't that I slept long, but more a matter of how deeply. No dreams, no rolling around in bed. I woke up in the same position I went to sleep in. Let me tell you, it left me stiff as a board. I took a long hot shower to work out the kinks, feeling Serena coming closer as I dressed.

It was warmer near ground than up in the air, but not by much, so I stuck with my fur-lined black leather jacket, top hat and thick red wool skirt. Under the jacket I wore my black corset with the red rose embroidery and the extra whalebone ribbing over a white blouse. Knee-high black leather boots, black leather gloves and a white silk scarf completed my outfit.

Of course, all that dressing just served as a distraction, since I desperately wanted to talk to Serena and she took her sweet time getting back to The Furies. When she finally arrived, I'd been pacing by the entrance to the Booty Bay for nearly ten minutes.

"Ah, there you are, Captain," Serena said as she led three vampyri aboard, as if she didn't know exactly where I was and exactly how impatient I was getting. But we'd also agreed not to speak of our link. Apparently it was some kind of big deal in Daxia.

"Allow me to present my siblings," she continued. "Dorit Bloodflower. Andras Demise. And Benedikt Scythe."

Dorit was dark-haired and dark-eyed, short and curvy, very pretty but not quite beautiful. Benedikt had oily black hair and a permanent two-day beard, made all the more starkly black against his pale skin, with startlingly pale green eyes, slightly buggy to either side of a hooked nose. His hands were rough, hairy and thick-knuckled. Tallest of the three, his stocky build made him seem even bigger.

Andras, though... Andras fell neatly into the stereotypical vampyri. Blonde hair neatly combed back, deep blue eyes like the colour of the sky under a full moon, lean of build and elegant of movement. Where Benedikt plodded, Andras glided.

Yeah, I could tell I was in trouble of serious spazzing, so I kept my attention on Serena.

"Welcome aboard The Furies," I said, shaking each one's hand. Dorit met my eyes, measuring me up, but both men bowed over my hand. I might have been imagining it, but Andras' hand lingered in mine a while longer than necessary. I cleared my throat and said, "Shall we discuss matters in my quarters?"

"That vill not be necessary, Captain," Dorit said. "Ve accept your terms. Ve vill bring this matter to the Blood Council tomorrow night. Vill you join us?"

I kept myself from glancing at Serena. "Just so we're clear, what terms do you agree to, exactly?"

"Ve vill attack Russankya, and any other ally of the Atlan swine, in exchange for certain concessions for Daxia and our freedom."

Benedikt said something in Vampyri, or Daxian, or whatever they called it, way too quick for me to catch with just a half-week of trying to learn Vampyri under my belt. Dorit looked and him and nodded.

"Ah yes. And the Anglic abominations must stop."

"Right," I said, glancing at Serena, hoping for some kind of explanation. I caught a whiff of caution? patience? something like that along our link and the slightest, almost invisible shake of her head.

I turned back to her so-called siblings. "Your terms seem very reasonable. I'd be happy to join you at your meeting with the Blood Council. What time is the meeting?"

"One hour past sunset," Dorit said.

"I'll be by vith my carriage," Andras added. "Until tomorrow?"

They said goodbye, we all shook hands, they each kissed Serena on both cheeks, then they left.

"That was weird," I said when I was sure they were out of earshot.

"I need a drink," Serena answered, heading for the stairs.

I caught up. "So what happened?"

"There vas a reason I left Daxia, all those years ago," she said. "Mainly to get away from them."

"For siblings, there isn't much of a family resemblance."

She laughed. "No, not much. Ve are not biologically siblings. Ve vere all turned by the same wampyri, a sadist who collected fledglings the vay some people collect books. Not for their content, but for how it makes others see him. Oh, so many books, they say, he must be very well read. A wampyri vith so many fledgling wampyri must be wery vealthy, wery powerful. Vonce, ve vere wery many. Now, only the four of us remain."

"Wait, I thought you said vampyri were born like normal humans."

"Ve are. But ve do not become fully wampyri until ve are turned. A master vill drain us. Feed us. Then ve become as I am now. Fully wampyri."

"What if you never get turned?"

"Ve age and die as a normal human vould."

"Okay. So uh, what happened to the rest of your siblings?"

Serena glanced at me. "They vere destroyed."

I got the very distinct impression that she didn't really want to talk about it, so I let it drop. "So what's up with those demands?"

Serena lifted a finger to ask me to wait as we entered the mess.

"Warm or cold?" Hilda asked her, wiping her hands on her apron.

"The first one, cold," Serena answered. "Varm the second, please."

Hilda's huge blue eyes widened at the order. Serena never drank more than one mug of blood in the mess hall, not without some sort of action coming up soon.

We sat at our usual table. Serena rubbed her face with both hands. "To understand the demands, you must understand the nature of our people. Despite the stories, ve are not immortal. How old vould you say I am?"

"I know you're over a hundred."

"Yes, but how old do I look?"

"I dunno. Twenty five?"

That surprised her. "So old? Really?" Then she laughed. "Ah vell. I vas sixteen vhen I vas turned. One of dozens of fledglings made by our sire, who vas, himself, one of thousands of wampyri sires. Vonce, Daxia stretched from the Night Sea across the Carpath Mountains all the vay to Etrusca and Bavardy. Vonce, ve ruled not just the night, but the day as vell. You know ve vonce kept slaves as blood herd, yes? Before I vas born, the practice had stopped. Legally, that is. Of course, illegal means vere found to keep the blood banks full. And naturally, ve need to feed. Humans required favours from us and paid in blood.

"But ve vere greedy and craved too much power. Atlan stepped in to 'rescue' the humans under our thumbs. And by the time I vas made wampyri, ve had been driven back across the Carpaths. Vonce, our population stretched across enough land, controlled enough humans, to sustain us. But vhen I vas made, ve vere being concentrated and our human population being offered freedom from our tyranny. Less food for us. More wampyri moving into Warnya every night.

"And so, ve varred vith ourselves. Sometimes open bloodshed. More often than not, alliances that shifted with the vind, secret murders in quiet alleys. My three siblings and I are all that vere left of the dozens of our siblings turned by our sire. A sire ve four could not kill ourselves, for such is the nature of sire and fledgling. But vhen the time came and ve saw him valk into a trap, ve fled, rather than assist him.

"After fifty years of manipulation and betrayal, I had had enough. I left Daxia on one of the last ships to be permitted unrestricted entry and departure."

"Whoa, wait," I interrupted. "We weren't restricted."

Serena waved her hand at that. "I bribed the dock officials to accept our papers."

"We don't have any papers."

"According to the dock officials, ve do."

Hilda brought Serena her second mug of blood. Serena accepted it with a smile. "So the wampyri society that had arisen from the so-called Invisible Var vas vun of machinations, dangerous alliances, and political manoeuvring. Nothing straightforward like a thrust to the heart. Everything vas plans vithin schemes vithin plots. And so many dead wampyri. Of course, our Atlan superiors had seen to it that the creation of new fledglings vould thenceforth be illegal. And who vould risk the creation of yet another rival for our dwindling supplies of blood?

"But not every human left Daxia. Gradually the humans and wampyri came to a truce. Or more accurately, a financial arrangement. And that has lasted until today."

"What does this have to do with your siblings' offer?"

"I am getting to that, Wal."

"Alright, fine."

"During the Invisible Var, Atlan military forces set up camp at our borders. To ensure the Var did not spill out beyond our borders, you see. But the humans manning the forts and patrolling the borders vere no match for our Wulka, much less a fully-blooded wiolent wampyri. So Atlan found a vay to keep us caged."

"Let me guess. Patchworks."

"Yes. Exactly. And since the majority of patchworks come from Anglica, my siblings seem to have some plot in motion to free Daxia from Atlan control. Vhat they vill do vith the country vonce they have shaken off the yoke of oppression, I do not know."

"They didn't tell you?"

"They do not trust me. I have only been home six times in the last fifty years, including this time. I send them letters vonce a year or so. It is so foolish,. Vhat could I do to their plans? And vhy plan, anyway? There are so few wampyri left, and ve are forbidden to create more."

"How few?"

"In the entire vorld, there are less than a thousand wampyri." She took a long drink from her mug, then set it down. "Unless..."

"Unless what?"

Her eyes went wide. "No. They could not be so foolish."

I resisted the urge to shake her. "How foolish?"

"The only reason they could vant to destroy the Anglic patchwork manufactories and agree to attack Russankya," she said. "They wish to breed an army of wampyri."

Chapter Twenty Three

Somebody Needs To Gag Me At These Meetings

We went to sleep at dawn and didn't wake up again until sunset. Again, no dreams, no rolling around in my bed. Head on my pillow, closed my eyes, woke up ten hours later. Starving. I ate four times as much as I'd normally eat while Domina and Hima got me dressed.

For my outfit, I went with reds and blacks. It seemed fitting.

Andras' carriage arrived ten minutes early, which meant I was still stuffing my face and stuffing myself into my clothes. Six black horses ahead of a black carriage with silver detailing. The man with the reins and whip kept himself hidden in a thick hooded cloak and leather gloves.

When Andras opened the door to the carriage, golden lamplight spilled out onto the darkened docks.

"Velcome aboard." His voice was silk wrapped around a dagger.

But I felt amusement from Serena so I climbed in. Serena sat next to me, both of us facing Andras.

Not spazzing out was pretty much my only concern as we made small talk. Or rather, I should say Serena and Andras made small talk, catching up on mutual friends, that sort of thing. They spoke in Atlan for my benefit, but since I didn't really have any interest in what they were talking about, I let my attention wander to the scenery we passed.

The town went about its nightly business. We were stopped at a checkpoint and questioned by patchworks wearing Atlan uniforms. Our forged papers seemed to be good enough for them, though, so they let us by. I found myself almost hoping they'd start something. A good fight would get some of the nervousness I felt out of my system. But they didn't seem willing to oblige. We soon were pulling up to the gates of a huge manor home.

Even this place seemed depressingly unwilling to comply with stereotypes. No colossal castle, complete with cobwebs and crypts, no. Bright light spilled from dozens of tall windows. Half a dozen carriages or so lined the driveway.

Inside, a human butler took our coats and cloaks and hats. Another servant, vampyri from the look of him, asked us to disarm. We obliged him by leaving a pile of weapons on his counter. I kept my two main gauches I'd strapped to my legs, though. Better to apologize later for any social gaffe, than find myself in a spot of trouble with nothing to defend myself.

We were led to a large circular hall, lit with both electrical lights and huge dripping candelabras. A huge round table occupied the centre of the chamber, surrounded by high-backed wooden chairs. I noticed there were no windows in the chamber. Vampyri and, surprisingly, humans stood around the room in groups of three or four, speaking to each other in quiet voices, a low murmur that blended into white noise. The doors closed behind us and people began to take their seats.

Andras bowed low over my hand and nodded to Serena, then went to his chair.

"So we sit on the floor?" I asked Serena.

She shrugged. "Ve stand. The chairs are wery uncomfortable."

A huge vampyri burst through another set of doors and announced something in Vampyri, loud enough to carry over the voices of anyone still talking. Everyone hurriedly took their seats.

"Vladimir Nightreaver," Serena muttered, glancing at the giant.

He stood head and shoulders taller than any other vampyri. Seriously, he was like, seven feet tall or something. Muscular, but not crazy buff. He wore his hair shaved short, dressed entirely in black, and carried himself as though accustomed to command, an attitude I knew well from the other pirate captains I'd known. When he looked at me, I got the distinct impression he wasn't impressed. Well, the feeling was mutual. It took more than being huge and ordering people around to impress me.

"So, Heartlace," he said in Atlan. "Returned once more? It has been many years since ve saw you here in the Council."

"Nightreaver," she answered. "I have been enjoying the liberty of the seven skies."

That got some mutters from people. I guess being trapped in your own country would make the freedom of travel seem much more attractive.

"And this must be the infamous Sunset Wal," he continued.

"That's me," I said, giving him my cheekiest grin. That scored me the slightest sliver of a scowl.

"Vhy have you asked to meet this Council, Captain Wal?"

"Lemuris needs help to overthrow Atlan oppression."

"So you come to ask our help?" asked an incredibly beautiful vamypri woman dressed in an incredibly beautiful green silk gown trimmed in white fur. Her black hair fell in ringlets all around her flawless face.

"Well, no," I admitted. "They sent me to ask the Zhou for help. But the Zhou won't help unless you join in the fight, too. Seems attacking Russankya before the winter snows have all melted doesn't exactly strike them as the easiest campaign. We need their help, and they need your help. That's why we're here."

"To convince us to help the Zhou?" an overweight human man asked. "Vhat have the Zhou done for us? They vill not even trade vith Daxia."

"Forgive me, but what does Daxia have that the Zhou would want?" I asked. "Besides one of the most feared military units in the world."

"It is true," Andras said, standing to address the Council. "Ve have nothing of value in the world of trade. Daxia, once proud, once great, a leader among nations, has been reduced to a backwater province, a protectorate of the Atlan Empire. Ve should throw off the leashes of our masters! Strike back and reclaim vhat vas rightfully ours!"

The room exploded in shouts and cheers and noise. Some people were nodding and shouting their agreement. Others were shouting for Andras to shut up, sit down.

Nightreaver stood and everyone shut up. "You're a fool, Demise. You think ve vould survive such a var? Let me tell you vhat vill happen. Ve go to var. Strike against Atlan forces. Von fully blooded wampyri is vorth ten Atlan soldiers, ve all know this.

"But they do not outnumber us ten to von. THEY OUTNUMBER US A THOUSAND TO VON! They vill send THOUSANDS of their soldiers to hunt us down! And vhat vill you do vhen sunrise comes and the slumber takes you? Vhen you are wulnerable to fire and stake and sword and the killing sun? Hmm?"

"Our allies vill protect us," Dorit said, standing beside Andras.

"Our allies," Nightreaver spat. "At best, they vill fear us as monsters. At vorst, they vill seek to use us as veapons and toss us aside vonce they have vhat they vant."

"Well, I mean, come on," I said. "Lemurisians are crazy, snake-loving murderers. The Union of Automatic Gentlemen are cold, inhuman machines. The pirate armada are a bunch of scavenging, murderous thieves. The Zhou Path of Three are criminals, thugs, and worse. You really think, in this group, you'll be considered monsters?"

"You're not exactly making a great case for our cause, Wal," Serena whispered, but underneath, I could feel she was fighting to keep from laughing.

"My point is this: we look out for each other. We have to! No one else will. And if we don't, Atlan will pick at us and pick at us until we're worn down to nothing."

Nightreaver just shook his head. "No. Ve entered into this... stalemate vith them to protect our vay of life. To protect the few wampyri who remain! If ve join this rebellion, Atlan vill have all the justification they vill need to swoop in and slaughter us all. You mortals vill be enslaved, or vorse, patchworked. Ve wampyri vill be hunted to the ends of Ayrth until ve are no more."

"You coward," Dorit accused him. Nightreaver leapt to his feet, baring his fangs, hands curled into fists.

"Wait! Stop!" I jumped up on the table. Everyone looked shocked

"Dorit, you're wrong," I said. "It's not cowardice to want to protect your people. Believe me, as an airship captain, I know. I'd love for all my girls to live to a ripe old age, surrounded by children and grandchildren and loved ones. I'd love for each and every one of them to die in their sleep on top of a bed of money and spent lovers!" That actually shocked a laugh out of some of them. "But we all know, that's not going to happen."

I turned to face Nightreaver. "And it's not foolish to seek a better life. Just because something worked years ago doesn't mean the same holds true now! When your people reached the stalemate with Atlan, were you confined to the borders of Daxia? Were you surrounded by patchworked soldiers, soldiers who are pretty much designed to fight vampyri? No blood, no pain, stronger than humans, faster than humans, nearly impossible to kill? Almost like they were designed to fight vampyri.

"Atlan has already changed the conditions of your arrangement. How much further can you let it go before the conditions become unbearable, unrecognisable from the original agreement?"

I spotted the fat human who'd spoken up before. "And you Daxians.

You're painted with the same brush, am I right? Restricted from travel. Denied trade. Because every Atlan knows you're just tools of your vampyri overlords and nobody wants to seem sympathetic to the vampyri. You're just as stuck here as them and for what?"

"It's true," he said. "The stalemate between the wampyri and Atlan has made Daxians everywhere the subject of scorn at best and wiolence at vorst. If a Daxian tries to leave the country of his birth, nowhere in Atlan is he safe. And so he must stay. Stay here, vhere year after year and generation after generation, ve try to scrape out a life for ourselves and our families. But how many generations can this continue? My vife and I vere blessed vith two children, a son and a daughter. My son... has the blood thinness. He can never have children. But my daughter is healthy! She vill have her pick of villing husbands, vhile my son vill live a lonely life and die childless. This is not the life I vant for him!"

"If you support this rebellion, he vill not live long at all," said a grey-haired vampyri sitting near Nightreaver.

"Not unless ve break the First Law," Dorit said.

The room went still. On every Daxian face, fear. On every vampyri face, cold calculation.

"Create more wampyri," a female vampyri in red said slowly.

"It is expressly forbidden," the grey-haired vampyri said. "Not just by the Atlan. Every nation in the vorld demands it of us."

"As do ve," one of the human Daxians said, a rough-looking man with a scar on one cheek.

"Yes, yes, ve promised not to make more wampyri, and you promised not to lead torch-bearing riots against us," the vampyri in the green dress said, waving her hand in annoyance. "It is an ancient compact, sealed in blood and honoured in tradition."

I felt a bit ridiculous, still standing on the table, so I hopped down.

"Let us say, each wampyri is free to create one fledgling," Dorit said. "That doubles our number. The fledglings vill be new to the hunger, eager to test out their power. Let us further agree that our mortal kin may even decide who shall be their master."

"How many of us even have children to turn, now?" a mustached vampyri asked. "How many generations grew old and died, because of the First Law?"

"There are enough," Dorit said. "Enough non-turned wampyri to double our numbers. And vhen the var is over, new children to raise... and in time, to turn into full-blooded wampyri."

Every vampyri in the room was thinking so hard, plotting so fast, that you could just about hear the gears turning in their heads. If this, then that. If that, then the other. The humans had settled back and begun to calculate for themselves, fear gone in the face of possible advantage. Everyone was trying to figure out the best deal for themselves.

So naturally, I had to open my big mouth.

"Look, it seems to me that the real problem isn't how few of you there are, but how many of your patchwork prison guards surround you. Right? I mean, as long as they can just make more replacement troops, it won't matter how many you kill. So why not remove their ability to make more?"

"And how do you propose to do that, Captain?" a woman said.

"Seems to me, if we shut down the patchworking factories, then you can slaughter them all and they won't be able to send in new patchwork troops. They'd have to send regular human troops, and you can take care of them, easy."

She laughed. "Just shut down the factories? They are in Anglica! And ve cannot leave Daxia."

"No, but I can," I said. Like I said, me and my big mouth.

"You?" Nightreaver sneered.

"Yeah," I said, grinning at him hard. "I'll go to Anglica, shut down the patchwork factories. You'll rise up against your patchwork guards, invade Russankya. The Zhou will join you and the Russ will be facing a two-front war against the most feared armies in the world."

Through my connection with Serena, I felt surprise, amusement, even pride.

Chapter Twenty Four

Living Life Is Hazardous To My Health

The arguing went on for a couple of hours longer, but the seeds had been laid and really all that was left was quibbling over the details. In the end, with dawn approaching, the Daxians agreed to allow the vampyri to create new vampyri. The vampyri agreed to attack Russankya, but only after they'd received confirmation that the Anglic patchwork manufactories had been shut down. Also, they insisted they couldn't leave Daxia unguarded, so they could only commit half their forces to the invasion. I was willing to bet that the half of their forces sent into Russankya would be the newly made fledglings.

To make sure the vampyri got their confirmation as soon as possible, they had one more stipulation to make. The Furies had to carry a squad of Vulka with us out of Daxia.

I hadn't been crazy about that idea, but without radio or telegraph to send information any faster, it really was the best option. Anyway, Serena had seemed keen on the idea, once they'd made it clear who they'd be sending with us.

We had to smuggle them aboard. I didn't know what was in the dozen huge wooden crates we hauled into the Booty Bay, but the patchwork dock officials seemed convinced they were filled with machine parts. The huge sides of fresh beef and pork, long strings of sausages and crate after crate of live chickens we brought aboard could have fed half my crew for a month. And the sacks of potatoes. Sack upon sack upon sack. The girls hauling the sacks joked we wouldn't be able to take off once all the hundreds of pounds of potatoes had been stored away. I just about believed them. When they rolled a half dozen huge barrels of beer into the Booty Bay, I began to wonder just how long these soldiers intended to stay. Mrs. Shorty just about had a fit, trying to find a place for everything.

Serena withdrew her entire fortune, hundreds of pints of blood, and stored it in our cold storage room. Made me think she might be considering never returning to Daxia, but she didn't seem inclined to talk about it.

Then the squad arrived, in the pitch of night, from the sea-side of the docks, away from prying patchwork eyes. We pulled them, naked and dripping frigid water onto our decks. A dozen tall, muscular, incredibly athletic women, joking about the water being just right for a night swim.

When the last of them had been hauled from the frigid Night Sea, we closed our bay doors and turned on the lights.

Every last one of them had red hair, pulled into tight braided loops.

Every last one of them stared at me, at my untamed mane of red hair, as they made their way past me into the ship. Even the shortest of them stood a good six inches taller than me. One of the crates we'd brought aboard held their clothes and personal gear. We'd brought them towels to warm themselves. Once they were dried and nearly dressed, Hilda handed out mugs of steaming beef broth.

"Who's their leader?" I asked Serena.

"That vould be me," the biggest one said, snapping to attention. "Olga Draganova, commander of the Wulka-rey."

I offered her my hand. "Welcome aboard, commander. Or can I call you Olga? We don't much stand on military protocol here."

She looked down at me. I mean, way, way down. She had to be six and a half feet tall, at least, and her feet were still bare. Piercing green eyes set to either side of a prominent nose looked me up and down. She took a deep breath. Then she took my hand and shook it, managing not to crush it to a bloody pulp though I'm pretty sure I heard my bones crack. She nodded once. "Perhaps in private, Captain. Your crew may not be military, but my vomen are accustomed to a more formal attitude."

"Alright, commander. We've got bunks set up for you and your, um, sorry, Vulka-rey? Is that right?"

"Yes, Captain. 'Air-volf'." She turned to her crew. "Ve hunt the skies, yes?"

The Vulka-rey all punched the air above them and howled. It wasn't a dozen human women howling, that sound. It was something that sent icy terror spiralling up and down my spine. It made me extremely glad they were on my side.

"Vhen do ve set sail, Captain?" Olga asked.

"As soon as possible."

"Excellent!" She gave a series of orders to her crew and they went to the largest of the crates we'd hauled aboard. Then she turned back to me. "Ve vill require the use of the flight deck for an hour or so, to see to our aircycles."

"Aircycles?"

"Ve vill show you. Vhen they are ready?"

I had the distinct impression I'd been dismissed. "Sure. I'll be back in an hour. We should be well under way by then."

"Excellent, Captain. Until then."

I went to the intercom and ordered the crew to get ready to make sail, then left the Booty Bay. The sounds of wooden crates being cracked open followed me up the stairs. My curiosity was killing me, but I went up to the Command Deck and ordered us into the air.

Serena joined me after a few minutes.

"They know how to make an entrance," I said.

"They are the most elite unit of the Wulka," Serena explained with a shrug. "And they know they are."

"Why are they all redheads?"

Serena folded her arms and leaned against the bulkhead. "Ah, so that is vhat is bothering you."

"I'm not bothered. Just curious."

"Of course you are," she said, raising a hand to her cheek and tapping an elegant finger against her temple, as if to say, *I'm in your head, remember?*

"Fine. Answer the question, please?"

"They are Wulka. In Daxia, the first sign that a child may be a Wulka is red hair."

"You gotta be kidding me."

"I kid you not."

"Look, not every redhead is a werewolf!"

"No, that is true. In Hibernia, in Eire, red hair is not a sign of the Wulka. Though in ancient times it vas considered a sign of the varrior rage. Before Atlan conquered them vonce and for all, the Eire berserkers and their highland kin in Hibernia vere among the most feared varriors in the vorld. Once Atlan conquered them, a century of denying anyone with red hair the right to breed, vell, they say it bred the berserk out of them. But vonce in a vhile. a redheaded Eire or Hibernian vill become a battlefield legend, a vild varrior."

"And in Daxia?"

"In Daxia, children with red hair are sent to live vith the Wulka. More often than not, sometime in puberty, the volf takes them, and they join the Wulka."

"Weird," I said. "So they think I might be one of them?"

"I have no idea vhat they think. However, it is most likely that they feel a certain relief that you may be von of their own."

We left the lights of Varnya behind us, with just the moon and stars to light our way. It surprised me how grateful I was to be back in the air, even if our mission so far hadn't yielded much success. So many variables, so many conditions, so many complications.

"Oh shit!"

"Vhat?"

"I forgot to write that letter to the Fist of the Path of Three! About Delicate Petal!"

Serena chuckled. "Relax, Wal. Tring made her write it and I posted it myself."

I blew out a huge sigh of relief. "Okay, good. Thanks."

While I waited for an hour to crawl by, Violette and I charted a zigzag course across Europa, keeping us well away from cities or major towns. We didn't want any trouble on the way to Anglica, though what we were going to do once we got there was another problem altogether. I had no clue how many patchwork manufactories there were and I had no idea how we were going to get them shut down.

But, first, we had to survive the trip to Anglica. Maybe I could track down the Tallyhos or Remy, get some ideas from them.

Finally an hour had passed, or near enough, so I headed back down to the Booty Bay. I expected it to be a complete disaster of opened crates and machine parts scattered everywhere. What I found, instead, made me stop short at the doorway.

The Vulka-rey had not only not made a mess of things, they'd actually cleaned up some of the mess we usually left lying around. Most of their crates were pulled apart and neatly stacked in a corner. As for what had been in the crates, well...

They kind of looked like motorcycles, but instead of a usual cycle engine their machines had these huge cylindrical engines mounted in front, on which were mounted eight-foot wide propellers. The tiny front wheel sat under the engine, and a leather saddle was mounted just behind. The rear wheel was much larger than the front, maybe six feet in diameter, and it was a solid disk, instead of a spoked wheel. Along either side of the vehicle were mounted these long brass... things. They're difficult to describe. They looked like bars of brass, ridged lengthwise, as long as the vehicle, about a handspan high and maybe twice that wide. They connected to the engine by way of a complicated hinged mechanism.

I climbed down the ladder to the Booty Bay just as Commander Draganova spotted me and headed over. The Vulka-rey all wore coveralls and fur-collared leather jackets, and hers were the cleanest, most spotless of the bunch.

"Ah, Captain, just in time," she said. "You vish to inspect the aircycles?"

"Uh, sure."

She led me on a tour of the aircycles, which looked well-used but also well-loved. Metal bits gleamed with loving polish; the leather saddles had been rubbed down with polish too. Even the few glass instrument gauges looked scrubbed clean. Draganova explained that each member of the squad was responsible for the maintenance and care of their aircycles.

Then she introduced me to her squad. Only a couple of them spoke any Atlan. One, Nikola, was introduced as their best mechanic. Another, Anya, spoke almost as much Atlan as the Commander. Anya was also the smallest of them, being only about six inches taller than me.

"Welcome aboard," I said to them all in Daxian. "I hope you are having safe journey."

"I don't," the one called Zora said while Anya translated. "Let's kill some Atlans, yes?"

I switched back to Atlan. "Tell her I said, I'll see what I can do about that."

Anya translated and they all laughed.

It was a sound I'd soon find familiar. Over the three days it took us to get to Anglica, they constantly traded jokes and teased each other. They laughed and sang songs. With my permission, they pretty much used the entire ship as an obstacle course, running through the halls, climbing up ladders and ropes and pretty much training and exercising whenever they weren't taking care of their aircycles.

Or eating. Could they eat! At the first meal we all had together, they ate about four times what even Inga could put away and drank gallons of beer on top of it. After the meal, they pulled out musical instruments and played for us. We moved the tables aside and everybody danced. It had been ages since we'd had any fun, so I allowed extra rations of wine and beer for everyone and it turned into a huge party. The only thing that slowed us down was sunrise.

Of course, after partying all night, the next morning was pretty rough on everyone. It didn't help that the sun shone brilliant and blinding from a pure blue sky without a cloud in sight. And to keep us from being spotted in that wide open sky, we had to fly closer to the ground, which increased the winds weaving us back and forth, up and down. Some of the girls were pretty hungover, and the privies reeked with the stink of vomit. Almost bad enough to make us regret the night before.

But not the Vulka-rey. They got about four hours sleep and then Commander Draganova had they up and running laps around the ship. I'm sure the sound of their booted feet thundering by didn't help anyone's pounding head.

They worked hard, they ate hard, they drank hard and they partied hard. Some of my girls tried to keep up with the partying but after three days of it, no one seemed keen to keep trying. The Vulka-rey just had us outclassed in the partying category.

I mentioned it to Serena while we watched Commander Draganova arm-wrestling with Inga. Both wore expressions of intense concentration while bets were placed on both sides and shouts of encouragement came from every direction.

"They are an elite military unit," Serena answered. "They know at any moment they vill be called upon to put their lives in danger. Vhat you call partying, they vould call... living life to its fullest, because at any moment, it could end."

"That's depressing."

"Perhaps. Or food for thought, yes?"

I shrugged. "I guess."

Serena put a hand on my shoulder, just as Inga slammed Draganova's arm to the table, much to the shock and amazement of the Vulka-rey and the cheers of my crew.

"You are young, still, Wal," Serena said quietly. "Live a little."

"I'll have plenty of time to live after the war's over, Atlan's destroyed, and the slave trade ends."

Serena looked into my eyes. "Vhat if you don't live that long?"

I hadn't thought about it. Or more like, I had completely avoided thinking about it. Across the room, my crew and our guests lined up to try to take Inga on. Draganova poured a mug of beer for her victorious opponent. Serena sauntered off somewhere. Miss Merryweather, Mrs. Shorty and Brunhilde were enjoying a bottle of sherry. Doc Regan and a few crew were playing six-card. Gigi and Nikola were talking about their engines, a very animated conversation involving a lot of gestures, since neither spoke the other's language. Everywhere around me, women were living life.

I admit it, I didn't like to think about the chance that I might not survive the war. That I might not live a normal life, ever again. That I might never get back home. None of those thoughts helped me deal with what I had to do. Call it denial, if you like. It got me through the day, that's all I knew. Kept me focused on the mission, on running the ship, on the greater goal of ending the slave trade. And push hope of anything else, anything more, deep down inside me.

Anyhow, whatever.

The third day saw us crossing the sea to Anglica. We could see it, a dark smudge on the horizon.

Commander Draganova found me on the Command Deck. "Captain?"

I turned toward her. "Yes, Commander?"

"The Wulka-rey vere vondering if you vould like a demonstration of the aircycles."

"Sure," I said. I'd been wondering how they worked.

"Anya has offered to carry you vith her."

"Wait, me get on one of those?"

"Of course! How else to experience the joy of flying an aircycle?"

From the safety of my command deck? Instead, remembering my conversation with Serena, I said, "Why not? Sounds like fun."

Next thing I knew, I was standing next to Anya's aircycle as she gave me a whole bunch of technical gobbledygook about stuff I couldn't possibly begin to understand. Then she helped me step over the brass bar things and settle myself onto the cycle's saddle.

"Where are the straps?" I asked.

She saddled up just in front of me, a tight squeeze but manageable. "Vhat straps?"

"The ones that keep you strapped to the aircycle?"

Apparently this was the funniest thing she'd ever heard, because not only did she laugh, she repeated it, in Daxian, to the other Vulka-rey. They all laughed, too. Not exactly the best beginning.

Commander Draganova gave the signal and one of my girls opened the portside Booty Bay doors. Wind whipped through the Bay, making my hair flutter into my face. I quickly pulled on my aviator cap and slipped my goggles over my eyes.

The Vulka-rey with their braided hair had no such problems, and they'd already all donned their goggles. Each and every one of them looked eager to get airborne.

Anya stood hard on the starter pedal and the engine roared to life, shaking and shuddering beneath me. She walked the aircycle into position and one by one the Vulka-rey launched themselves out into the open air. I spotted a major, huge, titanic problem right away, but terror gripped my voice until it was our turn to jump out the Bay doors.

"The propeller's not turning!" I yelled over the thundering roar of the engine.

"Of course not!" Anya said over her shoulder. "It vould smash to pieces against the deck! Hold on!"

And with that, she pushed us out into the empty air.

We fell for like, forever. My heartbeat halted. My lungs laboured to breathe. The ocean rushed at us, closer, closer.

Then Anya flipped a switch and the propeller sputtered to life, whirring away over the thunder of the engines.

And still, we fell.

I had a brief paranoid idea that the entire thing, the vampyri agreeing to our deal, getting the Vulka-rey aboard, all of it, had been an attempt to kill me. Maybe even the Zhou were in on it, refusing to attack Russankya, forcing us to go to Daxia.

Then Anya flipped another switch and the brass bars along either side of the aircycle folded out and folded out again and again and again, a hundred times, becoming feathered wings spread out to either side of us. Anya pulled back hard on the twin control levers and suddenly we weren't falling any more. We were flying.

We leveled out probably a hundred feet over the ocean but I could have sworn I felt the sea spray on my face. Anya had slipped her feet into stirrups to either side, which she used to help her stand in the saddle. The engines roared even louder and the propeller's whine climbed and suddenly we were really booting it through the sky, climbing, climbing, as she pulled on the controls. She let out a whoop of delight.

I'd flown in ornithopters and with our batwing backpacks before, but this was something else entirely. The sheer speed made breathing bothersome. I panted through clenched teeth. The shuddering roar of the engines and the purring mechanical drone of the propeller made conversation pretty much pointless, too. And the vibration, well, my insides were being turned into a milkshake. Or a Valshake, I guess.

Anya pointed off to port and I looked. The other Vulka-rey were already in formation. She pushed hard on the left lever and pulled on the right. We banked to port, and joined the formation, a V-shape like birds flying south for the winter. Commander Draganova held the point of the V.

Suddenly a pair of sharp cracks rang out over the roaring drone of the aircycles. I knew that sound really well. Gunshots. But from where? I whipped my head around, trying to see who could be shooting at us.

Turned out, Commander Draganova had been the one to fire. See, although they were shaped like bird's wings, the aircycle wings didn't flap, the way an orni's wings did. Aircycle wings were pretty much fixed in place, though I did notice the metal 'feathers' constantly adjusted to keep us steady. And the forward edge of the wing held something just outside the range of the propeller. Guns, of course.

Anya flipped the covers on the handles of the control levers, revealing a pair of thumb triggers. In perfect sync with the other Vulka-rey, she fired off a couple of shots. With our guns cleared, Commander Draganova put us through a series of manoeuvres. Spiralling and sweeping and banking and spinning, splitting into two groups of six, three of four, four of three. The whole time I kept my arms wrapped around Anya's waist and my knees clenched on the saddle.

At one point we levelled out and did a huge banking turn around The Furies. She was a beauty, all red and brass, as graceful aloft as a bird. Okay, maybe more like, as graceful aloft as a whale was underwater. Anyhow, I realized then that I loved that ship, my ship, our ship, more than I'd ever loved anything in my life. Even more than the coat I'd made for myself, even more than my grandfather's top hat.

A bunch of crew had gathered at the rails to watch us in flight. I spotted Restless waving at us frantically and risked waving back. Of course, that was exactly when Draganova ordered us to split into two groups and circle the ship in two different directions. I grabbed at Anya's waist just as we began to climb.

And that's when I saw her. A figure, crouched low near the tailfin. Dressed all in grey, it had been nearly impossible to spot her against the overcast sky, but against the balloon, she stood out clear as day. Hooded and masked, I couldn't tell who she was, but she lifted something skyward and just as we began our descent, I spotted a rocket flare fly into the sky and explode with green light in the clouds.

Then we were under The Furies and I was facing the wrong way to see what else the mystery woman did. It didn't much matter, because as we began to climb again, I saw the results.

The rocket flare had signalled an Atlan cruiser to come out of hiding.

Chapter Twenty Five

Werewolf Women Are Crazy Bitches

"Get us back to the ship! Now!" I screamed at Anya.

"Now? But the battle has not begun yet!" she yelled back as she flew us into attack formation with the other Vulka-rey.

We flew straight at the enemy vessel. From where I sat, she looked to be one of their Barracuda fast-attack cruisers. Tough and quick in a fight. The Furies had taken Barracudas on before, but you never knew when a capable commander might earn his way up the ranks, instead of buying his commission. It had been known to happen in Atlan Aerial, not often but not rare, either. The idea ranked pretty highly in my list of nightmares I hoped never would come true.

She'd come out of the clouds just out of our firing range and from her angle I guessed she was trying to cross our T. But Draganova had something to say about that.

The Commander led us straight in, nose to nose. Gunshots cracked out in the open air as we were ordered to open fire. I couldn't see how it could possibly have any effect at this range, but they seemed to know what they were doing. Atlan soldiers, startled to find open opposition so soon, dove for cover.

"I have idea!" Anya said. "Take controls!"

"WHAT?!"

"Is easy! Push right, go right, push left, go left, stand go faster, sit go slower, push both forward go down, pull back go up. Yes? Triggers vork guns. Now take controls!"

She stood in the saddle and stepped over me, forcing me forward. Her hands left the handles, and I grabbed them to keep us from crashing into the ocean. Balancing on the seat, she shucked off her boots and jacket, storing them in one of the compartments behind the saddle. Then, just as Commander Draganova led us over the Barracuda's main deck, firing the whole time, Anya jumped.

I was so stunned I watched her fall and land on the deck instead of trying to watch where I was flying. But it paid off when I saw her change from crazy lady to enraged werewolf. Her jumpsuit bulged and stretched and tore. She grew about a foot and a half, all long and lean and fur and claws and fangs. Suddenly the crew weren't worried about the dozen aircycles circling back for another firing run. They had a snarling, whirling predator to deal with.

Then I couldn't see her any more and it hit me: I was flying the aircycle. It was a lot trickier than flying the batwing backpacks. The controls weren't as responsive, for one thing, so I had to anticipate and plan ahead a lot more. But I got the hang of it soon enough, and focussed on not crashing. I hoped someone would show me how to land, assuming we survived the battle.

The second strafing run took us across the length of their balloon. This time I was confident enough in my piloting that I chanced a few shots. Feeling the kick of the guns through the controls was a rush, but even better was seeing the gaping holes opening up in their balloon's protective metal mesh exterior.

Draganova broke formation and swung back to come alongside me. "Go back to ship!" she yelled at me. I barely heard her over the crash and thunder of battle and the roar of our engines.

"I don't know how to land!" I yelled back. "And Anya, she's still on their ship!" I turned to point.

My hand leaving the control? Bad idea. I suddenly spun away from Draganova and the formation, spiralling out of control. The ocean rushed up to smash me to bits as I fought to gain control of the aircycle, grabbing at the lever and hauling back on both. Standing to gain even another ounce of leverage only made the aircycle go faster, but it also gave me enough strength to pull out of my dive.

And, you know, shoot straight up again. I passed right in front of the Atlan Barracuda's bow, and the few soldiers not entirely occupied with a rampaging werewolf took a couple of pot shots at me. I didn't even have time to duck or react at all, because I flew past them so fast it wasn't until much later that I realized how close one of them had gotten – a bullet hole clean through the sleeve of my jacket. Of course, I couldn't let that kind of thing go unanswered. You let people shoot at you without doing anything about it and next thing you know, everyone's doing it.

I levelled out, got my bearings and then banked hard to port, swooping down, fingers clutching down on the triggers of my guns. Bullets filled the air, racing ahead of me as I swept across the deck. Some of them hit home. Screams filtered through the thunder of battle.

And then I passed them, hurtling toward The Furies. Behind me, the Barracuda fired off a full broadside at my ship. It'll give you an idea of how slow airship battles really were, knowing the aircycles had pretty much been able to make three strafing runs on the Barracuda before she'd gotten her guns trained on my ship. Anyhow, The Furies had their T well and truly crossed. I pulled up hard at the sound of the Atlan cannons. Good thing, too.

See, an experimental lightning cannon being fired in a thunderstorm? Not such a good idea. But in a relatively clear sky? Pure. Awesome.

The Barracuda exploded in mid-air.

Not completely, because that would be way too convenient, but you know, enough to make them think twice about ever flying again. Probably because the blast of lightning The Furies fired off got caught up in all the cannonballs heading their way.

Anyhow, the Barracuda had a huge hole blasted through their hull. I mean, right through. The keel started to buckle in the middle and that's when bodies started falling out, or jumping off, abandoning ship to risk surviving in the frigid ocean beneath us. I'm a little embarrassed to admit that's the first time I thought about Anya being still on board.

But that was pretty much when she landed on the seat behind me. Yes, I screamed and nearly lost control of the aircycle. I glanced up and spotted the Vulka-rey formation about thirty feet above me. Then I risked a look behind me at Anya.

She'd reverted back to human form, not a scratch on her. Her jumpsuit, though, was full of holes, basically reduced to rags. Later she explained that the shifting back and forth from her wolfish form could heal any injury. But right then, laughing, she grabbed her jacket out of where she'd stored it and pulled it on. Then she stepped around me and took back the controls.

"Having fun?" I asked, angry.

"Of course! Aren't you?"

"Not really!"

She just laughed harder.

Chapter Twenty Six

Old Friends In New Places

We made it back to The Furies in once piece, which is more than I can say about the Barracuda. While we were landing in the Launch Bay, she cracked right in half. Fires raged and soon took over their balloon, which then exploded in beautiful orange flames. She sank rapidly toward the ocean. We heard the hiss of the fires extinguishing even from where we hovered, high above her.

And let me tell you, if I thought the Vulka-rey partied hard before, that was nothing compared to the insanity that followed the battle. Singing, dancing, feasting, drinking, you name it, it happened. I tried to stay relatively sober, but every single Vulka-rey wanted to toast me at least once. At some point they started calling me "Captain WAL-ka-rey!" and so they toasted themselves for their cleverness and toasted me for being one of them and toasted Inga for being such a crack shot with a lightning cannon and toasted The Furies for being such a fine ship and toasted the Vulka-rey for being such fierce warriors and toasted Anya for being so brave, so daring, so stupid, so, so, so... Well, you get the idea. A lot of toasts meant I got very, very toasted.

They pulled out a bottle of a very clear liquid that smelled a little like prunes and a lot like floor cleaner. I don't remember anything after that. I guess someone put me in my bed, since that's where I woke up. Not Domina, since she would probably have taken off my boots and corset. Let me tell you, waking up with a pounding headache, sick to your stomach, after spending the night asleep wearing a corset, isn't my preferred method of waking up. I took off my corset and boots, threw up in my chamber pot, drank half the pitcher of water to get the taste out of my mouth, then collapsed back asleep. Yeah, remind me not to party with werewolves any more. I spent the day in bed, hungover and sorry for myself. Or I would have if Doc hadn't shown up around noon.

She sat me up and handed me a mug of something that looked vile and smelled worse. "Drink this."

"What is it?" I asked, though it came out more like "wazzit".

"Hangover cure," she answered.

I moaned. "Can't you just put a bullet through my brain?"

"Sure, an' we wouldn't want to waste a perfectly good bullet."

I moaned again for purely self-pitying reasons and took the mug from her. I took a deep breath, then chugged the entire concoction.

Doc Regan pulled out her watch and checked the time. She glanced at me, snapped the watch shut and passed me the chamber pot.

"What's this for?" I asked. So far, the so-called cure hadn't done anything for my pounding head.

"Shush now," she answered, checking her watch again.

"Doc," I began, then I threw up everything I had ever eaten in my entire life. I swear there was baby food at the end there.

"That's the cure?!" I complained, spitting to clear my mouth of the foul taste.

"How d'ye feel?" she asked, taking my pulse.

I opened my mouth to yell at her, to call her every name in the book, then I realized that the pounding headache had disappeared, that the urge to empty my guts was gone. "Uh... hungry?"

"Good! Ye're fine. Time t' get out o' bed, Cap'n," she smiled at me.

"This is a miracle. You're a miracle worker."

Doc Regan raised an eyebrow at me. "That's one o' them words means somethin' back where you're from, don't it?"

Right. No religion meant no miracles. "Uh, you just made the impossible possible."

"Bah. Tis jus' chemistry, Cap'n."

"When the war's over, your chemistry will make us very rich."

She laughed at that, then left me to get dressed.

I didn't much feel like wearing a corset and anyway Domina was nowhere to be found. I guess she didn't merit Doc Regan's Impossible Hangover Cure, being so far down the command structure or something. Anyway, I put on my comfiest clothes and went looking for breakfast.

I helped myself to a huge bowl of Brunhilde's bacon potatoes and a steaming mug of coffee. There were fresh baked apple turnovers, too, so I had two of those. I scarfed them down and was just helping myself to a second cup of coffee when Restless found me.

"Cap'n Cap'n Cap'n!"

"Restless Restless Restless!"

"There you are!"

"Here I am."

"Message for you, Cap'n."

"Okay. Wait, why aren't you on duty?"

"Not on 'til sundown, Cap'n."

"What's the message?"

"Miss Wolfwood compliments, Cap'n, and 'if you're finished stuffing your face would you kindly get your arse to the bridge?'"

I laughed. "Molly said that, did she?"

"Yes'm."

"Okay, go tell her I'm on my way."

"Aye aye, Cap'n."

Restless ran off. I swear, I never saw that kid walk anywhere. I followed her, carrying my mug of coffee with me. Mrs. Shorty had told me we were running out of real, fresh Merinasy coffee beans. I wanted to savour the supply we had left. Maybe once we were done with this mission we'd head on back to Libertia and pick up some more. First things first, though.

Molly looked like she'd been up all night, listening to people partying. Which, come to think of it, was very probably what she'd done. Don't know why she didn't join us. Serena had been on duty, mildly pissed off that she'd missed the entire daylight action. I think Molly's prosthetics made her self-conscious about being around too many people. But I mean, we had other women on board with artificial prosthetics, like Inga's new eye. Maybe Molly just didn't like parties, I dunno.

Anyhow, she looked at me from where she stood up by Argenta and the radio. Relief washed over her face and she practically jumped down the spiral staircase that led up to Argenta's station.

"The bridge is yours, Captain, you deal with them," she said, heading out without another word.

"Them who?" I asked Argenta.

"Coo-eeeeeeee!" came a familiar voice over the radio. Even with the crackle and static, I recognized her. I felt a huge grin split my face as I ran up the stairs.

"Tallyhooooooooo!" I answered into the voice cone.

"Ducks, wherever have you been? It's simply been an age!"

"Tell me about it. Where are you?"

"Just at the limit of the wireless, wot? Portside-ish of you."

I looked out to port and saw a black speck in the sky. "Your lookout's got good eyes."

"Well, you are somewhat noticeable, haw haw!"

"How goes the war?"

"Not here, pet, too many ears might be listening. Did you know an Atlan Barracuda went down not far from here?"

"I heard something about that. What's this about others listening?"

"Follow us home. We'll discuss it over tea."

I heard another, similar voice break in over the radio. "We should have a fete!"

"Oh Gwen," the first voice said, making her Guinevere. "We simply haven't the time for a fete."

"But the pavilion's already up and Bunny won't mind."

"The pavilion and our dear brother are entirely beside the point. We haven't any dancers, any musicians, any fire breathers or jugglers and anyway, it's barely Spring!"

"Oh tosh!"

"Tosh yourself. Sunset, follow us, won't you?"

"On your stern," I answered, then relayed the orders to...

"Cobra?"

"Yes, Captain?"

"Why are you piloting my ship?"

"I asked Miss Wolfwood if I might take the helm, Captain. I had never done it before." She glanced over her snakeskinned shoulder at me. "It has only been an hour or so. Do you wish that I stop?"

"Yeah, um, it might be better for a real pilot to take us in. Landing's a little trickier than keeping her steady in a calm sky."

She looked disappointed but said, "As you say, Captain."

One of the new girls replaced her, an Afric pilot named Alliya. She guided us toward the Tallyho Sisters (the ship, not the girls) and fell in behind them.

We followed along for an hour or so. Then, just as the sun was setting, way off in the distance I saw a filthy grey cloud, low on the horizon. Violette had joined me, so I asked her, "What do you think that is? Is it heading our way?"

She glanced out the window. "I should hope not," she answered. "That's Albion."

"What? Is it on fire?"

"After a fashion. Coal fires, gas fires, the crematoria. Oh, and the very poor tend to burn horse droppings."

"That's totally disgusting."

"But inexpensive, Captain."

"I guess. Wait, crematoria?"

Violette took a sip from her mug of tea. "Mm-hmm. Where they dispose of the leftovers."

"Leftover what?"

"From the patchwork manufactories. The unusable... bits."

"Yep, still disgusting."

"You asked."

"So I did. Argenta, raise the Tallyho Sisters, please."

Argenta spoke into the voice cone, as I climbed the spiral staircase to the radio station.

"Tallyho Sisters, Captain," Argenta said. I took the voice cone.

"Ahoy, the Sisters," I said. "I thought we were going to Albion."

"Ahoy-hoy yourself, ducks, we are. Not in our airships, though. Be snatched up in a jiff, wot? Notorious pirates and all that rot."

"Oh yeah. So where are we headed."

"You just stay on this heading, pet. We'll be running dark as soon as night falls, so do try to keep up."

"Okay, got it."

Night fell, creeping along from grey to black, a long slow fade into darkness. Violette, seeing that her services weren't required, headed off to supper. Serena woke up just as the Tallyhos shut off all their exterior lighting. I passed Alliya a pair of our special see-in-the-dark goggles and put on a pair myself. Serena, I knew, didn't need any help seeing in the dark.

"Argenta, give the order to run dark."

"Aye Captain."

"Ve are not going to Albion," Serena said.

"No, the twins think we'd be snatched up by the authorities the second we flew overhead."

"The price of notoriety. I have always vanted to be infamous."

"I'm starting to think fame might be overrated."

"So vhere are ve going?"

"No idea. The twins said something about a pavilion, and someone named Bunny? Their brother I think."

"You did not ask?"

I shrugged. "You know how they are when they get going. Sometimes it's hard to figure out how much of it is just an act. I usually just go with the flow and try not to pay too much attention to them."

Serena shrugged. I swear, nobody could say as much in a shrug as she could. This particular shrug said, *They're your friends and I don't care enough to argue about it* and *You're probably right, the Tallyhos can be a bit dizzying at times with all their babble.*

As hard to follow as the twins were, following their ship proved pretty easy, deep into the heartland of Anglica. We soared over rolling pastures. Once in a while we'd see the silver line of a road, or the brilliant white meandering of a stream or river. Occasionally the golden glow of a public house at the centre of a small village. Finally we came to a foggy moor. Wisps of mist rose up from the ground like silvery ghosts in the moonlight. The last patches of winter snow coated the ground in... well, patches. And there, in the heart of the moor, rose a huge old manor home, like a black battleship in a sea of white. A few yellow lights still burned inside the manor.

The Tallyho Sisters led us around the manor toward a thin stand of tall trees. Pretty smart of them, I figured. Anyone flying overhead would probably see our balloons, but anyone riding or driving past would just see trees. We could spread nets of tree branches over our balloons if we were really worried about being spotted from above.

Anyhow, we weighed anchor, got ourselves locked down, then I went off with Tring and a couple of her girls to meet the twins.

"Hallooo!" Gwendolyn cried, arms spread wide to give me a warm hug and a kiss on both cheeks.

"Wherever have you been, darling?" Guinevere added, taking her turn at hugs and kisses.

"I'll tell you when we get somewhere warm," I answered. "Where are we, anyway?"

"This?" Guinny said, waving a dismissive hand at the looming manor. "The ancestral manse, pet. Frightful old thing, wot?"

"I say, Sunset's right, let's get inside and warm up," Gwen said, shivering dramatically. "Hot toddies for everyone!"

"I'll just stick with tea, thanks," I answered.

The twins each took one of my arms, looped it around their own and arm-in-arm we walked through the foggy moor toward the manor. From the air it hadn't seemed quite so big, but as we got closer I realized the place was huge. Three storeys, multiple wings kind of huge.

I couldn't keep the amazement out of my voice. "This is your family's home? Why would you leave?"

"Dreadfully boring, doncha know, darling."

"And can you see the pair of us as dutiful, meek little wives? Haw and haw again, pet."

They had a point. Dutiful and meek were the opposite of the twins.

A man spoke from the shadows of the door we were headed for. "Certainly I could never imagine such a thing."

Chapter Twenty Seven

A New Friend In An Old Place

Everything blurred. Tring was in front of me. Li was behind me. Jin, Yue and Bao rushed ahead of us all.

The man, I'm not joking, giggled. "How quite impressive, my very, very deahs."

"Oh Bunny," Gwen laughed.

"You rascal!" Guinny added. "Hiding in the shadows. You scamp!"

The door opened behind him, golden lamp light spilling out, warm and inviting, and I got a good look at him. He was so handsome my eyes hurt just looking at him. Dark hair, twinkling blue eyes. A gorgeous smile he hid behind a raised hand. A dark three-quarter length coat and a white silk scarf.

He gave his sisters a group hug, then turned his eyes on me. I felt myself turning into a complete, hopeless spaz when he looked at me.

And then he spoke.

"And is this the little girl who's causing so much trouble? She's an absolute doll, dahlings, a absolute and utter treat!"

And a miracle happened. The spaz died a horrible death.

She didn't do me the common courtesy of closing my mouth for me when she went, though. It hung there, slack-jawed at his comments. I forced myself to assume he meant them as compliments and forced myself to close my mouth.

"Captain Sunset Val, of The Furies," I said, offering my hand.

"Of cawse you are, my very deah, who else would you be?" he answered, taking my hand in his and bending to kiss it. I found myself wishing I'd worn my gloves, or at least washed my hands.

"Bunthorne Bartholomew Tallyho, esquire. Y'service," he said, looking me in the eyes. He turned away. "Well, don't let's stand out heah catching our deaths of chill. Come in, come in!"

Bunny ushered us into the family home. You can probably imagine how gorgeous it was inside – rich dark wallpapers, countless family portraits and paintings and pictoriographs, thick intricate carpets. Bookcases everywhere, filled with leather-bound tomes, statuary, and knick-knacks of every possible description. Automaidons scurried here and there, carrying covered silver trays that perfectly matched their silvery bodies. And finally we reached a comfortable drawing room, with armchairs and side tables and oh well you get the idea. A crackling fire danced in the ten-foot wide solid granite fireplace. Over the mantle was a family portrait, very nearly life-sized, painted when the twins were still little girls and their brother a serious-looking tween. The artist was very good, capturing the mischievous sparkle in the twins' eyes and smiles. Electric lamps sat in the corners of the room, giving light without taking away from the fire's golden glow.

A robot butler led in a parade of automaidons, offering us every manner of food and drink. I took a cup of tea with three lumps of sugar. I couldn't usually have three lumps, since Brunhilde needed our sugar for our baking. If you'd ever had one of her pastries, you'd have given up your sugar allotment too.

Bunny and his sisters kept up a steady stream of small talk about people and places and events I'd never heard of, so I didn't pay very much attention. I just sat and enjoyed the sound of my own language. Well, as much as Anglic sounded like English, anyway. It surprised me what a weight off my mind it was, not having to follow along in a foreign language.

Finally, though, I had to interrupt. "Sorry, girls, but does Bunny know about your... um, occupation?"

The three of them laughed.

"Isn't she precious? Piracy could hardly be called an occupation, my deah," Bunny answered for them. "In the family, we refer to it as the twins' 'little indiscretions', doncha know."

"Oh. Okay then. Um."

"What is it, pet?" Guinny asked, polishing her monocle.

I glanced at Bunny and said, "Well, we need to talk about um, you know. Stuff."

"I'll leave you to it, then," Bunny said, rising out of his chair. "Not for me, this business. Piracy, now, that's full of brilliant adventure. War, though, that's a different thing altogethah."

"You don't approve of a war to end slavery?" I asked.

"Ending slavery is a noble goal, my very deah. But war, now, that's another bucket of cogs, wot? I'm a dedicated pacifist and truth be told a bit of a coward in martial realms. Absolutely abysmal at the Academy. War holds no appeal to me whatsoevah. I'll have Platinuma bring in moah tea, should you like. Or something strongah, p'raps?"

"We'll take care of it, Bun-bun," Gwen said, shooing him out of the room. "Let us girls talk now."

Long story short, I told them everything that had happened since leaving Lemuris, the deals I'd had to make, the saboteur on The Furies. You already know all that, so I won't go over it again.

They told me about the war. Things had ground to a halt in Afric, neither side gaining much ground. Lemuris forces had liberated a major city called Q'ardum, wherever that was. They'd been using it as their new base of operations, but the land forces in Afric had been reduced to fighting from trenches dug along a thousand-mile front while the aerial forces pounded away at each other. Admiral Salamander was getting desperate, throwing troops and ships into worse and worse situations, trying to break the stalemate.

"That's how we lost more than a few of the pirate armada," Guinny said, shaking her head.

"Including a couple of ships outfitted with the communicatrons," Gwen added.

My mouth hung open, my mind filling with all the problems that would create. "So now the Atlans have radios of their own?"

"Well, Doctor Zero has insisted that it will take them some time to sort out the inner workings of the communicatrons," Guinny said, sipping from her tea. She wrinkled her nose and set the cup aside. Getting up and going to the sideboard, she added, "More likely they're listening in, trying to discover our movements and plans. Remy's got our folk spinning all sorts of tall tales to get the Atlan bastards to bite, but so far, no luck. Port, anyone?"

"No thanks," I said.

"A double for me, there's a dear," Gwen said.

"How is Remy?" I asked.

"Well enough, though truth be told I suspect the crown lies uneasy on his head," Guinny answered, coming back with two crystal glasses filled with dark amber port.

"What crown?"

"Oh, some silly thing some of the other captains cooked up," Gwen said, taking her drink from her sister. "Said if Remy was going to act like a pirate king, he might as well be one in name as well."

"So they all got together and voted Remy the King of the Pirate Armada."

"You don't vote for kings," I said, shaking my head. "And anyway, he should be Admiral of the Armada, not King."

"Oh, semantics, luv, it doesn't mean anything," Guinny laughed.

Gwen sipped her drink and got serious. "Your news of sabotage, though, now that does mean something."

"Oh rather! Not the first we've heard of it, have we, Gwen?"

"Not the first by a long shot, Guin."

"Really? Other pirates, you mean?"

Both of them nodded.

I sank back into my chair, arms crossed. "Nice to know I'm in good company."

"Oh, ra-thah! At least half a dozen pirates have had problems aboard their ships. Engine failures, fires, thefts, even some cold-blooded murders."

"Guess we got off light," I said, horrified. Murders? "Any ideas who's behind it?"

"Got to be Atlan spies, but none's been caught yet."

"Great."

"Indeed."

"Of cawse, it would be easier to slip a spy into your unruly lot than into the rigid military," Bunny said from the doorway.

Gwen slapped her thigh in annoyance. "Bunny! How long have you been eavesdropping?"

"Terribly gauche of me darlings, I know, but I simply cawn't help meself. This sort of gossip will keep me fed for weeks, doncha know."

I tried, I really tried, to keep the sneer off my face. "Fed?"

"Invites to soirees, my very deah," he answered with a flip of his hand. "The meat and potatoes of the society set, you might say, a-haw-haw, a-haw-haw-haw."

I waved my hand around the room. "You have all this and you're worried about having enough to eat?"

"Oh tosh," he answered, waggling his finger at me in a way that made me want to draw my sword and send that finger into the fireplace. "The food itself is secondary to the gossip, deah heart. Gossip is where fortunes are made."

"You've already got a fortune here," I said through clenched teeth.

"Oh, but for how long? The Tallyho fortune, that is, the legitimate, legal fortune, is based on our herds of aurochs. Vital for the airship industry, doncha know. But one bad case of hoofrot or some other disease could wipe out one of the bigger herds and then, well, all this fluff needs upkeep, my precious. It's too too expensive, being so rich. Appearances and all that rot, wot?"

I frowned, not getting it. "So you what, go to these parties, find out gossip about people, then blackmail them?"

The three Tallyhos laughed like I'd said something hilarious. I was ready to throttle them all.

The twins sipped their ports. Bunny pulled a lace handkerchief out of his pocket and wiped at his eyes. "Blackmail! What a hoot! How very much a pirate you are my deah, how so very very."

"Isn't she just?" Gwen said.

"We knew you two would get along smashingly," Guinny added. I gave her an *Are you nuts?* look, but she didn't notice.

"No my deah, gossip is best applied to business. Alliances are made and broken through the choicest bits of gossip. For example, the fact that there are spies and saboteurs among the pirate armada means that someone, somewhere views you as a threat. That little tidbit is enough for me to surmise that the pirate armada is a legitimate player on this particular field. P'raps enough of a player to merit an alliance, wot? After all, should the Atlan forces prove unequal to the task of putting down your little rebellion, why then, we should all find ourselves in a brave new world, doncha know."

I think some of my surprise must have shown on my face, because Gwen leaned over and patted me on the arm.

"Don't let his foppish facade fool you, pet," she said with a wink. "Beneath it lies a mind as sharp as a tack when it comes to applying gossip to the family's advantage."

"You're too too kind, my deah."

"Not at all, I insist."

"Thenk yew evah so."

"And a good thing, too," Guinny added. "Otherwise the family would be absolutely impoverished. Bunny here keeps the family name from flying away into piratical obscurity, all while feasting on the society set's foibles."

"When it comes to gossip, y'see, I am both gourmet and gourmand, a-haw-haw," Bunny explained. "I simply must consume everything I find, and yet, I much prefer the choicest bits." He sat next to me and patted my knee. "So tell me, what's your goal heah in dear old Anglica?"

I frowned at him. "I thought you were eavesdropping on us the whole time?"

"Not the whole time, alas."

"Okay, well, we have to figure out a way to shut down the patchwork manufactories for good."

Bunny wrinkled his nose and rolled his eyes. "Dreadful places. Cawn't imagine why they had to be set up heah in Anglica. Why, do you know, when the wind is right you can see the smoke from our third floor balconies? Such a shame. Albion was once such a pretty city. At least, so I've seen in the family's albums and paintings and such."

"You know perfectly well why, ducks," Guinny said. "A ready supply of parts, a willing workforce and to keep the populace in line. What better way to rule than through the terrible notion that stepping out of line will wind one in a patchwork?"

"Criminals wind up patchworked?" I asked.

"Not all criminals, but some," Gwen answered.

"And debtors, my very deah," Bunny added. "Lest we forget."

"So we've got to shut them down."

Bunny tapped his chin with his forefinger. "Well, you should know. There's a man in Albion, a rabble-rouser, who's running a dangerous game with the authorities, looking to do exactly that, doncha know."

"Sounds like my kind of guy," I said, grinning for the first time since I met Bunny.

He stared at me. "I say. My deah, you simply have the most dazzling smile. You must let me sketch you sometime. Do say it will be soon?"

"Yeah, sure. Tell me about this guy."

"Well. They call him the Hooded Fox." Bunny wrinkled his nose. "Bit dramatic, doncha think? Weahs a mask and all that, wot? Does terrible things in the name of justice or some such thing. Don't see how it's just to deprive the workers of their livelihood. Why do you know, only last week, he freed an entire stockyard of dangerous criminals into the streets of Albion? They shut down the manufactory for an entire day, because the patchworkers had nothing to chop up or sew togethah!"

"I'm sure the patchworkers can find other jobs somewhere," I said. "Anyway, what they do is pretty horrible."

Bunny shrugged. "I suppose."

"Oh Bunny, I know!" Guinny said, hopping in her seat excitedly. "Should we succeed in shutting down those horrible manufactories, you could buy the buildings and convert them into slaughterhouses for the family aurochs! And tanneries, too, wot?"

"T'ain't as though the neighbours would complain of the smell, a-haw-haw!" Bunny joked, but I saw his eyes light up. "And the workers would have new jobs, brilliant!"

"Okay, so that's one problem solved. Now, how do we meet the Hooded Fox?"

Bunny tapped his finger against his chin again. "There's a soiree I've been invited to in Albion. I hadn't planned on going, but there just might be someone there we can speak to about arranging just such a clandestine meeting, wot?"

"We?"

"Oh, well, you'll have to come with me, darling. I couldn't possibly plead your case with as much eloquence and verve as you yourself would. Besides, it might be best if I weren't too thoroughly implicated."

I frowned, glancing at Tring, who'd settled herself in a corner of the room, standing watch. "I dunno. I mean, I can't go anywhere without a platoon of bodyguards these days."

"Quite so," Gwen said. "You're too too important, pet."

I shrugged. "I don't see how I'm any more important than any other pirate captain."

Guinny leaned over and put a hand on my knee. "Oh but you are, love. You're the face of the rebellion, doncha know! The ex-slave turned pirate captain turned revolutionary? It's the stuff of legends! And... Oh dear, she doesn't know!"

Gwen stared at her twin. "Doesn't know... Oh!"

"She doesn't know what?" I asked.

"When Remy was elected King of the Pirates, there was a conclave with the other captains. There was some discussion about the likelihood of your mission to Zhou succeeding. After much heated debate, Remy applied the full weight of his complete confidence in you."

I felt a lump in my throat and my eyes stung with tears. No one had ever given me so much support. "Oh. Wow."

"Well, tell her the best part!" Gwen said, shoving her twin.

"He said, in front of the entire conclave, that if you proved successful in your mission, he would name you his second-in-command of the entire pirate armada."

My head spun. I couldn't believe it. I'd never even wanted command of a pirate ship, much less the entire armada. The girls had voted me captain and now Remy wanted to make me second-in-command?

"But... I... why?"

Gwen grinned. "He says that he liked the way you don't let precedent influence your decisions, that you stick to what's right no matter how entrenched the wrong idea may be."

"I'm not even sure I know what any of that means."

"Not to worry, pet," Guinny said. "It doesn't mean anything unless two things happen, wot?"

"What two things?"

"Well, something's got to happen to Remy, for one. And second, you've got to succeed in this mission."

"Oh yeah, that. Just shut down all the patchwork manufactories so that the vampyri will invade Russankya so that the Zhou will attack too. No big deal."

"I say, that is a load to bear," Bunny said. "Three goals in one mission? Although, if you succeed, why then, you'll be a legend in your own time."

I shrugged. Unlike Serena, my shrugs just basically said, *whatever*. "I guess. First things first, though. Who do you know at the party?"

"My very deah, I know everybody at the party. But the one to whom I refer, who may know someone who may lead us to the Hooded Fox, is a certain personage by the name of Periwinkle Spearsharpe."

"NO!" the twins exclaimed.

"YES!" Bunny exclaimed back. They laughed themselves to tears.

"Oh my," Gwen said, wiping her face.

"It's too very," Guinny added, tossing back the last of her port.

"Isn't it just?" Bunny said.

"What did I miss?"

Gwen turned to me as Guinny went to the sideboard and brought back the bottle of port. "Darling little Winkie was a childhood friend, doncha know."

"A pixie at a party, imagine the possibilities," Guinny added, pouring herself another glass and topping up everyone else's.

"I don't have to imagine, I can tell you, it's simply a hoot," Bunny said. "They're so delightfully delicious."

"Pity we shan't see her, it would do us a world of good," Gwen said. "All this serious war business, eh wot? A spot of hijinks might lighten the load, so to speak?"

Guinny gave her twin a look. "Now Gwen, you know that if we were to show our faces in the society set, we wouldn't even make it past the entree before the authorities had been summoned, notorious pirates that we are."

Gwen sighed. "Alas, too true. How fortunate for us dear Bunny escaped the scandal."

"Indeed," Bunny said, raising his glass in salute to his sisters.

Chapter Twenty Eight

A Pretty Perilous Party

Turned out the soiree was the next evening, so I managed to convince Tring that Serena would be enough bodyguard for a society party, left Molly in charge of the ship with special orders to hunt down the saboteur and let the Tallyhos dress me for the party.

First, let me say this. They had amazing taste in clothes. The dress they found me, a shimmering navy satin gown with ruffles and bows aplenty, fit like it had been made for me. It even completely hid the dagger and tiny two-shot pistol I strapped to my calves. My assorted accessories came from my own collection of sapphire and silver jewellery I'd obtained in our piratical adventures and it turned out Hina had hidden hairdressing talents. Hair up, pinned in place, bejewelled and bedazzling, I felt every inch a society lady. The fact that I wasn't remotely familiar with the rules of etiquette didn't seem to faze the Tallyhos in the slightest.

Second, and pardon the pun, but bustles? Total pain in the ass. Strap a bird cage to your behind sometime and try walking around without making it wiggle. And forget about getting comfortable sitting down, it's impossible to lean back. So the steamcoach ride from Tallyho Manor and the train ride to Albion and the auto-horse carriage ride to the party were really, really uncomfortable for me.

Why a train, instead of one of our ships? Because Bunny had "a dreadful fear of heights, doncha know." Cue much eye-rolling.

So I arrived in Albion tired, sore and cranky. Not really in any mood for a party. At least the trip had been quick – a half hour of careening over frozen dirt ruts, bumping along; an hour on the train, chug-chug-chugging; a few minutes in the auto-horse carriage, clattering along cobbled streets. But I mean, you spend two hours sitting on the edge of your seat while your vehicle does everything it can to knock you off.

Listening to Bunny.

That, I think, was the worst. He went on and on about who had done what with or to whom. Names flew past my head so fast I found myself wishing for a good bit of action, just to compare it to bullets whizzing past me. And I couldn't even tune him out, because he had some kind of sixth sense that let him know when I'd start drifting away and he'd ask me direct questions that would draw me back into the conversation. I started to think that he was doing it on purpose, seeing how quickly I'd tune out and pulling me back in again just as quick.

Albion was smelly, dirty, cramped and basically a big grey let down. The cobbled streets were lit with gaslight, which did little to dispel the fog, just casting gloom and making shadows dance. A thin grey snow fell from the cloudy sky. When I asked about it, Bunny shuddered.

"The crematoria only run at night, my deah. Thus, the cloaks."

When we'd arrived at the train station, Bunny had produced long grey hooded cloaks for us to wear over the beautiful fur coats he'd also provided.

"That's ash out there?" I felt my stomach want to empty itself.

"Alas," was all Bunny answered.

I stared out the window as the auto-horse clip-clopped down the mostly empty street, its hooves pounding the ash into slush. I shook my head, more determined than ever to shut down the patchwork manufactories. I pushed down my anger from a boil to simmer in the background, not wanting to cause too much of a scene at the party.

The carriage eventually turned up a private drive and headed for a huge manor, three storeys tall and lit from below with electric lights. Through the window I saw other carriages pulling up to the main doors to drop off their occupants, so we had to wait our turn.

"Everyone ready?" I asked.

"Of course," Serena said. She'd drunk quite a bit of blood before we'd left, not knowing if there would be anything for her at the party, so her cheeks were still a little pink. She, of course, was flawlessly gorgeous in a gold gown and black fur coat. Her normally straight pale hair had been styled in thick ringlets and pinned back. Gold and ruby jewellery sparked from her ears, neck and fingers. I knew that somewhere in the folds of her gown and under her corset she'd hidden enough weapons to start a small war. Neither of us were taking any chances.

The auto-horse pulled up to the front doors. Bunny got out first and offered us his hand, helping us down from the carriage. As Serena and I pulled our cloaks around us, making sure none of the grey ash touched our fine gowns, Bunny paid the auto-horse. Then he turned to us and offered us both an arm, ignoring the flecks of ash falling onto the sleeves of his fur coat.

"Shall we, my deahs?" he asked, then led the way up the stairs and into the manor.

Bunny presented his calling card and we'd given off our protective cloaks and fur coats. A snooty butler escorted us through the entry hall and up a sweeping marble staircase. A crystal chandelier hung from the ceiling high above, glittering with electric lights. The walls were papered in intricate patterns of blue and gold. No paintings or portraits, but there were alcoves set into the walls with marble busts of stern-looking men. They all had a certain family resemblance, so I assumed they were the ancestors of our host.

From the top of the stairs came laughter and music, spilling out from a pair of tall wooden doors, polished to a mirror shine. The butler-type gave Bunny's calling card to a man at the doors, who glanced at it and tossed it onto a silver tray already loaded with other, similar cards.

"Mister Bunthorne Tallyho and..." The guy at the door glanced at me and Serena.

"Guests," Bunny said pleasantly.

The guy gave him a tiny smile. "Very good, sir." He turned to the room and announced, "Mister Bunthorne Tallyho and guests."

There were actually a few cheers and somewhere a man shouted, "Now the party can finally start, wot?" to the general laughter of the people around him.

We spent the next hour being introduced to everyone there. Bunny told people I was "Miss Victory Venture" an actress from Yoke, wherever that was, while Serena was "Mistress Syren (pronounced the Gallic way, 'See-wren') Marigold" a vampyri tourist to Albion. We were both under strict instruction to speak only when asked a direct question. The men we met all bowed and kissed the air over my gloved hand. Many of the women we met complimented my hair, asking how I achieved such a realistic colour. I didn't quite know what to tell them. Bunny stepped in and told them it was a trade secret. Part of my life as an actress.

The whole actress thing puzzled me when he'd first suggested it on the train, until he explained that it might be best to have some kind of story in case someone recognized me from my wanted posters, or by the descriptions in the dreadfuls. Not that anyone in the society set would ever admit to reading anything so base as a novel about airship pirates.

A real live human servant passed by with a tray of drinks. Bunny snatched up two long flutes of champagne and passed me one. The servant glanced at Serena and nervously asked if she would care for anything. Serena shook her head politely.

"Ah, Bunny, there you are," a woman said.

Bunny turned and spread his arms wide. "Here I am, m'deah!"

She was tall and imposing, with nearly black hair arranged in curls behind her head, and bright blue eyes. Her dress of crimson silk and about nine yards of ruffles was a work of art. Her jewellery was all diamonds, glittering from every conceivable location. I could have fed my entire crew for a month on the cost of those jewels.

Bunny bowed low over her gloved hand and kissed the air above it. "Lavender Touchstone, my sparkling diamond, allow me to introduce Miss Victory Venture and Mistress Syren Marigold, two very deah friends of my recent acquaintance. Ladies, this magnificent specimen of femininity is our hostess."

"Miss Venture," she said, offering her hand. I hoped she didn't expect me to kiss it, so I took it in a very soft handshake. She turned to Serena, offering her hand. "Mistress Marigold." Serena smiled and took her hand, squeezing slightly, then let it drop.

"I don't believe we've evah had the pleasure of hosting a vampyri," Lavender said with a polite smile. "Bunny, you scamp. You should have told me you were bringing guests. We would have made arrangements for Mistress Marigold."

"Do not trouble yourself on my account, please," Serena said. "I've already dined tonight."

If Lavender reacted, I didn't see it, except a slight tightening of her smile. "Of course you have. How wonderful. Do enjoy yourselves this evening." She turned and nodded at Bunny. "Bunny."

We watched her move off to greet her other guests.

"Oooo, I do believe I stepped in it this time," Bunny muttered behind his flute of champagne. I glanced up at him. He tried, without much success, to hide his mischievous joy.

"What do you mean?"

He looked down at me. "I've brought someone to the party she can't possibly top, my precious jewel. No one heah will prove to be as remotely interesting as our deah Syren heah. An actual vampyri? I'll be the talk of the town for weeks to come."

Anger flared inside me. "That's why you were so keen for me to bring her? Not for my protection, but so you could set society a-twitter with gossip?"

"Well, your protection did factor into it, dearest one."

I rolled my eyes and finished my drink. "Is there anything to eat here? I'm starving."

"Of cawe you are, my deah. Let's seek out the buffet, shall we?"

We wandered through room after room. In one, a quartet of musicians played soothing music while the party-goers ignored them. In another, card tables had been set up and several people were playing various games. I recognized the six-card table and that was about it. Finally we came to the buffet, a long room filled with people crowded around a table in the centre. The table was loaded with an obscene amount of food. Fruits and cheeses fought for room next to cold roasts and platters of pastries. I managed to get a plate and set a few slices of cheese, some bread and half a dozen cherry tomatoes on it. I was absolutely determined not to stain my gown or the gloves that reached up almost to my shoulders. Good thing, too, since the short sleeves of my gown barely covered up my slave tattoo or my various scars.

After eating, we wandered some more. In one room a man in a pith helmet and rumpled suit was giving a lecture about the possibility of flying to the moon. He was simultaneously trying to smoke from a pipe and drink from a crystal glass filled with a green liquid I recognized as absinthe. Next to him stood an orangutan with what I thought was a goggle strapped over one eye; after watching the pair of them for a while, I realized the goggle wasn't a goggle, it was an artificial eye.

"The Professor's in fine form tonight," Bunny said as we left.

"He looked a little wild-eyed to me," I said.

"Well, the line between genius and madness is often blurred, wot?"

"I guess," I said. "Was he serious?"

"About going to the moon? I expect so. His plans always seem quite ludicrous but then he makes it work and comes back to tell us the most outrageous tales. What a lark!"

"He won't get there in a balloon," I said. "He'll need a rocket."

"I'll be sure to tell him so," Bunny said, leading the way into yet another room.

And that's pretty much how it went, flitting from room to room and conversation to conversation. Bunny collected bits of gossip here and there. Very little of it seemed all that important to me and none of it concerned the war. You'd almost imagine they didn't even know there was a war going on.

Eventually we settled in one of the quieter rooms. Bunny had attracted quite a few followers and hangers-on by that point, so I pulled Serena off to one side and found somewhere to sit. My feet were aching.

One of the guys who'd followed us from the ballroom – there was a ballroom, with fancy dancing, did I tell you that? Bunny asked me to dance but I let Serena take my place. When they danced it got everyone's attention. Anyway, this guy raised his glass in Bunny's direction. "Oh Bunny, you simply must recite that amusing little poem you wrote!"

"Yes, do!"

"Please do!"

"I say," Bunny answered, standing. "If you insist."

"We do, we do!"

I watched Bunny take a deep, much-put-upon sigh. Then he smiled coyly. He obviously enjoyed the attention, but the rules of etiquette clearly demanded he not enjoy it openly. I rolled my eyes.

Bunny struck a dramatic pose, one hand outstretched before him, then recited:

"The Hooded Fox, by Bunthorne Tallyho, Esquire:

Look for him, look for him, wherever you can.

    You'll never find that Mysterious Man.

Look for him up, look for him down.

    They say he might be in Albion town.

Will he land in the Pit or just in the stocks?

    First you must catch... the Hooded Fox."

As the others applauded his pretty cheesy poem, I clapped politely then turned to Serena. "What's the Pit?"

"Blackiron Prison, vhere the government places its most dangerous criminals. It is a coal mine in the heart of Atlan itself. Its location is a closely-guarded secret."

"Why don't they just execute them?"

Serena shrugged. "These criminals are the vorst of the vorst. Multiple murderers, crime lords." She smirked and added, "Insurrectionists and seditionizers. Suffragists. Traitors. Pirate captains, sometimes."

I grinned back. "Sounds like our kind of people."

"Mm. Perhaps. But they are the kind of people who the government vould not vant to make martyrs of, yes?"

"I say!" Bunny said, mincing over to us. "You two seem to be engaging in some sort of frightfully serious and very dull conversation. Allow me to rescue you."

I couldn't help myself. He was just so infuriating. "The day I need rescuing by you, Bunny, is the day I retire from piracy."

He just laughed, one hand circling limply at the wrist. "I certainly hope so, darling, a precious jewel like yourself should be pampered and treated to the finest life has to offer."

I rolled my eyes again, gritting my teeth. "Bunny..."

"Precious jewel?"

I stood up with unladylike speed, not caring who noticed, stepped in close to him and glared up into those deep blue eyes of his. "Call me that again and I'll make you bleed."

And he laughed. Again. "Of cawse, my dear. Never think upon it again. A thousand thousand apologies and all that, wot?"

I swear he was doing it on purpose. I swear he was trying to make me mad. And I could not, for the life of me, figure out what it was about him that made me so angry. Maybe it was because behind their flippant facade, his sisters were simply steel. Bunny, however, was all facade with nothing beneath, a fake, a phony. A perfect society gentleman, with no substance or capacity whatsoever. Pretty much useless, as far as I was concerned. If only he wasn't so blasted gorgeous.

I know, right? Where did that come from? But that's the first time I began to suspect something more was happening between us. Anyhow, I think I actually growled a little at him, because he stepped out of my way instead of forcing me to push him aside as I left the room.

The manor, you can imagine, was pretty huge. The layout wasn't exactly maze-like, but the sheer number of people at this "little" soiree made making my way through it all kind of a hassle. Which I suppose explains how I walked right into a nightmare.

Chapter Twenty Nine

A New Nightmare

I pretty much stumbled right into Lavender, pushing my way through a crowd of people, murmuring my apologies and smiling politely. She turned from her conversation to see who had bumped her. Her glare melted from outraged to politely amused when she saw it was me.

"Ah Miss Venture, there you are," she said. "Join us, won't you?"

I tried to find an excuse to keep going but couldn't. My brain had stopped, shocked into silence.

Tall. Thin. Crooked teeth. Dressed in dark military greys and blacks, a bland and boring contrast to the kaleidoscope of colour around us. If he wasn't Captain Crow come back from the dead, he had to be related.

"Commodore Crow, may I introduce Miss Victory Venture," Lavender said.

"Miss Venture," he said, his voice the one from my nightmares.

No hope for it now, I thought. I forced a smile and offered him my hand. "Commodore. How do you do?"

He took my hand and did the whole bowing and not quite kissing thing. "Exceedingly well. And you?"

"Very well, thank you."

"What a striking colour your hair is," he said.

"Thank you. My hairdresser will be ever so pleased."

"And your accent. I cannot quite place it."

I forced a light laugh. "How very strange, Commodore, I was just thinking the same about yours!"

"I am from Ys," he answered, pronouncing it to rhyme with 'grease'. "Prior to the unpleasantness in Afric, I was governor there."

"Governor! How exciting for you. I've heard Ys is very beautiful."

"It is."

A servant passed by with a tray of drinks and I snagged one. The Commodore didn't take a drink.

"I still cannot place your accent," the Commodore said.

I sipped my wine. "Well, I am originally from Yoke, but I've found it best for an actress to cultivate a more neutral accent in order to appeal to a broader audience." Yeah, I don't know where I got that load of ballast from, either, but there you go.

"An actress?" he said, looking to Lavender. "How very scandalous of you, my dear."

Lavender laughed without opening her mouth. "Thank you, Commodore, but I assure you, it wasn't my idea."

"No? And whose was it, may I ask?"

"Why mine, of cawse," Bunny said from behind me.

If it's possible to be simultaneously utterly relieved to see someone and utterly infuriated to see them and even more infuriated to be relieved and also slightly embarrassed to be infuriated, then that's what I was. Also more than a little queasy, with all that adrenaline pumping through my system.

The Commodore and Bunny introduced themselves and Bunny flagged down another servant, helping himself to a drink.

"Now," he said once he'd sipped. "What were we talking about?"

"We were discussing Miss Venture's very unusual accent," the Commodore said.

I smiled, trying to remember the load of ballast I'd just unloaded. "Right! Yes, right. Well as an actress of course I... You see."

"I don't suppose you let it slip?" Bunny asked me.

"Let what slip?" I asked, a sinking feeling in my stomach.

"Your accent?"

"What about my accent? I've tried to form an accent that is pleasing to the widest possible audience, Bunny, I told you that."

Bunny frowned, not understanding. Fear filled my guts with lead. Bunny wasn't following me at all. How drunk was he?

"You never told me any such thing," he said. He turned to the Commodore. "The reason you cannot possibly place her accent, old bean, is because she's not an actress."

"Bunny, shut up," I said through clenched teeth.

"If she's not an actress, who is she?" the Commodore asked.

Bunny grinned. "She's Sunset Val, the notorious pirate!"

Chapter Thirty

Tallyho To The Rescue

Everything seemed to happen all at once after that, so let me see if I can put it in proper order.

Lavender glared at Bunny, hands on her hips. "Really Bunny, you don't mean to say you brought an actual pirate to my party? Wasn't bringing a vampyri enough?"

"Sunset Val is known to travel with a vampyri bodyguard," the Commodore said.

I wonder what Serena will think of being called my bodyguard, I thought, then: *Hey, where is she, anyway?*

The Commodore, somehow, managed to move right up next to me. Probably while I was glaring daggers at Bunny.

"Pirate? Or actress, my dear?" The Commodore loomed over me.

I switched my glare from Bunny up to the Commodore, refusing to give ground. "It's one of Bunny's silly jokes, of course. Look at him, he's drunk."

"A man in my position can't take that risk," the Commodore answered. "It's simply resolved, though. Let us see your left shoulder."

He looked at me. I looked at him. Pretty much at the exact moment I was going to say no way, his hand whipped out and grabbed my poofy sleeve. He started to lift it, and caught a glimpse of the tattooed crow, his dead brother's insignia. His eyes flashed with triumph.

I spun my arm away, ripping the sleeve. Dropped down. Reached up under the skirts and petticoats of my gown. Came back up with a dagger and tiny two-shot pistol. *Dagger first,* I thought, my mind racing like lightning. *Pistol will alert the whole house.*

I brought up the dagger, aiming for his collar bone. He grabbed my wrist with one hand, quick as a whip, his other hand holding a scrap of my torn sleeve. I pressed the pistol to his throat, just behind the jaw. There were screams then, I think. I don't really remember.

The whole thing had taken less than two seconds.

"At this range you're dead, Crow," I said through clenched teeth.

He was panting and not just from exertion. Fear glittered in his eyes as they flickered from mine to the hand holding the pistol.

"See here, unhand her, sir!" a man said. From the corner of my eye I saw the Professor from before, pushing his way through the crowd.

But Bunny just applauded, laughing. "I say! Too marvellous, wot?" The other party-goers looked at him. Some applauded, confused. Crow and I broke our eyelock and stared at Bunny.

"What a magnificent performance, my very very deah," Bunny said. "Exactly the type of excitement, adventure, dare I say, passion, we might all see at the upcoming presentation of your latest play, Sunset Val's Aerial Adventures, wot?"

It might have taken me a couple of seconds to clue in to what he was going on about. I dunno, I was still pumping adrenaline and filled with murder. Bunny gave me a look that pretty much said, *Take a hint and follow my lead, dummy.* It startled the urge to kill right out of me.

I broke away from the Commodore, spinning my little gun and twirling my dagger, smiling as brightly as I could. "Of course! Dear friends, I do hope I didn't alarm you with my little theatrical display. And I hope you'll all come to see me in Sunset Val's... um."

"Aerial Adventures!" Bunny finished for me, leading the applause again. More people clapped this time and a few even laughed.

"Oh I say!" the Professor said, grabbing Bunny's hand and pumping it up and down. "Well done, old man! You can rest assured that Professor Elemental will want two tickets! At least!" Then his eyes went wide as he spotted something in the next room, and left, yelling, "Geoffrey! Put him down this instant!"

"But the tattoo!" the Commodore argued.

Bunny licked his thumb and rubbed my shoulder, smearing something black all over my tattoo. Everyone stared at the mess, including me. It looked exactly like he'd just smeared my tattoo into oblivion.

"An astonishing bit of cosmetic artistry my deah Commodore, nothing more," Bunny answered, grinning the whole time. "Now I'm sure our little actress requires refreshment after her performance, don't you my very deah?"

"What?" I looked up from the smeared mess of my tattoo. "Oh. Yes. Of course."

"Of cawse she does!" Bunny said right into the Commodore's face. Bunny pointed at the Commodore's hand. "You don't need that, do you old chap?"

"What?" Commodore Crow asked, refusing to step back.

They both looked down at the scrap of my sleeve, still stuck in his claw. Fist. His fist.

"Of course not," the Commodore said, handing it back to me.

"Of cawse not, Commodore Crow, of cawse not."

Was it just me, or was Bunny making fun of Crow's name, cawing like a crow? Must have been the adrenaline, making me wonky.

"Rest assured, Mr. Tallyho, I shall make inquiries into the legitimacy of this... play," the Commodore said.

"Of cawse you will, of cawse, of cawse!"

Okay, now that convinced me he was teasing the man I'd just nearly killed. Not the best idea I'd ever heard of. Pretty dumb, really, but I had to admire Bunny, just a little, right then. Sometimes dumb and gutsy are pretty similar. From the way the Commodore glared at Bunny and the totally oblivious way Bunny returned the stare, I'd say it had definitely been more gutsy than dumb.

"Bunny, dear, I do feel the need to retire for the evening," I said, taking Bunny's arm and breaking the staring contest.

"Of cawse you do, my beautiful dove. Good evening to you, Commodore."

Bunny led me back the way I'd come, heading in the general direction of out. I grabbed a glass of wine off a tray and downed it quick.

"I say, you pirates really know how to drink," Bunny murmured.

"Not really. I'm planning on throwing up in your carriage."

For some reason this struck him as hilarious and he laughed, a real, honest laugh, not that fake 'a-haw-haw' thing he normally did. Something inside me liked the sound of his real laugh, but liking a part of him that he hid under the fake foolish fop only made me angry.

I took my arm away from him. Not rough, but deliberate. Then I took the scrap of sleeve away from him, too, and wiped at the tattoo.

"So what did you smear on me, anyway?"

He leaned in close to murmur, "Just a bit of caviar jelly, my deah."

"Fish eggs? Ew."

"Only the best for you, my dove."

"Can we go?"

"Do let's. I love to make an entrance but I never make an exit."

On our way out, I saw something that made me stop short. Or rather, someone. My stopping pulled my hand off of Bunny's arm. He turned to look at me.

"What is it, my dove? You look like you've seen a ghost."

I kept staring through the open doorway. "Who is that man?"

Bunny looked. "Which one, pet, there's evah so many."

"The one arguing with Professor Elemental."

"Tall skinny chap?"

"Yeah."

"He's a Doctor Sweet-something. Sweetwild? Sweetwelder?"

"Sweetwater."

"That's the one. Do you know him? Shall we make our way...?" Bunny looked away from the room and down at me. "No, I see by your face you've no intention of conversing with the man. Let's be went, shall we?"

My mind whirled. Maybe it was the adrenaline and maybe it was the alcohol, but I think it was mostly the man in that other room. If Sweetwater was in Albion, that meant that Eve was somewhere here, too. And if Eve was somewhere here, that meant I could rescue her. Because I had no intention of leaving her in the hands of the madman who'd planted hypnotic commands into her mind. But how was I supposed to find her?

I had to think about something else, because worrying about Eve and how to save her would drive me crazy. So once we were outside, I said, "You know it'll take about five minutes for the Commodore to find out that there's no play called Sunset Val's Aerial Adventures, or any actress named Victory Venture."

Bunny handed a card to a stablehand and smiled coyly. "What makes you think there isn't?"

"What?!"

"Vhat vhat?" Serena asked from behind me.

I turned on her. "And where were you?"

"Talking to Periwinkle Spearsharpe. And you?"

"Trying to kill Commodore Crow and compromising our cover completely."

"Vhat?!" Serena hissed, if it's possible to hiss a word with no 's'.

"I'll tell you on the way back."

I caught Serena up with what had happened and she told me about meeting the pixie we'd actually come to the party to meet. It annoyed me that I'd let my temper get the best of me, making me miss meeting our contact. I blamed Bunny for it.

Anyway, Serena had managed to set up a meeting with a friend of Periwinkle's, someone who supposedly knew something about the Hooded Fox, or at least, knew someone who was involved in the anti-patchwork movement. Seems the vampyri weren't the only ones with an axe to grind against the patchwork manufactories. The faerykin of Anglica, Eire, and Hibernia didn't much like the practice either.

"Oh, aye, I coulda toldya tha," Moonchance said, at our crew chief meeting that morning.

"Why didn't you tell us that?" I asked.

"Din't arsk, didya?"

I closed my eyes, took a deep breath and let it out slowly. "Does anyone know any way to shut down the patchwork manufactories? Feel free to speak your minds. Anything?"

Wren raised her hand.

"Yes, Wren?"

"Faerykin ain't much 'appy 'bout 'em patchworks, Cap. Moight be wurf arskin' 'em 'bout it."

The three pixies giggled. I resisted the urge to knock their heads together.

"Why do faerykin have anything against patchworks?" Miss Merryweather asked.

"Takin' our jobs, ain't they?" Apple answered. "'ard enough, tryin'a find work for you 'umans. Finkin' we's too wee and such ta do it right an' propah."

Moonchance lit her itty bitty cigarette. "But buy yerself a patchwork and tha's about the end of it, roight?"

"Too roight!"

"Okay, we'll take it under advisement," I said. "If we can't get the Hooded Fox to help us, maybe we can get the faerykin to stage a revolt or something."

"We knows some faerykin who's fair revoltin', eh?" Wren laughed.

"Any other news?" I asked, looking around the table.

Molly said,"We found a cache of combustible materials by the powder stores,"

"What?!"

"It seems clear we nearly caught our saboteur in the act," Miss Merryweather explained.

"There is no way she could have hidden that stuff there for more than a few minutes," Inga added. "I have been checking the stores myself every half hour ever since we first started having the troubles."

"You must sleep," Mrs. Shorty said.

"I sleep next to the powder. None can pass without waking me."

"That sounds pretty uncomfortable, Inga. But thanks."

"It is nothing."

"Keep looking," I said to the others. "We've got to find that bitch before she kills us all."

Python burst into the room, rattling off a long string of Lemurisian. I could tell we were all pretty stressed, because we all jumped. Molly and I even went for our weapons and Tring nearly tackled Python.

"We're in a meeting, Python," I began, but she interrupted.

"Blight take your meetings!" she spat, angry tears spilling down her cheeks. "Tama is dead!"

Chapter Thirty One

Investigation & Interrogation

Tama's throat had been slit. Her body had been hidden in a barrel in the Booty Bay. The last time she had been seen was after breakfast that morning, when she'd gone to the showers. After that, it had been her turn to work with Mrs. Shorty. She hadn't reported for duty.

"I'd been planning on mentioning something to Miss Merryweather when you called the crew chiefs' meeting," Mrs. Shorty explained.

"She's not been dead long," Doc Regan said. "No rigidity yet."

"She wasn't killed here, either," Molly added, looking at all the shelves around us. "No blood. Wound like that would have sprayed all over the place."

Doc Regan pulled Tama out of the barrel and laid her out on the floor. Miss Merryweather knelt beside the body. She took one of Tama's hands and turned it over. Then she looked closely at Tama's face.

"I believe she must have known her killer," Miss Merryweather said. "No defensive wounds on her hands."

"The cut goes from right to left," Doc Regan said. "Someone behind her would have been left-handed."

"Someone behind her would have left bruises on her face," Miss Merryweather argued. "No, the killer was right in front of her. Surprised her with the attack. If we assume the killer and our saboteur are one and the same, then we must assume Tama stumbled upon the killer, engaged in some act of sabotage. She was killed to keep her silent."

"The murder couldn't have been far from here," Gigi said. "There's no way someone could have carried Tama that far without attracting attention."

"Alright, enough," I said. "Doc, take Tama and figure out what sliced her throat open. If we're lucky, we might figure out who the killer is by what kind of blade she used. Molly, organize search parties to look for the blood. Like you said, Tama must have bled out somewhere. All that blood didn't just disappear and the killer likely hasn't had a chance to mop it up yet. Miss Merryweather, will you assist Molly, please? Gigi, see if there's some way to sneak a body into the Booty Bay. Everyone clear? Good. Tring, hang back a minute."

Everyone scattered, leaving me alone with Tring. I told her about Dr. Sweetwater being at the party. Her eyes widened a little, but that was her only reaction.

"We need to find him," I said. "Find him, we find Eve."

"You wish to return to Albion?"

"Yes. We'll find her and save her."

"No. You must stay on target. You have a meeting with the Hooded Fox, do you not?"

"Not exactly, but sorta, I guess."

Tring nodded. "Who else knew Eve?"

"Gigi, Argenta, Serena..."

"Very well. Leave this to me."

I had to pause. "Really?"

"Of course. Why?"

"This isn't really very bodyguardish, that's all."

"A quest into unknown territory to save a missing comrade from a madman, or a few drinks with a criminal whose personal vendetta seems to lie in the same direction as our mission. Which do you think is more dangerous?"

"Yeah, okay, good point."

As I watched her leave, I had to admit she was right. Much as I'd rather go rescue Eve, I had a mission. Sometimes life throws a lot at you, and you can't always get to do what you want to do. I had a missing friend to rescue, a murderer to catch, a criminal to find and convince to work with us, the patchwork manufactories to shut down, the Zhou and the vampyri to invade Russankya and the Lemurisians to rendezvous with. Oh, and figuring out how to work the aetheric portal to send me back home. On top of, y'know, running a pirate ship. Although that last one pretty much handled itself. And anyway, we weren't exactly pirates any more, not really.

I know what you're thinking. You're thinking I should have gone off to rescue Eve. If I had my choice, I'd go find Eve, then hunt down the murderous bitch on my ship, then deal with the patchworks, because...

"The patchworks!" I yelled. The crew around me jumped. "Gigi!"

"Yes, Sunset?" she answered from somewhere deep in the shelves.

"Never mind that right now!"

"What? Why?"

"Come on!"

"Where are we going?!"

"To the lab!"

When we got to the lab we found Tring and Argenta waiting for us. I sent Tring to get Doc Regan. Gigi and I hooked up what was left of the patchwork assassins to the machines that would revive them and keep them awake and aware without any bodies.

Doc Regan and Tring arrived to help with the final connections.

"Are ye sure ye're wantin' us t'do this, Cap'n?" Doc Regan asked.

Gigi glanced up from the wiring she was attaching to the backs of the patchworks' heads. "It's just, you seemed a bit put off by our experiment, Sunset."

"That was before," I answered. "Hurry up. Please. Tring, can you go ask Bunny where you could find Dr. Sweetwater? I'm sure he's got some idea."

Tring left without a word.

"What was that about?" Gigi asked without looking up.

"When she gets back, you're going with Tring to rescue Eve."

"Just us? Just like that?"

"And Argenta. Why, is there anyone else you'd like to bring?"

Gigi shrugged. It sort of said, *Sure, but I can see you're in no mood to argue*. I think she must have been taking shrugging lessons from Serena. "There! Doctor, would you like to throw the switch?"

"Don't mind if I do," Doc Regan said, moving to the console.

Gigi, Doc and I put dark-lensed goggles over our eyes and Doc threw the switch. Bare electricity crackled around the patchworks' craniums. Gurgling go gushed through into thick tubes. Bellows began blowing air into their airways.

As one, two pairs of eyes opened. The heads began to breathe. The eyes scanned the room, us, each other.

"You may as well kill us again," the first one who'd attacked me, the one who'd destroyed my bed, said.

"We have nothing to say," the second one said.

"I'm going to offer you a deal," I said.

They both laughed, sort of. It sounded really creepy, two disembodied heads trying to laugh through the machines that replaced their lungs. Airy, raspy. Disturbing.

"I won't ask you anything about who sent you, or why," I continued. "I need information about the patchwork manufactories. If you answer my questions, I'll make sure your heads are re-united with your bodies."

Gigi and Doc Regan knew enough to keep their mouths shut at my bluff, but Argenta said, "But, Captain Val," before I cut her off with an angry "Quiet!"

I felt bad about that, but I didn't have time for the possible hurt feelings of our automaidon. "Tell me how to shut down a manufactory."

"What makes you think we know anything about manufactories?" the first one asked after a few seconds of silent staring at his... His what, his brother? Let's call him his brother, it's easier.

I raised a doubtful eyebrow at him. "You mean to tell me you were made by a private hobbyist? He must have really hated you guys to mix and match you all up on purpose like that."

"No," the second one said. "Though we were created with specific purpose, we come from a manufactory."

"Sort of a custom job, right?"

"Right," First said.

"So these manufactories, I hear they're pretty terrible places."

"That depends on your point of view," Second said. "It was our second birthplace, after all."

"Fair enough. But see, I need to shut them down, permanent-like. How do I do that?"

"Get rid of the source of supplies." First grinned an evil grin.

"Supplies? Oh. You mean, human bodies."

"No more humans, no more patchworks."

"Right. Let's just say that the complete eradication of the human race isn't on the table, here. How else?"

"What about the revivification fluid?" Doc Regan asked. "Sure an' if we get rid of that, there can't be any more patchworkin'."

First looked like he was trying to shrug, then settled on rolling his eyes. "The fluid is made of several different chemicals. Some are as common as the blood of the primary donor. Others come from extracts of rare plants or the specific glands of exotic creatures. The pituitary and adrenal glands of a specific breed of salamander, for instance. And most have substitutes."

"Every manufactory has their own fluid formula," Second added. "You wouldn't be able to take out a single supplier and... Hmm."

"Hmm?"

"Well. A manufactory needs three things. A steady supply of donors. A ready supply of revivification fluid. And a constant supply of electricity."

"That's true," First said. "Private generators don't provide enough power to fuel the revivification process. For instance, all the manufactories in Albion are supplied by the Aldgate Amalgamated Aelyctrix power plant. They're all cabled together."

"Shut down the power plant and you've crippled the patchwork industry," Second said.

"Thanks," I said. "You've been incredibly helpful."

"Our bodies?" First asked.

"You'll get them," I said, then I threw the switch and shut down the machine. The heads died again.

"Ye're not really gonna give 'em their bodies back?"

"I never said anything about re-attaching their heads, did I? We'll bury them on some deserted rock somewhere."

"Why not just dump them overboard?"

"I don't want to risk them floating ashore somewhere and someone well-meaning putting them back together again."

Just then Tring returned. "I know where to find Dr. Sweetwater."

"Go," I answered. "Gigi, Argenta, you go with her." I turned to Doc Regan. "Any luck finding out what killed Tama?"

"A straight-edged, tapering blade, about so long," she answered, holding her hands about eight inches apart. "It was very quick. Not slit across from behind like we t'ought earlier. Punched across, from the side. I imagine there was a lot of blood, though, so wherever she was killed, there's bound t' be a mess."

"Punched across?"

"Aye, like so." She moved to my right, then mimicked punching me in the side of my neck.

"A punch dagger," Tring said.

"But the only person aboard ship who uses a punch dagger is..."

"Python," I finished.

"Impossible," Gigi said, shaking her head. "Python loved Tama. Python is the one who reported the murder!"

"She was visibly upset when she did so," Tring said. "Could she have been acting?"

"No," Gigi answered. She tapped her little cat nose. "Humans smell differently with different emotions. That kind of anguish cannot be faked. Python was truly grieving her friend's death."

"Sure an' she might not have needed t' fake her grief," Doc Regan said. "If her secret mission is t' sabotage us and Tama came across her doin' somethin' t' that end and Python was forced to kill someone she's known her whole life, could be the grief was real enough."

Gigi frowned. "Why report it to us, though?"

"Argenta, you're being pretty quiet," I said.

She turned to face me. "As per your order, Captain Val."

"Oh yeah. Right. Sorry about that. I just didn't want you to give anything away in front of our talking heads here."

Her eyes flickered as she thought about it. "Yes, I see."

"Anything to add to the current discussion?"

"No, Captain Val."

I turned to Doc Regan. "Doc, go and tell Molly about the murder weapon, please. You three, get going. Save Eve."

As the others left the lab, Gigi put a hand on my shoulder. "What are you going to do?"

I sighed. "I have to go and get dressed. Bunny and I have an appointment with Periwinkle Spearsharpe and the Hooded Fox."

Chapter Thirty Two

A Momentous Meeting

We made it back to Albion much faster than the night of the party. The steamcoaches and trains ran more frequently during the day than in the evening, Bunny explained, not that I cared. It was just me, Bunny and the Tallyho sisters. I'd worn something a little more practical, this time: tan riding skirts, an emerald corset over a white blouse and under a long green coat (which also served to hide a couple of main gauches and a pistol), my black bowler hat. No bustle, thank you very much. The twins wore similar outfits, with their trademark top hats. Bunny was delighted and scandalized. Or maybe he was delighted to be scandalized, it was hard to tell.

We arrived in Albion just in time for tea, which had been our intent. We met Periwinkle Spearsharpe at an out-of-the-way pub called The Merry Clockmaker. The décor, you can imagine, consisted entirely of clocks. Big clocks, little clocks, clocks built into the beer taps, clocks built into the tables and chairs. The ticking and tocking and sporadic clinging and clanging (because the clockmaker was "merry, not accurate") made conversation very difficult. More importantly, it made eavesdropping impossible.

Periwinkle Spearsharpe was maybe the biggest pixie I'd ever seen, standing nearly two feet high. She had curly lavender hair that she'd threaded and braided with dozens of red ribbons. Her eyes were red, too. She wore a tiny dress under a tiny coat, slit up the back for her wings.

We shook hands. "I do so love your hair," she said.

"Thanks," I answered, sitting in the chair Bunny held for me. "Yours is very pretty."

"Do you really like it?" she asked, shaking her curls. Red ribbons shimmered in the dim light.

It surprised me that her accent was so clear. I'd been expecting an entire meal trying to decipher an accent like Moonchance and the others, "fick as pea soup, guv'nah".

"I do," I answered, but then she turned to the twins and they spent the next half hour catching up and reminiscing about people I didn't know and places I hadn't been. I tried to pay attention but it rapidly got annoying so I kind of zoned out. At some point a waitress took our orders and brought them to us; I'd ordered a pint of cider and nursed it.

I tried not to think about my friends who were out there, trying to rescue Eve. I tried not to think about the other friends I'd left back at The Furies, searching for a murderer. I even tried not to think about, you know, the reason I'd come to Albion in the first place.

"But enough about us," Periwinkle said, finally, after the waitress had taken our tea orders. I'd mistakenly thought that 'tea-time' meant, you know, drinking tea and maybe eating pastries or cakes of some kind. Apparently 'tea-time' meant 'early supper', so we'd all ordered the special, lamb stew, plus biscuits, plus another round of drinks.

"Tell me, Captain, to what do I owe the pleasure of this reunion?"

"Sorry?"

"She means, why are we here, luv," Gwen answered.

Why didn't she say that, then, I thought. "Oh. We need to find the Hooded Fox."

"Ah," Periwinkle said thoughtfully, sipping at her dewdrop. At least, that's what the drink was called, although the sheer number of other pixies in the pub made it seem likely that they'd actually carry and serve real dewdrops.

"And what makes you think I might know anything about that remarkable individual?" she asked, finally.

The twins and I all pointed to Bunny.

Periwinkle slapped at his arm. "Bunny, you spoil all my surprises."

"Oh come now, my delightful doll, my jewel, you simply cawn't expect a man to keep a juicy secret like that to himself, now can you?"

Periwinkle crossed her arms and pouted prettily. I restrained myself from the urge to roll my eyes. After a few seconds, she grinned at him, "No, I expect not. It really is too choice, isn't it?"

"It is! But I nevah did heah how it was you met the gentleman," Bunny said.

"Oh I say, do tell us," Guinny said.

"Oh yes, do!" Gwen added.

Periwinkle leaned in. We all followed her lead. She dropped her voice nearly to a whisper. With all the clocks tick-tocking and the general hubbub of an afternoon crowd in the pub, I could barely hear her.

"Well. It all began one evening as I flying home. All of a sudden, out of an alley come running dozens of humans! Being chased by patchworks! Well, I thought it some sort of grand game, so I followed them. But it wasn't a game, the patchworks were guards from the nearby manufactory and the humans had escaped the stockyard. Then, out of nowhere, a mysterious figure drops down on one of the patchworks. Bing! Bang! Boom!" Here, she punched at the air, miming a fight. "And the patchwork is down for the count. Another patchwork goes to help his friend. But the Hooded Fox, for it was none other, is too quick for them. Bang! Boom! Pow! And the second patchwork is down. The others hadn't stopped, they'd kept after the escaped humans. The Hooded Fox launches a sort of rope and claw thing at a nearby roof, climbs the wall quick as a squirrel and takes off across the rooftops. I followed him. And then he jumps off the roof! Takes out two patchworks faster than I can tell the tale. But while he was fighting them, a third patchwork pulled out a stick, cranked a knob on its side and it starts sparking. Electrical, doncha know! And he's about to stick it to the Hooded Fox! Well, I didn't think that was very sporting, so I dove down and flew straight in the patchwork's ugly face."

"No!" the twins said together.

"Yes! And screaming like a banshee, I don't mind to say! Well, that distracted him long enough for the Hooded Fox to turn around and see him. Whoosh! He kicks the stick out of the patchwork's hand. Bam Bam Bam! And the patchwork falls, beaten." She paused to take a sip of her drink. "Then he turns to me and says, 'Thank you for the assistance, Miss.' 'Think nothing of it,' I replied. 'Can I help with anything else?'"

"You didn't!" Bunny said.

"I did! Bold as brass, me!" she laughed. "'Nothing right now, Miss. But should you ever require assistance yourself, well, you know the statue of The Hunt in Empire Square?' I nodded to indicate I knew the statue of which he spoke. 'Leave a note in the fox's mouth. I'll get it.'"

"Oooohhh," Bunny said, disappointed. "So you don't really know who he is."

"I don't believe I ever said that, Bunny," she huffed. "I just know how to contact him. And now I'm not sure I want to contact him."

"Oh come now, Peri," Gwen said. "Bunny's sorry."

"I don't know that I am," Bunny answered, just as huffy as Periwinkle. "I don't think much of her story, quite honestly. Three or four blows to take down a patchwork? Show me a human that strong. I'm told that even the weakest patchwork is quite resilient to injury!"

"There are other ways to take down a patchwork," I said. "Electrics, for one. Anyhow, this is entirely off topic. Look, Periwinkle, will you help us, or not?"

She looked shocked. "Well, I never. If you're going to be like that, then why don't you tell me what it is, exactly, you're wanting the Hooded Fox to do for you and leave it to me to decide whether or not it's important enough for him to get involved in."

"Peri, don't be that way..." Gwen started.

"No, it's fine," I answered. "We need the Hooded Fox's help to shut down Aldgate Amalgamated Aelyctrix."

From the expression on her face, that confused her more than anything. "Why d'you want to shut down Aldgate Amalgamated?"

"Because that'll shut down the patchwork manufactories."

Her eyes widened and she flashed a huge grin. "I say! You really are that pirate lass."

"What makes you say that?" I said, not looking at Bunny.

"Well, that's rather a dramatic course to set, isn't it? Everyone knows how passionate she, that is, you, are about ending the slave trade and winning the war and toppling the government and all that. But stopping the patchwork manufactories from making all those soldiers from the parts being shipped back from the front? Oh I say, that is rather amusing isn't it? Back from the front?"

"Yeah, I see what you did there," I said, stalling for time as my mind raced to catch up to what we'd just learned. Soldiers from the war were being sent back to Anglica to be remade into patchwork soldiers. I would have bet that the people still to be slaughtered in the stockyards were being sewn into soldiers, too. More than ever we had to shut down the manufactories. "So is this important enough for the Hooded Fox?"

"Oh no, this is much more important than some masked vigilante," she answered, twirling her fingers in her red ribbons. "I know some lads who would be more than happy to help you achieve your goal."

"What lads would these be, then?" Guinny asked.

She smiled coyly. "Let's just say they're my kind of people, but not my kind of people, if you follow me."

I glanced at the twins, who glanced at each other.

"No," Gwen said, shocked.

"Really?" Guinny asked, scandalized.

"Who?" Bunny added, then, "Oh! Oh I say!"

"Anyone want to fill the new girl in?" I asked.

"We'll tell you later," Gwen said, shaking her head. "Best not speak of them in public."

"Too bloody right," Guinny added, calling for another round. Even Bunny looked upset.

"You know those people?" Bunny asked Periwinkle.

"Of course I do," she snapped. "Those people are my people, Bunny."

"No. I mean yes, but." He let out a worried, sigh. "I suppose."

"So these lads, they'll help us?" I said, trying to get the conversation back on course.

Periwinkle nodded. "For a price."

I rolled my eyes and nodded. "Of course. And what's their price?"

"Eire," the three Tallyhos answered before Periwinkle could.

"What, the whole island?"

"Yes," Periwinkle answered. "The whole island."

Chapter Thirty Three

Something Goes Really, Really Right For A Change

"Who are they?" I asked as we walked along the crowded streets.

"Peri's kind."

"Fae folk."

"They want to establish an independent Eire, freed from human interference. A homeland for the Fae."

"What, all of them? Moonchance is from Albion. And Doc Regan's from Eire."

"Not all of them," Bunny answered, keeping his voice low. He even looked over his shoulder to make sure no one around us could eavesdrop. "Peri's speaking of a militant branch of Fae known as the Redcaps. They want all the humans out of Eire and all the Fae to go live there."

"But wouldn't that, you know, cause a lot of problems?"

"They do tend toward the shortsighted, doncha know."

"Okay, so, what are our options, anyway? Give them Eire to shut down the manufactories?"

"They'll need to do much more than that to gain a homeland," Gwen said. "One criminal act hardly merits that kind of reward, I'll tell you that much for free."

"Eire is one of Atlan's main shipbuilding sources," Guinny said. "What if Peri's lads shut those down as well?"

"And they'd have to help out in the war, not just safe behind lines in Albion," I said. I looked around, spotting a huge grey monolith of a building at the end of the cobbled street. "Is that it?"

The twins nodded and we continued walking, avoiding hawkers selling everything you can imagine, women too old and worn out for the pleasure houses selling themselves, children begging for pennies, piles of garbage and other, nastier stuff just lying in the gutters. The noise was incredible, the stench unavoidable.

We came to a corner and were about to cross when Bunny grabbed my arm and pulled me back, hard. An auto-horse nearly collided with a real horse, both pulling little two-seat carriages. The real horse reared up and caught itself in the harness. The sole occupant of the two-seater spilled out into the muck of the street and landed hard on the cobbles. Even from where we were standing, with all the noise of the street, I heard the sick wet snap.

A fluke accident. Neck broken. Dead before he knew it.

Everything went still around us. I recognized it right away. The sort of calm that comes before a big fight.

The horse trotted away, trailing its empty two-seater behind it.

The dead man stayed still in the street.

Suddenly, everyone had a knife in their hands. Except us.

I'll never know who moved first. When it all happened the Tallyhos surrounded me, keeping me from the chaos. I saw enough, though.

The locals rushed in and started pulling the corpse to pieces, fighting over the scraps. The Tallyhos pulled me well away from the melee, but I saw men and women beating each other for the dead man's hands, legs, chunks of meat I took to be organs. I saw a bunch of beggar kids running away with the head, tossing it between them like a football, while a pair of very angry men chased them.

When it was all over, there was nothing left of the dead man but a bloody smear on the cobbles. Not even a scrap of clothes.

"What just happened?" someone said. It took me a few seconds to realize it had been me.

"They sell the parts to the manufactories," Bunny said, his voice low, angry, and deadly serious.

I looked up at him. He was staring at the bloody smear. Gone were all traces of the foolish fop. His eyes gleamed with unshed tears and something more – determination. His lips were pressed into a thin line of barely-restrained rage. It struck me again, how incredibly gorgeous he was. If this angry, determined man had been the Bunthorne Tallyho I'd met just a few days ago, I'd have spent the last few days being a complete spaz around him.

He looked down at me, saw me looking at him. Something electric between us happened then, but it happened so fast I couldn't be sure it wasn't my imagination. Anyway, his face changed back to the fop and he pulled out a handkerchief to wipe his eyes.

"Come my deahs, we should be going," he said, all traces of anger gone from his voice. "Let us see Aldgate Amalgamated and be went. Don't want to be late for suppah, wot?"

I sighed and rolled my eyes. A man was just killed and hacked to pieces and Bunny was worried about being late for supper. Everything I'd thought I'd seen in him must have been from the shock of seeing a man torn to pieces.

Aldgate Amalgamated Aelyctrix loomed into the evening air, a huge grey brick building, surrounded by a high grey brick wall. The electric plant was three storeys tall, with windows only on the top floor. Only one gate led in through the wall and it was guarded by two huge animen – a rhino and a lion – its gate doors shut to the public. A bit of a crowd had gathered outside, but they gave the guards a wide berth, chatting or eating hasty meals out of lunch pails.

Electric lights were spaced evenly around the wall, at least, as far as I could see. Overhead, thick cables hummed, spreading out in every direction, carried away atop wooden poles, some with as many as six crossbeams.

"Can't climb the wall, the whole town would see you a mile away," Gwen muttered.

"Cross on the cables?" Guinny offered.

"Can't be sure they wouldn't fry you in a heartbeat."

"There is that."

"Mmm."

A steam whistle blew three short bursts, and as one, the crowd turned toward the gates. After about a minute, the gates opened.

Bunny sniffed his handkerchief. "Just in time for the shift change."

I watched as the crowd shuffled in reluctantly and other workers, men and women, shuffled out, obviously exhausted. Even though the winter air was chill, most wore open coats, their faces grimy and sweaty under soft caps or kerchiefs. Some had a thin scarf wrapped around their throats. All of them wore thick-soled work boots.

As they filed past us, most without even giving us a second look, I noticed something. "Why are there so many patchworks?"

"That's how the manufactories pay for their electricity, my dove," Bunny explained. "Each manufactory pays Algdate Amalgamated. one patchwork a month."

"There have to be hundreds of them," I said, watching them pass us.

Very few human men, and no human women. The only women I could see were patchworks. "The A.A.A. owns them? Like slaves?"

"They're paid a modest sum. Enough to rent a room and feed themselves."

"That's horrible."

"Cheaper than hiring humans, animen or faekind, though."

"It's still horrible," I said. "I've seen enough. Let's go."

I had no idea how I was going to shut down the A.A.A. or the manufactories, but if I had to spend one more minute in that horrible, awful, terrible city, I was going to puke.

The train and coach rides back to Tallyho Manor were quiet. I stared out the window and tried not to think. I couldn't remember the last time I'd slept a full night's sleep. I'd only been on Ayrth for a few months, but it felt like years since I'd been just a high school kid, worried about boys and grades and missing my favourite shows. I felt worn out, ground down.

"Come have supper with us, ducks," Gwen invited when we finally pulled up to the manor.

"A few drinks, a few laughs and in the morning we'll start plotting the downfall of Aldgate Amalgamated," Guinny added.

"No thanks, girls, I'm for my own bed," I answered, forcing a smile. "I'm about done in."

"Alas, my very deah," Bunny said. "Do rest. You've important business to be about, wot?"

"I know, Bunny," I said, resisting the urge to punch him. "G'night."

I trudged through the new snow that had fallen while we were gone, heading for the stand of trees where we'd hidden The Furies. No lights escaped the ship, but the faint sounds of music led me straight to her. Guess the Vulka-reys had broken out their instruments. As I got closer I could hear laughter, too.

I paused, resting my hand on the ship's hull, gaining the strength to be a pirate captain again and not just a tired, stressed out teenaged girl a long way from home.

I took a deep breath and shook it off. Go time.

I banged on the Launch Bay doors and a couple of girls who'd been standing guard let me in. I made my way through the ship, avoiding the party in the mess hall. I didn't feel much like partying. I checked in with Serena, who was on the command deck.

"Get some rest," she said to me. "You are exhausted."

"Tell me about it."

I climbed the spiral stairs up to my room. Inside, I found Tring and Gigi waiting for me.

"What are you doing here?" I said, tossing my hat on my dresser. "I told you to go find Doc Sweetwater and rescue Eve."

"We must regretfully report we could not find Dr. Sweetwater," Tring said with a little bow.

"But about that other thing?" Gigi said, then stepped aside.

"Hello, Miss," Eve said, standing.

She looked skinnier than I remembered. There were dark smudges under her eyes, making her look about as tired as I felt. Her clothes were worn and dingy, like she'd slept in them for a week, maybe longer. I rushed into her arms and gave her the biggest hug I'd ever given anyone I'd ever known.

Chapter Thirty Four

Catching Up

There were tears, I'm not ashamed to admit, more than a few, and not just from me. And laughter, so much happy laughter. And babbled conversations. I asked Domina to bring a meal up for everyone and we settled ourselves with mugs of tea and glasses of wine.

"Tell me everything," I said, pulling off my boots, giving me immediate and considerable relief.

"We arrived at the address provided by Mr. Tallyho," Tring said. "When no one answered our bell ringing, we allowed ourselves entry."

"She kicked in the back door," Gigi translated, sipping her wine.

"A thorough search of the house revealed Dr. Sweetwater to be absent."

Eve cupped her mug of tea in her large-but-somehow-delicate hands. "They found me in the basement. Father often... chained me there as punishment."

"Eve, you've got to stop calling him that," I said.

"He is my father, Miss."

"No he isn't. And you've got to stop calling me that, too. Just... Sunset, okay?"

"Alright, Sunset, I'm sorry. But he is my father."

"Eve, he made you from a kit and a bunch of parts."

"Not just a bunch of parts," she said, shaking her head. "Most of my parts, my primary donor? Actually was his daughter, Evelyn Sweetwater. She died in a steamcoach accident. It drove him a little mad, I think."

"Bloody blight," Gigi said.

Eve shot her a quick, I-know-how-you-feel smile.

I held out my hand and she took it. "Anyhow, it's all over now and you're back here safe, right?"

She smiled at me and said, "Yes. Thank you."

Tring set her mug of tea aside. "If I may ask, why were you being punished, Eve?"

Eve gave a little half-shrug. "Father... That is, Dr. Sweetwater doesn't seem to need much reason, these days. Any little sign of resistance or rebellion and he chains me in the basement, in the dark. I suspect Evelyn was afraid of the dark, although that is speculation on my part. Personally, I don't mind, especially. It's certainly better than accompanying him to the manufactory."

"A patchwork manufactory?" Gigi asked.

"Yes. He's been working there, developing new patchworks. Seeking a means to cross the speciative divide."

"The what?"

She turned to me. "The reason why patchworks cannot be made from vampyri, animen, or faekind. Or any other species than human."

"Has he had any luck?"

"Not yet. I suspect his employers are less than pleased, which is why he's been so harsh with me. He's even mentioned sending me for reconditioning."

I laughed. "Is that where they wash your hair twice?"

Nothing. Not even a chuckle. No clue what I was talking about.

"That would have been funny, where I'm from."

"Sure, Sunset," Gigi said, patting my knee.

"Reconditioning is a process reserved for the most recalcitrant, rebellious patchworks," Eve explained. "The subject's brain is subjected to chemical treatment and localized electro-static application. It's designed to wipe the brain of any trace of rebellious impulse, rendering the subject docile and compliant."

"Wow," I said. "That's bloody horrible."

"Of course, if he subjected me to the process, he would lose his only assistant. Reconditioning also renders the subject imbecilic."

"So, good thing we saved you, eh?" Gigi laughed.

Eve nodded, tears spilling down her face. "A very good thing."

"What about that thing he did to you?" Tring asked. "The command that rendered you subservient?"

"Oh that," Eve said, wiping her face. I passed her a handkerchief. "A simple post-hypnotic command. When he began to lock me in the basement, I took the opportunity to hypnotize myself, determined the nature of the command and removed it. He wasn't especially happy about that, I assure you!"

Gigi's eyes widened. "You can do that?"

Domina arrived with bowls of thick vegetable soup, and we dug in.

Eve shrugged in answer to Gigi's question. "It was a fairly simple combination of meditative techniques and a specific chant, or mantra. In my case, 'remove the command' proved effective. And if I might speak ill of someone not present to defend himself, my fath... Dr. Sweetwater's activation word wasn't especially original."

I swallowed my soup. "It sounded like math to me."

"Well, that is, it was chemistry, actually," Eve said. "The chemical makeup of my revivification fluid."

"But any scientist or patchworker could have said that, in casual conversation!" Gigi said.

Eve shrugged again. "As I said, not especially original. But enough about me, I want to hear all your adventures!"

So we told her. About the Battle for Libertia and the war. About Lemuris. About our mission to recruit allies in Zhou and Daxia and finally here to Anglica.

"So if you're successful in shutting down the manufactories, you'll have three powerful allies for your side," Eve said.

"How do you figure, three?" Gigi asked.

"The Zhou, the vampyri, and these red hat people."

"Well, we haven't agreed to the Redcaps' terms," I said, setting aside my empty bowl and wishing there were more. "I'm not sure I can agree to forcibly evicting all the humans and animen from Eire so that the fae can have a home of their own."

"It is a question of politics," Tring said. "Not war. In war, decisions are made to ensure a specific, desired outcome and you live with the consequences, often because you had no other viable choice. In politics, every other choice is a viable choice and the consequences must be considered, weighed in balance to the desired outcome."

"Yeah," I said. "And I'm no politician. I'm just the captain of a pirate ship."

"Not true," Gigi argued, a huge grin on her feline face. "You are much more than that! You are the infamous Sunset Val! Books are written about you! The theatres of Albion echo with tales of your adventures. The Pirate King himself has named you his heir!"

Eve laughed. "You have been busy!"

"I guess. Anyhow, I'm not even sure we need the Redcaps. There's got to be some way to knock out Aldgate Amalgamated without them."

"We could just fly in and blow it out of the sky," Gigi said. "Or, land, I mean."

"I'm not sure even Inga has enough firepower to shut down that plant completely. I mean, we don't even know what's inside."

"Is there a way in?" Tring asked.

I described the building. No windows except for the third floor, only one gate, animen guards, the patchwork slaves, all that.

"If we can distract the guards I might be able to slip in."

Everyone stopped talking, and I turned to Eve. "You what?"

"Well, you said yourself the workforce is mostly patchworks, correct?" Eve said. "I want to help."

Part of me freaked at the thought of putting Eve at risk, so soon after rescuing her. I admit it. I couldn't lose her. Having her on The Furies meant more than I can explain. There was a bond between us, something more than friendship. I still have a hard time explaining it.

But another part of me, the captain part of me, the bitch part, thought it was a great idea, and wanted to go for it. To send one of my only friends into the enemy camp, into harm's way, all just to get the mission done. I don't know if it was from a sense of duty or personal glory, but that part of me, the part I'm not proud of, was willing to do whatever it took to win.

"I'll think about it," I said, knowing but not willing to admit that I'd already decided to do it. "Meanwhile, I think we need a plan for shutting them down, permanently."

"Well, if they are designed like most electrical plants," Gigi said, "there will be huge steam-powered dynamos inside. I'm surprised they're using power cables, though. Most places use broadcast electricity these days. Probably cheaper to use those cables. Tell me, were there any birds sitting on the wires?"

I thought about it for a second. "No, none."

Gigi nodded. "Cheap bastards. Those cables aren't nearly insulated enough. The local birds found out the hard way not to roost on the wires. Probably wound up in pies."

"That's all great, Gigi, but how do we blow up the place?"

"We might rig up some charges and set them under the dynamo's steam boilers. Although you might achieve the same effect by shutting down the pressure releases. But I assume we want to shut the plant down permanently?"

"Best destroy it completely," Eve said. "Otherwise they'd just be up and running as soon as they can repair the damage or remove the wreckage."

Gigi nodded. "Charges placed by the steam boilers and the dynamos would shut it down, but if you really want to blow the place to pieces, that's structural. Support columns and the like. Inga and I can devise some charges that would do the trick."

"I'd rather not kill the workers, though," I said. "We need a way to evacuate them before the bombs go off."

"A fire is generally accepted as a valid reason to evacuate," Tring offered. "If we can start a fire inside the building somewhere, the workers will flee for their lives."

"Why wouldn't they just put out the fire?"

"Patchworks have a particular horror of fire, Val," Eve explained. "The price of our resilience is the simple fact that we do not heal. Cuts and and other puncture wounds can be sewn up, broken bones can be splinted with metal implants, but fire damage can never be healed. Sometimes the damaged areas can be replaced with grafts from new donors, but... It's distasteful. Inasmuch as I know I am formed from several deceased humans, I've grown rather attached to the pieces I have. I dislike the idea of adding yet another human's parts to the ones I already have. It's a psychological issue with many patchworks, part of the process of waking up after our second birth and learning to use our new bodies. If you set a fire in the electrical plant, I guarantee you, none of the patchworks will risk further disfigurement or possible grafting in order to put it out."

"I didn't know that about patchworks," Gigi said.

"There's no reason you would be knowledgeable on the subject," Eve said with a gentle smile. "It's not really common knowledge."

"Is that why there are no partial patchworks?" Tring asked. "Why Miss Molly, for example, can never have another human arm or leg, to replace the one that doctor removed?"

"Well, that and the fact that we'd have to drain all her blood, effectively killing her, then replace it with the revivification fluid. And then the rest of the patchworking process removes all traces of memories of the donor's former life."

"Okay ladies, we're getting off course," I said. "If Eve sneaks in and gets a look around, we can decide what we'll do. But for now, I like the fire idea to force an evacuation and while the patchworks are panicking we'll set the charges and blow the entire plant to pieces. Sound good?"

They all agreed, and I asked Tring to help Eve find a bunk. Then they left and I got my first good night's sleep in days.

Chapter Thirty Five

Putting The Plan Into Action

The next morning I explained our plans to the Tallyho sisters. Bunny had opted out of our morning breakfast meeting, claiming that not knowing what we would be up to was his only defence, if anyone official came asking.

"I say, you never did plan anything small, did you, luv?" Gwen said around a mouthful of biscuit-and-jam.

"Blowing up the place on our own saves us the problem of dealing with the Redcaps and figuring out a way to shut down each individual manufactory," I said, spreading soft cheese on my biscuit. They'd been fresh baked that morning and they were every bit as good as Brunhilde's, though she'd probably poison me for saying so.

"Speaking of the Redcaps, we received this letter just this morning," Guinny said, tapping the letter with her tea spoon as she sipped her tea. "From Periwinkle."

"What's it say?" I asked.

"Just that she'd spoken to her people. They're eager to help out."

"That was quick."

"I suspect they'd already had something in the works, wot?"

"You think?"

"I do." Guinny shrugged. "We haven't agreed to anything."

I took a bite of biscuit-and-cheese and let myself enjoy the flavours before saying anything else. I washed it down with a sip of tea and said, "Probably for the best, right now. I'm not sure I've got the authority to make that kind of deal."

"You're second in command of the entire pirate armada, luv, what more authority do you need?" Guinny laughed.

"Political authority," I answered. "Ain't got none of that."

"So what do you need from us?" Gwen asked.

I thought about it. "Not sure. We're going to need to get Eve in, first. Then we'll see what we can do to sneak in the explosives."

Gwen nodded. "You've got what you need to make the charges?"

"Yeah, Inga said it was no problem. She looked really excited."

"Doesn't she always, when the opportunity to blow something up comes along?"

I laughed. "Yeah. Anyhow, first things first. We'll head into Albion and set ourselves up so that Eve can sneak in at the shift change tonight."

"Night shift?"

"Yeah. We figured, the less people around to ask her who she was and where she ought to be working instead of snooping, the better."

The twins nodded, with the exact same look of mischievous scheming on their faces. Then they looked at each other and grinned.

Gwen said, "We might be able to arrange your distraction."

"How's an airship chase right overhead sound?" Guinny added.

I grinned. "Like difficult to arrange but incredibly fun?"

After that it was just details. What time, how much of a distraction it needed to be, how soon before everyone could be ready. Luckily neither of our crews had been granted any shore leave. Too dangerous, here in enemy territory. But it left both our crews restless and looking for some action. The Furies would have to wait, but at least the Tallyho Sisters would be able to let off some steam.

I went back to The Furies and got ready. This time instead of going into the Aldgate area dressed like a posh lady looking to get mugged, killed and sold to the manufactories, I dressed like myself. Black slacks tucked into black knee-high boots, thick red leather corset, heavy red brocaded coat over top. Hair twin-braided. Bowler and goggles. And armed. No way was I going into that den of hacking, slashing, body-part-stealing psychos unarmed. But I limited myself to a couple of pistols and my main gauche / main droit pair. Oh and a couple of boot daggers. No sense drawing unnecessary attention. And to make sure we wouldn't get picked up at the train station, one of those awful grey cloaks over the entire outfit.

Tring and a couple of her girls came with us. Aldgate during the day was bad enough. Staying there overnight? Not smart for a person to be alone on those streets.

We got to Albion late that afternoon, with just enough time to grab something to eat from a street vendor selling roasted meat on a stick.

I almost asked what kind of meat, then decided against it. Sometimes ignorance is the best strategy. Anyway, it tasted alright enough and filled the hole in my belly.

We got ourselves a room at a local hotel, a couple of blocks from the Aldgate Amalgamated. The guy at the desk looked like he wanted to say something, so I asked, "Is there a problem?"

"Have to charge extra for 'em furriners," he answered, nodding at the Open Hands. "And no funny business. This ain't no pleasure house."

I slipped five times his asking price across the desk. His eyes went wide. "No problem," I said, even though he was a greedy, perverted, racist thief. "There's double that in the morning, if we're not disturbed."

He actually licked his lips. "Don't want no trouble is all."

"There won't be no trouble, if no trouble comes to us," I said, taking the room key from him. "We'll be back in a bit."

"Yeah, alright."

We headed out, down the cobbled streets toward Aldgate Amalgamated. I wasn't about to let Eve do this without backup.

"Really, I'm fine," she said for maybe the tenth time.

"I know you are, I just want to see what the twins have cooked up," I lied. I hated, hated, HATED sending Eve into there.

We got ourselves positioned in the square outside Aldgate Amalgamated and Eve shuffled off to stand near the workers who were waiting for the shift whistle to blow. And it blew. Just like the last time, the workers turned toward the gates. The gates opened. Tired workers walked out, night shifters walked in.

"They're late," Tring said.

"They'll be here," I answered, but she was right. The night shift crowd was thinning and Eve was still standing there, looking nervous. She started shuffling slowly toward the gates.

"She's gonna get caught," I muttered, then took a deep breath to yell at a passing carriage, our pre-arranged signal to call Eve off.

But just then a cannon fired, right overhead.

Well, it sounded right overhead, anyway. The boom echoed down the street and people shrieked and horses screamed and suddenly, a familiar airship rose over the buildings and swooped down the street, chased by a half-dozen ornithopters. I could have sworn I heard laughter from the Tallyho Sisters as they flew past.

The ornithopters followed and cannonshot flew ahead of them from their swivel-mount guns. Little three or four pounders, from the look of them, hardly enough to dent the Tallyho Sisters' hull. Probably even bounce right off the balloon's skin. I didn't quite see the point of firing at the ship until I spotted another pair of ornies join in the chase and another pair in the distance looking to cut the Sisters off. Their guns were basically signal cannons.

Just like that they were gone, off in the distance, cannon echoing in the evening sky.

I turned to see if Eve had gotten in. The guards were still staring up and pointing, trying to watch the chase. The whole neighbourhood had poured out into the street. No sign of Eve.

She had slipped past the guards and disappeared into Aldgate Amalgamated.

Chapter Thirty Six

And Of Course, Nearly Everything Goes Wrong

We went back to our hotel room to wait. I think we all know exactly how much I love waiting.

The room had a narrow bed, a single rickety chair and a rough, bare table. A single lamp filled with a foul-smelling oil gave off some light. Jin and Yue curled up on the bed and quickly fell asleep. Tring and I took turns sitting on the chair and pacing. Well, I paced. When Tring wasn't taking a turn sitting, she stood quietly by the window, looking out into the night.

During one of my turns on the chair, somehow I fell asleep, head resting on my crossed arms on the table.

A hand on my shoulder woke me. Someone had put out the lamp. Cold grey light on the horizon lit the room enough to see Tring standing over me.

I wiped the drool from my cheek and sat up slowly, working out the kinks in my back and neck. "What time is it?"

"Just after five bells," she said. "The night shift ends at six."

"Twelve hour shift," I nodded. "No wonder they all look so exhausted at the end of it."

Tring woke the other two as I stood and stretched. I really don't recommend sleeping that way. It felt like I popped every joint in my body, just standing up.

The guy at the desk was asleep, too, but I didn't mind waking him. He took the packet of money I gave him without even looking at me.

"We were never here, right?" I said.

"Never seen ya," he answered, counting the bills. I got the impression it was something he said often.

We went down to Aldgate Amalgamated and watched the day shift gather, hurriedly eating out of metal pails or handkerchiefs or from the carts of early-rising entrepreneurs. The shift whistle blew and the gates opened.

Night shift came out. Day shift went in.

No sign of Eve.

"Where is she?" I hissed through clenched teeth.

"Patience," Tring said, grabbing my arm.

The gates shut. Eve never came out.

I turned to Jin and Yue. "You two go back to the hotel, see if we somehow missed her, or if she got out early, or whatever. If we're not there in an hour, head back to the ship, tell Serena or Molly what's happened, then come get us. Tring, you're with me."

Jin and Yue never even glanced at Tring. They just nodded and left.

"And what are we going to do?" Tring asked.

"Figure out a way into that place," I said, "and find Eve."

Tring just nodded.

First we did a full perimeter search around the building. The stone wall went all the way around it, the front gate the only way through.

"So, we go over," I said, pointing at a nearby tenement building. Four stories high, built close enough to the power cables that we might be able to jump across. Assuming the cables had been insulated enough, we might survive rappelling across to Aldgate Amalgamated's roof.

We broke into the tenement with a well-placed kick by Tring, then climbed the stairs to the roof. I heard a baby crying from one room. A cat eating a mouse glared and hissed at us as we climbed past. Those were the only signs of life inside the building.

The roof had a rope strung up to for drying laundry, though drying their laundry so close to the chimney struck me as kind of stupid. Plus the ashfall from the crematoria meant a lot of very dirty clean laundry.

From the roof, the jump to the cables looked even further than it had from the ground. I let loose a string of curses.

"Be thankful there are cables at all," Tring said, measuring off paces from the far edge of the roof to the launch-off edge. "If they had invested in broadcast electricity, we would have to ride the air itself."

"Ride the air..." I muttered. Then it hit me. "Tring, you genius!"

I ran for the stairwell and down the stairs, not stopping until I hit the front door of The Merry Clockmaker. Panting, I looked around the room, until I found a likely suspect.

"You!" I said, pointing at a pixie in the corner. He had long hair tied back with a piece of red string. "I need to talk to you."

He looked startled and glanced around the pub. "Me? Got the wrong pix, luv. I ain't never seen you in me life."

"I know. Listen, you know Periwinkle, right? We were in here a couple of days ago."

"Never 'eard of 'er."

I snatched him right out of the air and brought him close to my face. "I don't have time to play games with you, Redcap! My friend's life is in danger! The longer you jerk around the likelier she'd dead, get me?"

"Captain," Tring said quietly beside me. I glanced at her.

We'd been very quickly, very quietly surrounded by faekind. All of them had red bits of ribbon or thread or leather tied into their hair.

"Good, I have your attention," I said, turning to them all. "I need your help. You know I was in here a couple of days ago, talking with Periwinkle. You know what we were talking about. You help me now, I'll help you out later. I promise."

That got them muttering to each other. The pixie in my hand said, "Oi! 'ow's about lettin' us go?"

"Yeah, sorry," I said, opening my hand and letting him fly off to join his kind in their conversational huddle.

I nearly lost my patience and almost interrupted them when one of the gnomes turned to me and said, "Deal. Shake on it, human."

I shook his hand. It was as hard as stone. When we stopped shaking hands, the assembled Redcaps all cheered. Some were even crying.

"Okay, look, as much as I'd love to stay and party, I need you to get me and my friend here into Aldgate Amalgamated."

"What for?" the pixie I'd grabbed asked.

"They've got a friend of ours trapped inside there somewhere."

"Why'd your friend go inside, then?"

"We're going to blow the place up, alright? Can we go?"

The cheering and crying all turned to laughter, then the pixie said, "Yeah, alright. Come on lads!"

And that was how I sold the entire island of Eire to the faerykin for a lift over a wall.

It took about a dozen of them, pulling on my coat and boots with all their might, wings buzzing like airship propellers, to lift me up and land me on the roof of Aldgate Amalgamated. Then they did the same for Tring.

"How are you planning to blow the place up?" the pixie asked.

"Start a fire to evacuate the workers, then place charges under the boilers," I said, not really paying him any attention. I was trying to find a way in while making sure that no guards were walking the wooden roof. "But we have to find our friend first and get her out."

The pixie laughed. "No problem. We're on it!"

"Wait, what?!" I said, but the pixies had already flitted away. *Okay,* I thought, *well, whatever.*

Tring caught my arm and pointed along the roof's edge. Halfway along, she'd spotted an open window. We ran to it and Tring helped me lower myself over the edge. I caught the window sill with the tip of my boot and hauled myself inside. Heat pounded at me, stifling compared to the cool air outside. I reached out and grabbed Tring's legs as she lowered herself down, pulling her inside with me. We squatted down, hoping no one had spotted our silhouettes against the window's light.

A quick glance down told me we didn't have to worry. Between the electrical lights strung above them and the fires from the boilers all around them, the workers were surrounded by light. They couldn't have seen us if we'd been wearing flashing signs that read "We're Pirates!"

The upper level we were on was basically a wooden catwalk all the way around the outer perimeter of the building, which was pretty much just a shell with very little inner structure. The roof was held up by huge wooden support beams, like squared-off trunks of trees, evenly spaced along the lengthwise axis of the building. Two stories below me, maybe two dozen dynamos hummed along, while below them giant steam boilers were being fed steady streams of coked coal by workers armed with shovels. Turning coal into electricity seemed like a big waste to me, especially with a river nearby, but hey, I wasn't there to spark an industrial revolution. I was there to save my friend.

We sneaked along the catwalk until we came to a stairwell, which we went down to the next floor. Still no sign of any guards, we made our way along that level. I spotted some doors at the far end of the building. Careful not to attract attention, we made our way over there, then checked the rooms one by one. They led to tidy offices with desks, chairs, filing cabinets, that sort of thing.

"Guess the office staff start later in the day," I said.

"Good place to start a fire," Tring muttered.

I nodded, thinking. Then I went to a nearby desk and picked up an oil lamp. "Surprised they don't use electrical lights."

"Any electricity they use is electricity they can't sell," Tring answered. "What are you thinking?"

"I'm thinking we're probably not going to get another chance at this." I heft the oil lamp, listened to the oil sloshing around inside it. I looked over at the wooden filing cabinets, filled with paper. Oil lamp. Filing cabinet.

I put the lamp down. "Find Eve first. There's no way we can do that if the building's on fire."

"And we do not have the explosive charges," Tring added. If I didn't know better, I'd say she was relieved I'd decided against doing something so reckless.

"Yeah, well, we could shut off the boiler pressure valves. That would wreck the machinery, anyway."

"Just the two of us? Shut down all the boilers while the building burns to the ground around us?"

"Yeah, you're right. Pretty crazy."

We left the offices the way we found them.

Chapter Thirty Seven

Frying Pans, Etc.

Sneaking down to the next level was a lot harder than getting into the building itself. For one thing, Tring and I didn't look anything like workers, who'd all put on these ugly grey coveralls. That problem was solved when we found a supply closet with coveralls. I ditched my beloved bowler and slipped my goggles into the pocket of my coat, which I kept on under the coveralls. And yeah, I was getting pretty sweaty inside all those layers. I hid my hair under a kerchief I found and Tring did likewise. Then we went out onto the shop floor.

All around us, patchworks and humans worked to keep the boilers fed. Some checked and rechecked the dynamos' output, fiddling with gauges and dials and switches. The noise battered my ears, thrumming from the dynamos, pounding from the steam engines, roaring from the boilers. Occasionally a steam valve would let loose a hissing blast of steam as the pressure built up.

Coal dust coated nearly everything and what wasn't coated in coal was covered in grease. Even the workers, who'd started the shift only a couple of hours ago, were already filthy.

Tring stayed behind me, in the shadows as much as possible. A Zhou in this crowd stood out like a patchwork in a park. I made sure to walk like I knew where I was going and was going there with a purpose. Nothing is more suspicious than someone who looks like their trying not to be noticed. The best way to hide was to hide in plain sight.

Or so I told myself. For all I knew, every person who saw me pass by stopped working and started pointing at me. I didn't look back.

A big guy, a patchwork, grabbed my shoulder as I passed. "Oi!"

I stopped, staring at the huge fist that had curled into the sleeve of my coverall. "Yeah?" I yelled.

"Fresh meat, eh?"

I attempted an Albion accent, atrociously. "Wot's it to ya, mate?"

"Nuffink, dahlin'. Maybe you and me can get a pint after?"

"Maybe!" I agreed, trying to get him to loosen his grip.

"Wassa rush, luv?" he asked, his patchworked face turning his leering gap-toothed grin into something genuinely gross.

"Don't want to get sacked me first day!"

He laughed. "Too roight! Off wi' ya, now!"

"Thanks!" I called, backing away. I headed to the outside wall, hoping to find some door or a stairwell leading to a basement or something. Walking along the outside wall would also keep me from the majority of the workers, since the boilers faced inwards, toward the piles of coked coal along the centre of the building. The coal was delivered in large buckets, running along an overhead rail that ran the length of the building. I followed the rail and saw that the buckets came up from, I assumed, the basement, using an elevator thing. At the other end, the end closer to me, they went back down an identical elevator thing.

I hurried to the elevator thing, getting there just as a bucket was heading into the basement. I climbed in and rode it downstairs. Tring followed along in the next bucket.

"Whatta you playing at?!" a big, bald, fat supervisor-type yelled at me, coming over with a red face and a clipboard.

"Fink thassa funhouse ride, do ya?" he yelled, grabbing my sleeve.

I was getting pretty fed up right about then, so as calmly as I could I reached into my coveralls and under my coat, then pulled out my revolver. He'd been so busy yelling at me he hadn't noticed me draw at all, but he noticed it when I jammed my gun in his mouth.

"Shut up or I blow your head off," I said.

I smelled him piss himself. He panted around the barrel, eyes fixed on my gun.

"Last night a girl sneaked in here, but she never left," I said. "You know where she is?"

He nodded.

"Show me where she is and I'll let you live."

I took the gun out of his mouth and turned him around, keeping the gun behind him. I knew enough not to jam it right in his back. Too easy for him to try and whirl around and grab it. Not that the tub of guts could have whirled if you paid him.

He led us past workers shovelling coked coal from barges into the passing buckets hanging about waist-high. Pretty smart of them, I thought, getting the coal delivered by underground river barges. The fishy, dead vegetation smell of the river made my eyes water.

Right about the time I expected, Tubbo found his nerve again, hidden in a pile of resentment at being unmanned by a little girl. He tried to whirl and take a swing at me, but of course Tring was there, too. She grabbed his arm mid-swing and twisted it so fast and so hard that I heard the bone's wet snap. He fell to his knees, howling in pain.

His screaming made the workers look up to see Tring holding him up by his broken arm and me pointing a gun at them.

"We're setting this place on fire," I said. "If you want to live, get on the barges and float downriver."

No one argued. Some of them even smirked at Tubbo's predicament.

That's when a couple of animen guards showed up. Without thinking I spun and shot at one, catching him right in the thigh. He went down, flat on his lion face in the coal dust and river slime. His partner, a gorilla animan, stopped short, crouching, ready to spring at me if my gun wavered even the slightest.

"They don't pay you enough to take a bullet," I said. "Pick up your partner and get on the barges with the others."

"Or what?" he rumbled.

"Or I shoot you and it'll be a toss up whether you bleed to death or burn up first."

He paused, straightening. "Burn?"

"We're setting the place on fire, gonna burn it to the ground," I said. "Think Sunset Val travels alone? My girls are upstairs right now, getting the place ready."

His eyes went wide. "Sunset Val?!"

It occurred to me right then, that maybe I could get used to this infamy stuff.

The workers on the barges muttered to themselves. I heard my name maybe a dozen times.

"Cast off, you lot!" I yelled at them without taking my eyes off of Ape-boy. "Tell the world, Sunset Val saved your lives."

I turned to Ape-boy, jerking my head toward the barges. "Your choice," I said, then cocked back the hammer on my revolver.

His waved his hands to stop me. "Wait wait! I'll go!"

He grabbed his partner and they got onto the last barge.

"What about me?!" Tubbo said.

"Show me where my friend is and I'll let you live," I answered.

He stumbled along discarded shovels and piles of coked coal as the buckets rumbled past, empty. "Why us, then, eh? Why Aldgate?"

"Because you use slaves," I said.

He turned to look at me. "Ain't no slaves 'ere!"

"What do you call all those patchworks sent here by the manufactories to work off their debt to you?"

"Only what's right an' propah! Give 'em our electrics, don't we?"

"Are the patchworks paid a fair wage?"

"A fair what?"

"Are they paid the same as you?!"

"No, o'course not!"

"Equal pay for equal work, you jackass! That's a fair wage. Now where's my friend?!"

Apparently I convinced him to shut up and stop stalling, because he led us to a room down by the far end. The small metal door was deeply set in the crumbling brick wall, but after much grunting and groaning, he managed to pull it open.

Faint lamp light spilled into the room, revealing Eve, tied up and gagged in the corner. She opened one eye as I entered. The other eye was gummed shut with some pus-like liquid and coal dust. Patchworks don't bleed, so they don't bruise, but it was pretty clear that she'd been roughed up. A gash in her pale cheek and colourless flesh revealed a bright white slash of bone.

I yanked the gag out of her mouth and she coughed, huge chest-racking coughs. I slit the ropes binding her with my main gauche and helped her stand.

"Sorry about this," Eve said.

"Not as sorry as me," I answered. "Can you walk?"

"Well enough."

I turned to Tubbo. "You. Swim for those barges."

"Oi, you said you'd let me go."

I lifted my gun and pointed it at his fat face. "No, I said I'd let you live. Be happy I'm in a good mood."

He jumped in, swimming as best he could with a broken arm.

"Now what?" Tring asked.

"Now we go back upstairs. Start a fire. Get the workers out, shut off the pressure valves, and hopefully this place will blow sky high."

"All by ourselves?" Eve asked.

"You think we'll get another chance at this? You two get to work on the pressure valves, I'll start the fire."

"I do not like the idea of splitting up," Tring said.

"And I'm not in a mood to argue about this!" I took a deep breath. "Look, I appreciate you're worried about me. I will do my absolute best not to be killed, I promise. Believe me, that's the last thing I want."

"Fire is very dangerous, Sunset," Eve said.

"I know, that's why I'll be careful," I said, slipping out of my coveralls. "Look, any second now someone's going to come downstairs to figure out why the coal buckets aren't being filled. It's go time."

I rode a bucket up through the hole in the floor. Once above the workers, who still had more than enough coal to shovel into the boilers, I ran along the conveyor rail to the far end of the building, where the offices were. I'm pretty sure some workers spotted me, but I didn't care. I was trying to make a scene and you can't do that without being seen.

Get it? Scene, seen? Alright, I know, get on with it.

I pulled out my guns and shot the ceiling a few times to make sure I had people's attention, then jumped from the conveyor rail to the balcony rail of the office landing.

"I'm Sunset Val!" I yelled to the people who turned to look at me. Most, amazingly, didn't, they just kept working. "I'm shutting this plant down! Equal pay for equal work!" I fired my gun into the ceiling again. "No more patchwork slaves!" Another gunshot.

They were listening now, most of them, even pointing at me and talking to each other.

"Yeah, that's right! Sunset Val, the infamous pirate! Now run, you bloody blighted bastards!" I fired into the ceiling again, then pointed my guns at the crowd.

They ran.

Once I saw that they were well and truly serious about leaving, I ran for the first office door. But when I grabbed the door handle to yank it open, it burned my hand.

Hissing in pain, I yanked the kerchief off my head and gingerly felt the door. The wood was hot. Burning hot.

And that's when I noticed the little flickering tongues of flames behind the window set above the door. Smoke seeped through the window frame and rose up toward the open windows along the catwalks above me.

"What the?" I couldn't help myself. I opened the door.

The office inside was an inferno. Desks, filing cabinets, chairs, walls, the ceiling, the floor, everything was on fire. The heat was so intense I could barely breathe. My first instinct was to try and close the door again, but then I realized: I wanted this. And somehow, it had happened.

The flames, now that they could escape, quickly engulfed the door jamb and began licking at the outer office walls. I ran to the next office, only to find it on fire, too.

Let me just say for the record, I had no idea the building would catch fire so easily, or that it would get so out of control so fast. Looking back it made perfect sense. I mean, it was so hot in there that the workers were always sweating, even in winter, which meant that all the wooden support beams and wooden floor boards and wooden everything would have dried right out, right? And with coal dust everywhere, well, that didn't exactly make things less flammable.

Every office I went to was on fire. The smoke was thick and stung my eyes, my throat. I coughed a few times, then held the kerchief over my mouth as I fumbled my goggles out of my pocket. Slipping them on one-handed wasn't easy, but I managed.

I glanced down at the shop floor, only to realize there wasn't any point, I couldn't see anything through the flames and smoke. I had to get out of there! But when I moved toward the stairs, a falling support beam rained flames and embers into my path, spreading the fire even more, blocking my way.

"Eve! Tring!" I yelled, coughing. "Get out! Get out now!"

I didn't hear any answers, just the roar of the flames, the hiss and crackle of old timbers splitting, the creak and groan of the building dying a fiery death.

My way down was blocked, but I could still go up. I ran for the stairwell to the catwalks above, trying to keep my head down to avoid the worst of the smoke. It was only when I got up to the catwalks and tried to find an open window that I realized my mistake. The fires had raced me to the windows, beating me there, sucking in air to fuel their destructive dance.

I was trapped.

Then a man behind me said, "Sunset Val, I presume?"

I whirled around. He was tall, dressed in browns and reds. He wore a hooded cloak. A mask, carved and painted like a fox's face, hid the upper half of his face, but his chin was strong and his smile was really gorgeous. The eyes behind the mask were dark blue.

"Who're you?" I asked.

"I should have thought it obvious," he answered. "Might I be of assistance?"

"You're the Hooded Fox?"

"I am," he said. Then he grabbed me by the waist and pulled me close. "But perhaps we might continue this conversation in more genial environs?"

And before I could answer he jumped off the catwalk, taking me with him. I almost fought him, but he did something I completely didn't expect and that's saying something considering a man dressed like a fox had just offered to save me by dragging me into a raging inferno.

What was so unexpected was this:

He kissed me.

On the mouth.

There may have been tongue. I'm not even sure, because of the, y'know, falling to a fiery death and all that.

Only we weren't falling, suddenly, we were swinging. And then we were swinging up. And then we crashed through a window, landing on an adjacent rooftop. Still inside the stone wall, but outside the main building.

"Great!" I coughed, shoving him off. "Do you have a plan to get us off this roof?"

"Not as yet, my deah," he said. Something about the way he said it, the way he was standing, the set of his jaw, the purse of his lips, and all of a sudden, I knew.

I rushed at him and shoved that fox mask up onto his forehead before he could stop me.

"Bunny?!" I yelled.

"I do wish you wouldn't call me that," he said, reaching up calmly and slipping the fox face back into place. "This is who I am. Bunny is... the mask."

"All this time, you were the Hooded Fox!"

"Guilty as charged, my deah."

"Stop calling me that! And you kissed me!"

"As I had longed to do since first we met."

"Okay, look! Bunny, Fox, whatever... Oh I see what you did there."

"Bunnies are cute, adorable. Most importantly, harmless. While foxes are somewhat more..." He paused and looked at me, and there was something, I dunno. Hungry. In his eyes. "...predatory."

And yeah, it got me hot, and not just because we were on the roof of a burning building. I may have leaned in. My lips may have pursed for a kiss. My eyes might have started to close.

But something inside the building blew up just then, shaking the entire roof and you know, bringing me back to my senses. And when I say blew up, that really doesn't say nearly enough. First there was a huge deafening thud. Almost at the same time, all the windows in the building shattered. Even the windows in the buildings across the street broke to bits. Then the roof shuddered, nearly throwing us off balance. I grabbed Bunny for balance just as he reached for me.

Then I shook off his offered hand, jabbed his chest hard with my finger. "This conversation is not finished!"

"Indeed," he answered, rubbing the spot I'd jabbed him.

We ran to the edge of the roof, which began splitting and collapsing behind us. Fires raged through the holes and soon the whole roof was caving in.

I stopped, right at the edge, and looked down. It was easily thirty feet to the cobblestone courtyard. I looked up at my rescuer.

"We'll not survive the way down," he said.

I was about to remind him of that swing line thing he had, but something over his shoulder caught my eye and a huge grin spread across my sooty face. "Then can I offer you a way up?"

The Furies had arrived.

Chapter Thirty Eight

Could My Life Get More Complicated?

The Furies swooped by, dropping a rope ladder. We just had time to grab on before the vicious updraft from the fire pushed The Furies back. Then we were dangling high above the city, getting higher and higher as the ship lifted off.

Rung by rung I climbed up toward the belly of my ship, her launch bay doors wide open and inviting as a mother's arms. I felt Bunny – Fox – climbing up behind me. I really didn't have time for emotions, much less sorting out everything that had just happened, so I focussed on getting into my ship as fast as I could.

I only paused when Aldgate Amalgamated Aelyctrix blew itself to pieces. Itty bitty pieces. Raining down for, reports later claimed, miles. Gigi figured out that the fires that had burned the building had super-heated the steam inside the boilers, even faster than the pressure valves could release. Eve and Tring had only been able to shut down about half of them before they'd run for it. The super-pressure inside them had turned those boilers into bombs.

Eve and Tring were already inside the launch bay, filthy with soot and sweat. They helped me in. A couple of other girls helped the Hooded Fox board our ship.

"He stays here," I ordered my girls, then headed for the bridge.

"How'd you know to come?" I asked Molly when I got there.

"We knew there'd be trouble, so Serena and I got the ship ready and lifted off at dawn," she answered, getting out of the command chair.

"Oh you just knew there'd be trouble," I said. "I like that. Thanks for the vote of confidence."

"We were right, weren't we? When have we ever not had trouble?"

"Fine, fine," I said. "You made good time, though."

"Easy when you're not land-bound like a train. We flew straight as the crow flies."

"The crow... Oh shit!"

"What? What is it?"

"The Commodore! Crow! He's in town, looking for us!"

But cannonfire interrupted my train of thought, just as a voice squawked over the intercom: "Atlan cruiser off the port stern!"

"Launch all ornies!" I ordered to Argenta, back in her spot at the radio. "Batgirls to the rigging! And someone find the Vulka-reys. Get those bitches in the air! Bring us about, hard to port!"

Restless spun the wheel as hard as she could while Molly ran to find the Vulka-reys.

"Inga! Fire at will!"

Argenta relayed my orders. I collapsed into my chair, wondering how much adrenaline one person could produce before breakfast.

"Why would he risk action over the city?" I asked myself out loud. "Civilians could be hurt."

"Maybe he don't care about that?" Restless answered.

"Clearly," I muttered, then shook my head. I turned to Argenta. "Argenta! Belay all orders! We're running. Restless, engines to full, set course due south."

"Aye, Captain Val."

"Aye aye, Cap'n."

Argenta turned to the intercom and Restless spun the wheel. I sat there, shaking my head, trying to figure out why he wanted us to fight him in a populated area.

"What's going on?" Molly asked as she stormed back onto the bridge. "You belayed the battle?"

"Why's he starting a fight over a city?" I asked.

"Because we're infamous pirates?"

"Too easy to damage civilians."

She thought about it. "Unless he wants to damage civilians."

"It would turn public sentiment against pirates. They seem to find us quaint, exciting and adventurous. They made a play out of me, right?"

"I dunno, I never saw it," Molly said. "But yes, any damage the battle would cause would get turned into our fault."

"We did blow up an electrical plant," Restless piped up. "Likely they won't be happy about that."

"But I made sure everyone escaped," I said. "That'll spread faster than the fire."

"The merciful Sunset Val," Molly smirked. "Nice ring to it."

I snorted. "I guess." I turned my seat around and studied the bank of screens. Scenes of the crew getting ready for a fight played on most of them, but two caught my eye. The first was a rear-view scene, off our stern, of the Atlan cruiser. We were holding steady, seemed like. The other screen showed me a small compartment door, which was unusual because previously the screen had shown a view of the surgery. Two girls, heavily armed, stood watch outside the compartment.

I realized I knew that compartment well. I'd been imprisoned there, when I'd been a slave. The Box, they'd called it then.

"You moved one of the cameras?" I asked Molly.

"Oh, right. Meant to tell you."

"Why?"

"We caught the saboteur."

I know, right? I bet you thought I'd forgotten about that.

"Who?"

Molly told me. It seemed obvious, then, considering when the problems had started. I just didn't understand why. And no, I'm not going to tell you just yet. It'll be more dramatic later and anyway, I had bigger problems just then. And we were interrupted.

The Hooded Fox stepped onto the bridge. "Problems, Captain?"

I glared at him. "I told you to stay in the launch bay."

"Your orders came down and everyone went into a frenzy of activity," he said, looking at the bank of screens, obviously impressed. "Quite professional, really. Your crew is to be commended."

"They let you leave the bay."

"Well, 'let' is somewhat incorrect," he shrugged. "I eluded them."

"Okay, fine, whatever."

"Should I take him back to the launch bay?" Molly asked in Atlan.

"No, it's fine. What do you want, Fox?"

"That list is quite long, I'm afraid," he said, switching to flawless Atlan. "Justice, liberty, equality, an end to the war...." Then he gave me a long look that said very clearly what else he wanted. And yes, part of me wanted to let him have that very thing. Another part of me wanted to toss him in The Box for lying to me all that time.

"You'll never outrun them," he said, changing the subject.

"The Furies is quicker than she looks."

"No doubt," he agreed. "But they have the force of authority and law on their side."

"What's that got to do with anything?" Molly asked.

"Uh, Cap'n?"

I turned. "What is it, Restless?"

"Constabulary ornies, up ahead."

"What? Where?"

"Them dots there, bobbing and weaving?"

"Bloody blight, you've got good eyes!" Fox swore.

I grabbed a pair of telescopic goggles from the rack of them we kept on the bridge and held them up to my face. I caught a glimpse of myself in the reflection of the lenses. Still covered with soot and sweat, my braided hair coming loose. Nasty. And here was this gorgeous guy who very clearly was into me. I sighed and rolled my eyes at the unfairness of the universe. Universes. Whatever.

I slipped the goggles on and scanned the sky, spotting the squat police ornies. Two-seaters, like ours, but where ours were long and lean and four-winged, the police ornies were built shorter and only two-winged. Less power, less control. And they had some kind of cage built on their rears, probably to carry arrested criminals. Against the backdrop of the grey Albion skies, they looked striped.

"Bit like bumblebees, eh Cap'n? Or more like, bobbin' bees?"

"Yeah." I turned to notice Fox standing right next to me. He'd done something to his mask and lenses now covered his eyes.

"You'll need a distraction if you want to outrun them," he said, not looking at me.

"I only need to get them away from the town," I said. "Then we turn and fight."

"A noble sentiment, my love, but you've a more important mission."

I turned to face him, hands on my hips. "Are you seriously telling me what to do on my own ship?"

He grinned at me, turning my insides to jelly. It was probably the most difficult thing I'd done all day, keeping a frown on my face while he smiled at me.

"Never, my dahling," he said. "Merely a reminder. And the sooner you complete your mission, the sooner we can be together."

No one had ever said anything like that to me. No one, as far as I knew, had ever felt that way about me. It turned my knees to water, my insides to fire, my anger to mist.

I looked away. "Don't be stupid. We can't know if either of us will survive the war. And anyway... I mean, I don't..."

"Shush. I would rather live with hope in my heart and no chance of it becoming a reality, than have my dreams dashed to dust."

"Fox..."

He touched a hidden button on his mask and the lenses hiding his eyes slid away, revealing those deep, dark blue eyes and everything that lay in them. "My love, we'll settle this once the war is over and that's all there is to it. Until then, you have your mission, I have mine and we're surrounded by the enforcers of a corrupt regime. Let us concentrate on one thing at a time and first things first. To whit, those ornithopters."

I took a deep breath. "Yeah, alright." I thought about it for a second. "We can launch our ornies, batgirls and the Vulka-rey, but that's a battle I'd prefer to avoid over a populated area. The Battle for Libertia taught me that."

"And the Commodore will catch up to you all the sooner," Fox said, leaning over a console to look down at the city. "Ah, there. Perfect."

"There where?"

He draped an arm over my shoulder and pointed. "How close can your ship get to Tall Paul?"

I looked, trying to spot what he was pointing at, when it became obvious: a huge, massive clock tower, with giant clocks on all four faces. Back home I would have thought it to be London's famous landmark, Big Ben; here on Ayrth, missing the Parliament buildings, and maybe five times bigger, Tall Paul loomed over the inhabitants of Albion, a daily reminder of the architectural skill and clockmaking talents of their Atlan overlords.

"Restless?" I asked.

She hopped up and down to get a look without leaving her post. "Oh uh... pretty close, Cap'n."

Fox nodded. "Very well, it shall have to do. My love, here is where we must part." He smiled a sad smile and my heart swelled and ached. Stupid heart! "Know that you dwell ever in my thoughts... and my heart."

"Alright, look, just... Stop. You're being... This is..."

He stepped close to me, close enough that I had to look up or continue talking to his chest. But looking up meant seeing him looking down, those deep blue eyes, that smile, and yeah we were kissing again. I wrapped my arms around his neck and felt him lift me and everything went dizzy headspinny woo. After a forever that ended way too fast, I felt the floor under my feet and realized he was putting me down and expecting me to stand on my own. I didn't trust my balance right then, so I leaned against his chest, my heart thudding in mine.

When my brain started working I looked up to see Molly giving me a 'do-we-really-have-time-for-this' look and Restless grinning so crazily I thought maybe her face would split in half.

I cleared my throat. "Alright. Um."

"Bring her down, Cap'n?" Restless asked.

"Right. Yes. That." I turned to Fox. "What are you going to do?"

"Jump ship," he grinned.

Chapter Thirty Nine

Nobody Gets My Jokes

I followed him off the bridge and through my ship to the launch bay, where all my pilots and batgirls and even the Vulka-rey had gathered, waiting for the word to launch into battle.

"Open the doors," I ordered. A couple of girls jumped to haul on the chain that opened the starboard launch doors.

"Do you want us to slow down?" I asked Fox over the sudden roar of wind.

He looked out the doors as we raced toward the clock tower at full speed. "No need. This should be fine."

"Hey, wait," I said, grabbing his arm. "I have a lot of questions."

"They may have to wait," he said. "We've not much time."

"Alright, um. How did you know to set the fire?"

"I didn't. I assume those pixies did."

"What pixies?"

"The ones that were leaving just as I arrived. I thought they were with you."

"So why were you there?"

"To find you, of cawse. I'd been nearby, orchestrating a prison break from a number of manufactory stockyards. Thought I'd pop in and see you in action. Didn't expect the fire."

"Oh. Why do you have such a hate on for the manufactories?"

"They've turned us against ourselves. You saw those ghouls in Aldgate. How they leapt to dismember a man, to sell his parts to the nearest manufactory. No one's been buried in the Aldgate cemetary for years. That's the fault of those bloody dehumanizing manufactories. And besides, it hurts the Atlan war effort, having the manufactories disrupted." He looked out the doors again. Tall Paul loomed huge ahead of us. "And now my love, I must go."

I grabbed his other arm. "No, wait, I feel like I just met you! The real you."

He pulled me close, wrapped his arms around me. I wanted to stay there forever. "And I've waited my whole life to meet you."

We kissed again, in front of the whole crew and everything. I didn't care. The Vulka-rey howled and pounded their booted feet against the deck.

And then he was gone. I opened my eyes in time to see him jump out the launch doors. My heart jumped after him. After about a second of freefall, using his cloak to slow himself, he pulled out a gun from a hidden holster and fired it at the clock face. I saw a line of something glittering reel out, wrap itself around the minute hand. That quick he wasn't falling any more. My urge to vomit disappeared, replaced with a rapid rush of relief. And just the tiniest bit of astonishment that it was only quarter past nine in the morning.

He swung around Tall Paul and disappeared from sight. I still didn't know what he intended, but I trusted him. I turned away from the open doors to find the entire crew looking at me, grinning.

"Don't you have work to do?" I snapped at them and they all hurried off to look busy.

I put my hand to my mouth, pressing the warmth of his kiss into my lips. Stupid. So stupid. I know, believe me, I know. I mean, I'd never been in love before, so I didn't know if this was it, the real thing. All I knew was, a man wanted me, said he loved me. I wanted him, too. Maybe that was enough. And maybe it was the war, making everything seem so urgent. Making me want to believe him. Making me want something for myself.

"Captain to the bridge, please," Argenta's voice rang out over the intercom.

I shook myself out of my dreams and hopes, pushing them deep down, away from here and now. Here and now, I had to be a pirate captain. Later, maybe, I could be a woman in love.

"All hands on deck, into the rigging, guns and rifles," I ordered. "Keep those bobbing bees off us."

"What did she call 'em?" I heard someone ask behind me.

"Bobbies, I think?"

I made my way back up to the bridge. "What is it, Molly?"

"Not sure." She was holding a telescope up to her real eye. "Look."

I noticed someone had ordered us to come about while I'd been off the bridge, because we were circling around Tall Paul. A glance through my telescopic goggles showed me a door open in Tall Paul's west face, just over the six. Something big and black moved there.

I heard cannon fire and someone yelled, "They're firing at us, Captain!"

"Argenta, tell Inga to stand down all cannons. Open fire, guns and rifles only."

"Aye Captain," she said, relaying my orders. Within seconds, the crack of pistols and the boom of rifles filled the air.

Outside, the bobbing ornies scattered, flying every direction. Off to our port, the Commodore's cruiser closed in. I slammed my fist against the armrest of my chair. We had their T crossed! A perfect shot and we couldn't take it.

"What about the lightning cannon?" Molly asked. "No ammunition to dump on the city."

"We'd probably hit Tall Paul there, instead," I said. "And anyway, flaming wreckage is worse than cannonballs that missed their target."

Molly growled in frustration.

"Come about due south, Restless," I ordered.

"Aye Cap'n."

"Argenta, tell Gigi she's got to get us going faster."

"Aye Captain," Argenta said. I could hear Gigi's reply clear down where I sat. Something about me getting out to push, only not nearly that polite.

The Furies came about due south and we left Tall Paul behind us.

"They're going to catch us, ain't they, Cap'n?"

"Maybe, Restless, but we won't go without a fight, civilians below or no."

"Maybe not," Molly said, pointing behind me. I turned.

There, onscreen, a giant cloud of fluttering black somethings spilled out of Tall Paul.

"What are those?" I asked, leaning toward the grainy grey image. "Bats?"

"The ravens," Molly said, wonder in her voice. "The great ravens of Albion."

We ran out on deck. The girls in the rigging had stopped firing at the bobbing ornies, staring at the huge cloud of ravens surrounding the clock tower. Up in the bow, I couldn't see much, so I made my way aft to the stern. Molly followed.

"There's got to be dozens of them," I said. "Hundreds, even."

Even from our rapidly growing distance, I could hear them cawing. Up close, it had to be deafening.

Up close. Exactly where the Commodore's cruiser was.

As one, the huge flock of ravens whirled and turned and swarmed the cruiser, the closest flying threat to their territory. The Atlan warship disappeared behind the black cloud.

"He did it," I whispered. "He did it! He stopped them! Yes!"

I realized I was jumping up and down, clapping my hands and laughing, only when I saw the looks on the faces of the crew. Some were confused, but most were various levels of amused.

"Oh come on, that's funny!" I said, hooking a thumb over my shoulder at the black cloud of ravens. "Commodore Crow, thwarted by ravens? No? Anyone?"

Some of the girls chuckled, at least.

"Back to your stations, girls," I shrugged. "Let's get out of here!"

Chapter Forty

Afric Accusations

Once we'd left Albion behind us, we swung southeast to rendezvous with the Tallyho Sisters. Luckily, they'd managed to pick up Jin and Yue. We raced over Gallia and past Bavardy. There were two reasons for all the rush. First, I wanted to report to the Lemurisians that the mission had been a success. That would end my mission and maybe I could sneak back into Anglica to I dunno, be with Fox some more and see if it was really real or just a lot of adrenaline-fuelled hormones.

Second, we were being chased.

Yeah, the attack by the ravens had slowed the Commodore's cruiser just long enough to let us put a healthy distance between us, but he hadn't given up that easily. And he'd found some friends. A half dozen or so other Atlan warships had joined the chase, rough odds for two pirate ships. So, we ran for it. She who fights and runs away, yadda yadda something. For a day and a half, we maintained a southeasterly course, crossing the Alpacian Mountains into Etrusca, where we were supposed to bid farewell to our Vulka-rey friends.

"Do not be silly!" Captain Draganova said, slapping me on the shoulder. "You vill need our help in the battle to come. Ve vill send three of our fastest Wulka-rey. They vill deliver the message that the mission vas a success, the patchwork manufactories are shut down and Daxia should invade Russankya, yes? Good!"

So Anya, Zora, and Aleksandra left us, kisses and hugs all around, promises to catch up as soon as they could. I had to admit I was sorry to see them go, but glad we kept the rest of the squad with us. Draganova was right. We would need them in the battle to come.

We almost lost the Commodore and his warships in a storm over the Europan Sea, but half a day into Afric Restless spotted them trailing behind us, one ship fewer than before. Better odds, but still too many for The Furies and the Tallyho Sisters to take. And another day would bring us to Q'ardum, the newly-captured Lemurisian stronghold.

Despite the Atlan forces' use of every underhanded, horrific weapon at their disposal, the Lemurisians had found unexpected allies in the Africs, hailed as conquering heroes whenever they liberated a town from Atlan control, joined by resistance fighters everywhere they went. Atlan was being forced off the continent.

We flew across the North Afric desert and past Aegyptia, following the Nil south. At sunset, the Commodore and his warships turned away, much to the cheering of my crew. Under the moonlight, we followed the silver ribbon of river until we came to the city of Q'ardum. Searchlights crisscrossed the sky and every once in a while we'd hear cannonfire, but for the most part the city was quiet and dark. Smallish shapes flitted through the air, circling the city. A quick glance through a pair of telescopic nightvision goggles revealed them to be Lemurisian ornies, guarding the skies.

One of them flew close and using a loudspeaker the pilot demanded we identify ourselves. Like our brass figurehead wasn't identification enough. I went out on deck, taking a loudspeaker of my own with me.

"Captain Sunset Val, of The Furies!" I yelled at him in Atlan through the loudspeaker. "Here to report to Admiral Salamander!"

"And your friends?"

"Tallyho Sisters, reporting to Admiral Jones!"

"Follow me!" he yelled back, then took up a position just ahead us.

We followed him down to an airfield hangar, where a dozen cannons were aimed at us. Another orny escorted the Sisters away, presumably to wherever Remy had his ship.

Things happened pretty quickly after that. We identified ourselves and once our claims had been verified, I sent a message to the Admiral, letting her know we'd arrived. A couple of hours later, an armed escort of maybe a dozen Lemurisian infantry came to get us. I left Molly in charge of the ship, grabbed Tring and a half dozen other girls, including Python. Most of them were busy carrying a large chest we filled with a gift for the Admiral. Serena came along, too.

We were brought before the Admiral pretty quick. She looked exhausted. Dark rings under her eyes, frown lines etched into her forehead and cheeks. She'd lost weight, too.

She'd made her headquarters in the biggest villa in town, a square house built around a central courtyard. It was lit with torches and oil lamps. Military aides rushed back and forth. The floor of the courtyard was a brilliant mosaic of tiny tiles set in geometric patterns.

"Ssunsset Val," the Admiral said, leaning back from a table covered with maps. "The ssstorriess about yourrr being able to ssssucceed at the imposssssible werrre not lying, werrre they?"

I shrugged. "I had a lot of help. A good crew and new friends."

"Indeed," she said, lifting a piece of notepaper. I recognized it as the message I'd sent her. "The Zhou and the vampyrrri, agrrreeing to invade Rrrrussssyanka? Anglic patchworrrk manufactorrriesss shut down? Rrremarkable."

"You called?" a booming voice rang out, filling the courtyard.

King Admiral Remarkable Jones stepped through an arched doorway, flanked by the Tallyho twins. Still huge, still bearded, still dressed in black. Royalty hadn't changed him, it seemed.

I ran into his arms for a great bear hug. It felt like coming home.

He looked down at me. "Good work, lass. You'll have to tell me all about it, over breakfast."

"And lunch and dinner," I agreed. "There's a lot to tell."

"Might I asssk forrr the abrrridged verrrsion?" Salamander asked. "I'm quite busssy, asss you can sssee."

"Sure," I said. "But first, we brought you a gift."

I waved the girls carrying the chest forward and let Python do the honours of lifting off the lid.

Inside, we'd bound and gagged Cobra. Python kicked the chest over and Cobra rolled out, unconscious.

Salamander shot to her feet. "What'sss the meaning of thisss?!"

"Oh you know," I said. "Sabotage, betrayal, treachery. The whole thing. We caught her trying to sprinkle the last of that acid she had on our balloon. Didn't quite work the way she expected. Copalum reacts differently with that particular acid, or something. I'm not a chemist. Anyhow, she told us everything."

"Oh?" Salamander asked, crossing her arms. "And what exactly did she tell you?"

"Oh come on," I laughed. "The one thing I couldn't figure out was the why. I mean, why send us on a mission, then add a saboteur to our crew? Why would you want the mission to fail?"

"If Captain Val failed in her mission, the Lemurisian war effort would be forced to withdraw their forces from Afric," Remy said. "Such a shame, what with your being so vocally in support of the war."

"A catassstrrrophic failurrre," Python spat. "A ssstain on yourr honourr and the honourr of dozensss of other Imperrrial family. No choice but to rrresssign. No hope for victorrry."

"These accusssationsss arrre rrridiculousss," Salamander spat back. "My entirre life hasss been ssspent in ssserrvice to the Lemurrrisian militarry! Why would I deliberrrately ssset myssself up for disssgrrace?!"

"Vhy vould you have stolen General Komodo's raptors and then set them loose at that party?" Serena asked. "The answer is obvious: to disgrace the General and then have sole dominion over the course of the var. And then, vonce the var vas lost and Atlan had conquered Lemuris, you could take your place as governor. Empress in truth, if not in name."

"Honourrrlessss," Python snarled. "To sssell yourrr people to the hated enemy. Betrrrayerr!"

"Yourrr wild accusssationsss arrre meaninglessss without prroof," Salamander said. "And the accusssationsss of a band of pirrratesss arre lessss than nothing in an Imperrrial court. Now if you will excussse me, I have a warrr to win."

Something clicked then. "Oh, now I get it. You didn't care one way or another if our mission succeeded. If Cobra managed to cripple our ship and the mission failed, you could sell out to Atlan and be made governor of Lemuris. And if we found her and what, executed her? And the mission was successful, you wind up with enough allies to really turn the tide in the war and you get coated in glory and honour, maybe enough to make you Empress one day. So you win, no matter what happens. Pretty smart, really."

Salamander smiled, but said nothing.

I smiled back. "But see, you didn't count on two things. First, the Afric uprising. You've been doing well, this past month, even with the Blighted roaming the battlefields. Gaining allies of your own without even trying. And now that the Zhou and the vampyri are in the fight and Atlan won't be making any more patchwork soldiers for a while, things just got a whole lot better."

"And second?"

"Well, second, the accusation doesn't come from us," I said. I pointed at Python. "It comes from her. As an airship captain, you outrank her. But as an Imperial princess, she outranks you. Pretty sure her accusations will stand up in an Imperial court."

I have to admit, I really enjoyed seeing that smug smile fade away, replaced by narrowed eyes and tight lips. I could almost hear the gears turning as she tried to figure a way out of the corner we'd backed her into.

Lucky for her and unlucky for us, explosions in the distance lit up the night sky.

Seconds later, a panting Lemurisian soldier ran into the courtyard.

Salamander snapped an order at him, in Lemurisian. He panted back a reply. Remy asked something, then nodded at the answer.

"What is it?" I asked.

"We're under attack," Remy explained, as Salamander gave out orders to her aides, pointing at a map of the city she had on her desk. "Land troops have breached the city's west wall. No sign of aerial reinforcement."

"So what do we do?"

"Not much airship pirates can do in a land fight, lass," Remy said.

"Nonsense, Remy," Gwen said.

"Tosh, in fact," Guinny agreed.

"You should see the amount of damage young Sunset here can cause without her ship, wot?"

"Too right!"

"Yeah, that's true," I said. "Look at the Battle of Libertia. The Furies got grounded and we were still in the fight."

"Not this time," Remy said, shaking his head. "They've got Blighted and aren't afraid to use them. Not worth the risk."

I frowned and crossed my arms. "So we let the Lemurisians and the Africs take all the risks?"

"That's not what I said, lass. There's only so much we can do. As shock troops the Blighted don't feel pain, and never rest. I've seen 'em drag themselves across a battlefield with their legs shot off. All they care about is their hunger. The only thing that stops 'em is the time it takes for them to feed. Down south I've heard tell that some Afric resistance fighters have taken to driving entire herds of water buffalo into the mobs of Blighted. The buffalo don't much like it but it gives the Africs a chance to make a break for it." He chuckled. "One group even drove a herd of elephants into the Blighted mob. That took the Blighted a lot longer to swallow, let me tell you, the elephants crushing them under their feet the whole time."

"Sounds pretty horrible," I said, sick to my stomach.

Then I had an idea.

"Give me a half hour," I said. "You'll have my ornies, my batgirls, even my Vulka-rey. They'll keep those Blighted busy."

"What are you going to do, pet?" Gwen asked.

I grinned at her. "Find something to crush them."

"What do we do with herrr?" Python asked, pointing at Cobra. "And Sssalamanderrr?"

"We'll finish this after the battle," I said. "Give Cobra to... uh. I mean, there's got to be some kind of military guard, right?"

"Yesss, if we trrussst them," Python said. She glanced around and barked out an order in Lemurisian. A couple of guards came over, picked up Cobra and dragged her off.

"I will ssstay with Sssalamanderrr," Python said, clasping my hand. "It hasss been an honour to ssserrrve with you."

"The honour's mine, Princess," I said, pulling her into a hug. "Be careful."

"I am alwaysss carrreful, Sssunsssset," she grinned.

Chapter Forty One

Bet You Thought The Last Book Had An Epic Ending

You know, I really wish I could have seen the faces of the Atlan troops when I came into view. It must have really been something to see me riding a giant Tyrannosaur off of the airfield and through the town.

And by giant, I really mean *giant*. Not the normal twenty feet tall type of giant. No, my idea had been pretty crazy, even by my own standards of wacky fun.

We'd reversed Gigi's shrink-o-matic machine, pumping it up so that Fluffy wound up close to three hundred feet tall. How did we keep her from, you know, exploding and stuff? Simple. We strapped the shrink-o-matic to a collar of ropes that we tied around Fluffy's neck. How did we keep the machine running, away from the ship? That's where those two patchwork assassins really came in handy. Or their portable dynamos did, at least. You know, the battery pack thingies they had on them to supercharge the first guy and power the second guy's electro-swords. We wired those things into Gigi's machine and kept Fluffy giant-sized.

Which was why I couldn't see anyone's faces as we thundered down the streets. Way up on giant-sized Mega-Fluffy's shoulders, I could barely see them at all.

Not that they would have had much of a reaction, I guess. The Blighted didn't know fear or pain. All they knew was their hunger. They didn't even notice Mega-Fluffy until she stepped on them, crushing them to paste between her toes. And the best part was that Mega-Fluffy's pebbled skin was so thick and hard that there was no way any Blighted would be able to infect her by biting her.

See, the Lemurisians had all kinds of Tyrannosaurs as a part of their land troops already. They used them as cavalry. Tyrannosaur cavalry, packs of trained raptors scouring the battlefield, armoured triceratops and stegosaur tanks, they had all kinds of dinosaurs for all kinds of different military roles.

But the Blighted had teeth, and a relentless need to feed. And no one wanted to see what would happen if a T-Rex got bitten.

So the Lemurisians had kept their most fearsome weapons, their dino division, away from the Atlan advance. Totally understandable, right? But it meant anywhere the Blighted were, the Lemurisians basically were out of the fight, restricting themselves to dropping oil on the Blighted from airships and then setting the Atlan shock troops on fire. It was pretty horrifying. Even as they burned to a crisp, the Blighted shambled around, needing to feed.

Stomping on dozens of Blighted with every step sounds terrible, I know, but we didn't have a lot of choice, not if we wanted to keep the city in Lemurisian hands. All I had to do was make sure Mega-Fluffy didn't eat any Blighted and she'd be okay. That's what we did, Gigi and me, at least. I steered Mega-Fluffy, Gigi kept that machine of hers working. Behind us came my two dozen batgirls, my four ornies and the nine Vulka-rey who'd stayed with us, raining death from above, dropping jars of flammable liquids on the Blighted, setting them ablaze.

Mega-Fluffy turned out to be a little harder to steer than I'd hoped, though, so maybe some buildings got crushed, too. My bad. At least we knew the buildings were empty. One word that the Blighted were coming and people scattered faster than chainshot out a cannon.

We'd pretty much cleared out most of the Blighted when something exploded off of Mega-Fluffy's port side. She roared in pain.

"Who is shooting at us?" Gigi yelled.

"Atlans?" I yelled back, staring out into the night to try and find who'd attacked us. Good thing I'd brought my nightvision goggles. I soon spotted our enemy. I pointed past the city walls. "There!"

Gigi looked, twisting the lenses on her own goggles. "Ah zut!"

A mass of maybe forty or fifty Atlan warcrabs were crossing the empty plains outside the city.

I grabbed the whistle I'd brought with me and blew as hard as I could. Almost immediately I was surrounded by batgirls.

"Weapons out, girls, fire at will!" I ordered, pointing at the warcrabs.

Their answering warcry was a blood-curdling shriek I'll remember my whole life.

The batgirls' shriek drew the attention of the ornies and the Vulka-rey and they descended on the Atlan forces with a vengeance. The harsh crack of gunfire filled the night. Once the Blighted had been dealt with, the Lemurisians let loose their dino division. Dozens of Tyrannosaurs thundered past us, followed by just as many Triceratopses – Triceratopsi? Triceratopsees? carrying armoured palanquins bristling with guns.

It was a slaughter. The Atlans never knew what hit them.

Of course, that had only been one wing of their attack. Barracudas had swooped in from the other side of town and the few airships on our side had been caught still getting ready. Except for The Furies, the Tallyho Sisters and Remy's Mistress O' Merit, who'd bought the Lemurisians enough time to get into the air and into the fight. I probably should have been there, instead of riding a giant T-Rex in the land battle, but they did fine without me.

Better than fine. When it was all over and the dust had settled and Gigi and I got back to The Furies with a very tired, normal-sized Fluffy, it turned out we hadn't had a single fatality in the crew. Plenty of wounds, sure. But not a single death. I wanted to weep with relief.

Dawn came bright and clear. Most of the fires had died out and there was pretty much nothing left but the cleaning up. Gigi and I hosed off Fluffy's very messy feet, making sure we got everything scrubbed off. I didn't want even a fragment of Blighted aboard my ship.

Then the alarms began sounding again. An aerial attack, this time. We left Fluffy in a stable with the other Tyrannosaurs and scrambled aboard The Furies.

I entered the bridge, eyes scanning the sky. "Where are they?"

"Behind us, Captain," Molly said, pointing at the viewing screen.

Hundreds of ships dotted the eastern sky, out of the sunrise.

"Restless, get us in the air!" I ordered.

But as the Lemurisian and pirate armadas took to the air to confront the attacking airships, we began to hear the all-clear air sirens sounding from the ships ahead of us. Then the sun rose behind a cloud and I saw the supposedly attacking ships for what they were: Zhou air junks.

"Captain," Argenta said. "They wish to speak to you."

"Me?"

"Yes, Captain Val."

"Uh, okay." I took the wireless from Argenta. "Hello?"

"Give me my daughter, you pirate!"

It was the Fist of the Path of Three. Don't ask me how he got a radiophonic communicatron, either. One of those things that just happen. A secret that useful couldn't stay a secret for long.

"Why aren't you in Russankya?" I blurted without thinking. The whole plan hinged on them attacking the Russ.

"Our troops are crossing the border as we speak," he answered. "Now give me back my daughter!"

"Uh, sure, Fist," I said, covering the microphone. "Find Delicate Petal fast!" I said to Molly, who ran off the bridge.

"Listen, what if she doesn't want to leave?" I asked.

"What do you mean? You kidnapped her!"

"No, she ran away to join us, Fist."

"Impossible!"

"Look, why don't you come over and we'll sort this out," I said.

It didn't take long for Delicate Petal to explain to her father why she'd done what she'd done. Whether he'd ever understand it is a different matter entirely. In the end, he agreed to give her a position aboard his ship, if she agreed to leave The Furies.

"Thank you so much," Delicate Petal said, bowing low to me.

I bowed back. "You're welcome," I said, not quite sure what she was thanking me for. Still, it seemed the simplest thing to say.

"So you're going back to Zhou?" I asked the Fist. "Because we could use you here, too."

"This force is but a fraction of the airships at our command," he answered. "I will return to Zhou, but perhaps we can leave you some of our ships to assist you, here in Afric."

"Thanks," I said. "I'm sure the we'll will be happy for the help."

When we got back to Q'ardum, we had another surprise waiting.

"What happened?" I asked Python.

She looked up from the hospital cot, where she lay with her shoulder bandaged up.

"The headquarrrterrrsss werrre... under attack. Blighted brroke thrrrough. Sssalamanderrr... essscaped in the confusion."

"Were you bit?" I asked, trying not to look at the bloody bandages.

"No. Gunshot. Not verrry amusssing."

"Yeah, I hear that," I said, rubbing the scar on my arm where I'd been shot once before. "You take care of yourself, alright? And we'll find Salamander. How far can she run, anyway?"

Python grinned her filed-teeth grin. "Not farrr enough."

I went back to The Furies, exhausted. All I wanted to do was fall into bed and stay there for a year or two. Instead, I visited my injured crew, talking with them each a bit, spending time with them. The last person I visited was Eve.

She'd been released from the sick ward and had settled into her new quarters, bunking down in Gigi and Molly's room.

When I found Eve, she was sitting on her bunk, reading. She'd stitched up her face, but a bandage covered her eye.

"Hey," I said from the doorway. "Can I come in?"

Eve sat up, shutting her book and tucking it away beside her. "Please do, Captain."

"You don't have to call me that," I smiled.

"Alright, Sunset," Eve said, smiling. "What can I do for you?"

I sat on the edge of Gigi's bed, which looked like it had never been made. "Nothing. Just wanted to see how you were doing."

"Fine, thank you. How are you doing?"

I took a deep breath and puffed it out. "I dunno. Fine. I guess."

"Clearly not." She swung her feet over the edge of her bunk.

"Oh Eve, your eye..." I said, looking up at her injured face.

One of her hands fluttered up to touch the edge of the bandage. "It... There was nothing Dr. Westmore could do, of course. I'm a patchwork, not a person. I mean, not a human. I'm sure it will be fine, if we can find, some revivification fluid. Until then, I suppose I can wear a patch."

"We can't outfit you with a prosthetic lens, like Molly or Inga?"

"No, the electricity that powers me would... interfere with the mechanism. Although that would make an interesting scientific challenge..." She paused, lost in thought. "Interesting. Sunset, if it wouldn't interfere with my duties, I think I might be able to sort something out."

"Your duties? You mean, as crew?"

"Yes. I assume I'm to be made one of the crew? That is, Dr. Westmore seems to have things well in hand, so I couldn't return to my previous post. It wouldn't be fair to her."

I laughed, but resisted the urge to hug her. "Eve, you're amazing."

"Am I? Goodness. No one's ever described me that way before."

"You are. Trust me on this. And as for you being one of the crew, as far as I'm concerned, you've earned your keep and more besides. You could sit here and read from now until the war's over and that would be just fine by me. As long as you stay safe, I'm happy."

Eve smiled at me, but crossed her arms. "You want me to stay safe aboard a pirate ship in the middle of a war. That seems to be quite contradictory."

I sighed again. "Yeah. I know. If I could send you, send all of us, somewhere safe while the war sorted itself out, I would."

"But you cannot."

"No, I can't. I kind of started this war, y'know? Convincing the pirate armada to stand and face that Atlan invasion of Libertia? So I've kind of got a responsibility to finish it."

"The war would have started sooner or later," Eve said. "All the elements were in place. Atlan oppression, the slave trade, military rumblings. Everything was primed. All that was needed was a catalyst. And that's you, Sunset. You're catalytic. You change things everywhere you go. So no, you didn't start the war. And no, you don't have to finish it. You always put so much responsibility on yourself."

"Well I am captain, you know."

"Because we voted you into the position, I'll have you remember."

"I guess." My leaned back against the hull wall and neither of us said anything for a few minutes.

"I'm so tired," I whispered, finally, closing my eyes. "I just want this war to be over."

"It's only been a few months," Eve said. "Some wars take years."

I opened my eyes and stared at her. "There is no way we'll survive years. I'm sick of seeing my friends hurt and my crew killed. If I had any sense at all, I'd take this ship as far away from here as I can. Keep you all safe. But apparently being captain means having no sense at all, since I keep bringing us back into danger."

"Being captain means having the most ruthless kind of sense," Eve said gently. "Knowing that one death might save ten lives, or a hundred. Or a hundred deaths might save thousands of lives."

I choked back a bitter laugh. "Hundreds? Thousands? Back where I'm from, there was this war. A world war. And it went on for years. And millions of people died. Millions, Eve. And the only reason the death toll wasn't any higher was because the side that won used a weapon so horrible, struck a blow to their enemies so devastating, that it seemed like no one would ever want to go to war, ever again. Until the next war, that is. Humans are stupid that way, I guess."

"Perhaps we should do that, then," Eve said.

Then I did laugh. "You know, that stuff about me being someone who changes things, maybe that's true, but there's no way I'm telling anyone on Ayrth anything about nuclear weapons. There's no way."

She shook her head. "No, of course. I agree. Best left unsaid. But there must be other ways to strike a devastating blow to Atlan and end this war."

"Like what?"

"I don't know," Eve smiled. "I'm not the catalytic one, remember?"

"So it's up to me, after all?" I laughed. "Think of something so huge, so terrible, that it will shatter Atlan once and for all? Sink every hope they have of ever winning..." I just trailed off then.

Eve waited a couple of minutes and said, "Sunset?"

I grinned at her, vicious and victorious. "I have an idea."

To be concluded in

Sunset Val's
Final Boarding

The Sinking
of Atlan

Other Series
by
Rob St.Martin

The Truthseekers Series

Welcome to Blackriver
Birthright
Level Up

***

The Princess Smith Saga

Princess Smith and the Clockwork Knight

***

The Squirrelman Books

Sins of the Past vol.1 - Calling All Crimefighters
Sins of the Past vol.2 - Endgame
The Amazing Adventures of the Sensational Squirrelman

Rob St-Martin is a Canadian author, editor, publisher, husband and father, not necessarily in that order. From his secret lair in Montreal, he writes fantasy novels with steampunkian flavour and strong female characters.

Since his first professional sale of a short story to the MISSPELLED anthology in 2006, Rob has edited an Aurora Award-nominated anthology (Ages of Wonder, 2009); written over a million words; published ten of his own novels and the two science fiction novels of Derwin Mak; been an Author Guest at over a dozen conventions; and become a husband and father. He lives with his wife (whom he adores), four children, two gerbils and a frog.

When not writing, Rob actively wishes he had more time to write.